KISSING MAX HOLDEN

KATY UPPERMAN

SQUARE
FISH

Swoon Reads | New York

SQUARE
FISH

An imprint of Macmillan Publishing Group, LLC

175 Fifth Avenue, New York, NY 10010

swoonreads.com

Library of Congress Cataloging-in-Publication Data

Names: Upperman, Katy, author.

Title: Kissing Max Holden / Katy Upperman.

Description: New York : Swoon Reads, 2017. | Summary: While both deal with problems at home,

one-time best friends Jill and Max, seventeen, kiss, and while Jill knows that was a mistake,

she struggles not to kiss him again.

Identifiers: LCCN 2016038314 (print) | LCCN 2017017893 (ebook) | ISBN 978-1-250-15896-3 (paperback)

ISBN 978-1-250-11115-9 (ebook)

Subjects: | CYAC: Love—Fiction. | Best friends—Fiction. | Friendship—Fiction. | Family problems—

Fiction. | Neighbors—Fiction.

Classification: LCC PZ7.1.U67 (ebook) | LCC PZ7.1.U67 Kis 2017 (print) | DDC [Fic]—dc23

LC record available at https://lccn.loc.gov/2016038314

Originally published in the United States by Swoon Reads

First Square Fish edition, 2018

Book designed by Rebecca Syracuse

Square Fish logo designed by Filomena Tuosto

10 9 8 7 6 5 4 3 2 1

FOR CLAIRE . . .
CHASE YOUR DREAMS, SWEET GIRL.

1

THE POUNDING AT MY WINDOW COMES LATE, and it scares me shitless.

A second knock quickly follows, rattling the glass in its pane and my heart in my chest. There's such force behind the rapping, I'm half expecting a bloodied, glass-encrusted fist to poke through my curtains.

Our house is silent and inky dark. The last of the trick-or-treaters have called it a night. My parents have stowed the leftover Snickers bars and checked the locks; they've been asleep for hours.

Another knock. More subdued, but still resolute. There's comfort in its persistence. Someone with deviant motives would be sneakier, more cunning. Fear gives way as curiosity blooms, and my stuttering heart resumes a steadier beat.

This knock, *his* knock, is familiar.

It's been years since Max visited me at night. Years since I let him crawl through my window and sprawl out on my carpet and talk himself gruff until early morning. It's been ages since we've talked at all, really, but I can't ignore him. It's not in his DNA to give up—he'll keep knocking and eventually he'll make enough noise to wake my dad, who'll come to investigate. Max is little more than a peripheral figure in my life these days, but Dad'll be pissed if he finds the neighbor boy lurking outside my window like a creeper.

I flip on a lamp and slip out of bed, straightening my skewed pajama pants as I pad across the carpet. I catch a glimpse of my disheveled reflection in the mirrored closet door and pause to adjust my tank top and smooth my ponytail. I jump when he knocks again, an agitated pummeling of the glass, like he's sensed my ill-timed vanity.

He's there as I draw the curtains back, peering up at me from the poorly lit side yard. The sad slope of his shoulders and the hard set of his jaw do terrible things to my heart.

Max Holden used to be equal parts zesty and sweet, like lemon meringue pie. Bright and jovial, so brilliant I once had to squint when I looked at him. Now, his dazzle has dulled, flattened like a biscuit that refuses to rise. Still, I can't help but hope for his once-trademark grin, the one that says, *I knew you'd come.*

Of course I'll come. He's Max and I'm Jillian, and that's how it's always been.

But he doesn't smile—he barely makes eye contact. He looks tired, defeated, and deeply unhappy.

I unlock the window and push it up. I don't officially invite him in, but he braces his hands on the sill and hurdles through the opening like a cat burglar. He stretches to his full height—several inches taller than my five-seven—and I look him over, one eyebrow lifted in unconcealed shock: I've never seen him so eccentrically unkempt.

His feet are shoved into tattered moccasin-style slippers—castoffs of his father's, probably—and he's thrown on faded McAlder High sweats, ratty things he wears to wash his truck, another hand-me-down from Bill. His torso is draped in a blousy white shirt with a black, jagged-edged vest over it, a skull and crossbones embroidered over his heart. His dark hair is spiked in every direction, like he recently ditched a too-tight hat. He runs a hand through it when he notices my scrutiny. And his eyes, a gray-blue so deep they're capable of drowning the unsuspecting, are rimmed in liner, thick and black and smudged.

Max isn't a makeup kind of guy.

I stare, perplexed. I look away. Then, because I can't help myself, I peek again.

"What?" he asks.

"Um. You're wearing makeup."

He shrugs. "And you're not."

"It's the middle of the night, Max. What are you doing here?"

He sinks wearily—and without answer—to the floor. He leans against my bed, unfolding his long legs across the eggshell carpet my stepmother, Meredith, had installed a few years ago. His eyes fall shut. His breathing is shallow, disturbingly irregular.

I stand over him. Now that his eyes are closed, I regard him again, turning over the facts I've collected. He's likely drunk. He went to Linebacker Leo's Halloween party, like the rest of our school's population, and from what I heard, his girlfriend, Becky McMahon, accompanied him. Who could blame him if he drained a keg to tolerate her presence?

A draft eddies in from my open window. It doesn't appear to bother Max, but I'm cold in my thin pajamas. I'm also self-conscious in my thin pajamas, which is absurd. It's not as if he hasn't seen me dressed for bed. We've been neighbors for ten years and our parents are close. When I was thirteen, I spent a week with the Holdens while my dad and Meredith honeymooned in Maui. But this—*this*—is different. We're seventeen, and we're alone.

The air suddenly seems gelatinous. Does he sense it? Probably not. He's slouched against my bed, eyes still shut, features pinched in a scowl. He looks seconds from sleep in his wacky getup.

My brain cranks into overtime. . . . Max Holden is in my bedroom, shouldering an air of gloom like heavy armor. The gloom isn't implausible or even surprising, but what *is* surprising is that he's come here. Though I've tried plenty of times, he hasn't willingly engaged with me—with *anyone*, as far as I know—in months.

Shivering and desperate for practical action, I step over his idle legs and push my window shut. He's staying, at least for now.

He opens his eyes to the quiet click of the window latch, gazing up at me from beneath heavy lids. "You let me in," he states thickly, as if he's just now realizing.

"You didn't give me much choice. You would've woken my dad if I'd left you out there beating the glass, all drunk and disorderly."

He smirks. "You're glad I'm here."

He doesn't deny the drunk or the disorderly, I notice. "You think so? I was in bed. We have school tomorrow, in case you've forgotten."

"Is that why you weren't at Leo's? 'Cause it's a school night?"

Leo, a huge middle linebacker whose father owns the Chevrolet dealership in town, is one of Max's closest friends, and I wasn't at his Halloween party for a variety of reasons. First, I hate the limited selection of costumes available to girls my age (slutty nurse or skanky angel . . . no, thank you). Second, I hate social gatherings that include more than my core group of friends (Leo invites half the school over anytime his parents go out). Third—and probably most significant—I hate watching Becky paw Max like he's a scratching post.

I don't feel compelled to explain any of this, though. Max and I may have been close in another lifetime, but I don't owe him anything now.

"Leah missed you," he says, folding his hands behind his head. The toothed edges of his vest ride up around his ribs.

"I'm sure she had a fantastic time." Leah goes out with Jesse, another of Max's football buddies. I helped her with her peacock costume, an indigo leotard we glued iridescent emerald and violet feathers to. Though she and Kyle, my best friend and McAlder's All-District quarterback, did their damnedest to convince me to go to Leo's, I didn't get the impression my absence would have much bearing on their fun meters. Besides, there was no way I was going to squeeze into the black cat "costume" Kyle pointed out during our trip to the local party supply store.

I eye Max's attire, lips pursed in contemplation. "Don't tell me . . . Jack Sparrow?"

"Nah. Just your general parrot-toting, sword-wielding, beer-guzzling buccaneer." His words are perfectly pirate-slurred.

"Sounds like all you got right was the beer guzzling."

He sneers. "Becky was my wench."

"Speaking of your better half, where is she? Oh! Wait! Did she walk the plank? Was she swallowed by a giant squid?"

His laughter, low and uninhibited, surprises me. It's the sound of my childhood: leisurely afternoons spent tossing a football back and forth in the street between his house and mine, gross-out comedies in the Holdens' big bonus room, dripping fudge pops devoured on summer evenings. His bloodshot eyes crinkle at the corners and his head tips back. A small, selfish part of me is flattered that he's here, with me, sharing a chuckle at Becky's expense.

But when his laughter dies, he looks uncomfortable, like he might feel guilty at having experienced even the tiniest bit of joy. He studies his watch, a vintage thing on a worn leather cuff that belongs to his father. Bill has no use for it these days; Max is the one who wears it unfailingly.

He shakes off the memory he fell into and says, "Becky went home." He makes a swilling motion, as if throwing back a drink. "I might've had one too many. Think I pissed her off."

"You *think* you pissed her off?"

"I spilled beer on her costume. Maybe in her hair. But yeah, she's definitely pissed. She made a big scene and then she left, which was shitty, because she's the one who begged me to go to Leo's in the first place. 'Blow off some steam, Max.' And then, *poof*"—he swoops an imaginary magic wand through the air—"she was outta there."

"Wow. Some girlfriend."

"Right? For all she knows, I tried to drive home and ended up in a ditch."

I blink away the image of Max's F-150 mangled on the side of a dark road. "She really left you without a ride?"

"Yeah, but Ivy brought me home."

Of course. Ivy Holden is a year older than Max and me, a grade ahead of us in school. She and Becky might as well be affixed at the hip, but that doesn't keep her from watching out for her brother. "Does Becky know you're here?"

He snorts. "What do you think?"

Honestly, I don't know what to think. . . . He ticked his girlfriend off, caught a ride home with his sister, then stumbled across the street to my house. How scandalous. Yet there's something right about his visit, even after all this time. I shiver again, though the window's sealed tight. Sure, Max is blitzed, but he came to *me*.

He captures my gaze, inhaling like he's preparing to admit

something of utmost importance. He's so serious, so un-Max-like, I stoop down to give him my full attention. Quietly he says, "I don't wanna be at home, Jill. I hate home. I've hated it since . . ."

His voice shrivels, but I know what he intended to say: *since my dad's stroke.*

He pretends to be impervious. He slogs through his classes, working just hard enough to maintain a GPA that'll keep him on the varsity football roster, then boozes it up with Becky on the weekends. He acts like he's fine, like he's handling it, but those of us who know him, *really* know him, see how much he's changed.

It's been almost six months since Bill Holden—patriarch, football fanatic, and my dad's longtime friend—collapsed while pushing his mower across his front lawn. Max, the only other Holden home at the time, found him unconscious in the grass. He called 911, and then he called my father. Dad and I stood in the yard with him while Bill was loaded into an ambulance, an experience profound in its gravity. Poor Max—he was a little boy all over again: scared, sorry, close to caving under the weight of my dad's hand on his trembling shoulder.

Later, at the hospital, we learned that Bill had suffered a hemorrhagic stroke, the result of an undiagnosed cerebral aneurysm that burst and caused bleeding in his brain. The damage is, for the most part, irreversible. He'll never again be the vital, active man he was, no matter how much his son drinks. No matter how desperately Marcy, his wife, prays. No matter how often his daughters—Ivy and Zoe—act out or micromanage.

The impact of Bill's stroke was instant, and instantaneously unraveling.

Since my dad's stroke . . . It's there, loitering in the air, ominous as a storm cloud.

Max's jaw is clenched and his eyes are inflamed and I'm horrified.

He's had too much to drink, and now he's battling emotion he's kept corked for months. I should let him say what he needs to say. Just spit it out and fall apart and be done with it. But the idea of tears trailing down his face guts me.

I reach toward him, brushing my fingertips along smudged charcoal liner. He exhales, but stays still. There's beer on his breath. Something warm and spicy, too—cinnamon—and it's inexplicably appealing. I have the briefest, most inappropriate thought ever: *I wonder what he tastes like?*, before I remember how damaged he is. Tonight he needs a friend, not a neighbor with indiscriminate hormones.

My fingers shake as they skim the kohl line of his eye. Touching him tangles my emotions—surprise snarled with self-awareness, embarrassment twisted with wonder. We've barely had physical contact over the last couple of years, but I committed the velvety quality of his skin to memory long ago.

He sighs, and I come to my senses. The last thing I want is to disrupt the trust he's instilling in me, but there's only so far I'm willing to go. Max has a girlfriend, one who'd breathe fire if she knew I was touching him. Besides, in the morning, after hours spent anxiously obsessing, this whole experience will seem dreadfully bizarre.

As my fingers drop away, he opens his eyes, catching my hand as it falls. I try not to fidget as he stretches it open, holds it close to his face, and studies my palm like he's reading my fate. My fingertips are stained an odd carrot color because I spent Halloween the same way I spend most evenings: baking. The orange food tint I used to color marzipan for pumpkin cupcakes is evidence. Layered over the orange, accentuating the dips and valleys of my fingerprints, is the black liner I lifted from his pirate makeup.

He folds my palm into the web of his and drops our knotted fingers to his lap, like the two of us holding hands is the most ordinary thing in the world. "Why are you being nice?"

"I'm always nice," I say, distracted by the heat of his hand against mine.

"Remember when we were friends?"

"Max. We're still friends."

"Not like we used to be."

"Nothing's like it used to be." The admission makes my chest ache.

"Remember when you used to hang out with me, not Kyle?" There's a sharpness to his voice that's alien, not to mention confusing. There's no reason to be jealous of Kyle, and Max knows as much. But if Kyle's not the issue, what is? Is he trying to provoke me? Has his never-ending series of fights with Becky turned him mean?

Whether he intends to or not, he's proving my point—*nothing* is like it used to be.

"Remember when you used to hang out with me, not your team-mates?" I counter, tossing my ponytail over my shoulder. "Not *Becky*?"

Predictably, he ignores my rebuttal. "Why don't I ever see you anymore?"

Because you're always playing football, or partying, or out with your girlfriend, I want to say, but I sense those words won't help. Instead, I tell him a different truth. "We grew up."

"That's such bullshit."

All at once, I regret letting him into my room. I tug my hand out of his. The lost connection combined with the bite of his tone make my stomach roil. "Don't put this on me," I say. "A lot has happened, stuff I've had no control over."

"What? You mean Becky?"

I mean his father, but the hurt he wore a few minutes ago flashes in my mind and I can't bring myself to mention Bill, who's had to leave his half of the Hatz-Holden Logging management responsibilities to Marcy. Bill, who's confined to a wheelchair, who needs help eating, dressing, using the bathroom. Bill, who has a hard time communicating a simple *hello*.

I stand. The ghost of Max's touch makes my palm tingle, but I feel better now that I've put some distance between us. I'll go to my desk, littered with cookbooks and recipe cards. I'll read my latest issue of *Bon Appétit*. I'll get ahead on my English lit assignment. I'll ignore Max until he sobers up, and then I'll send him on his way. I'll pay for these late hours tomorrow, but there's no way I can get comfy in bed with Blackbeard acting all wasted on my floor.

I'm stepping high over his legs, fuming at his audacity—his *idiocy*—when he grabs the hem of my pants. I lose my balance, wobbling on one foot like a dizzy flamingo, until I'm forced to give in to the inertia of his pull. I drop into his lap, landing with an embarrassing *oof*. Judging by the look on his face—chagrin swirled with a generous dash of unadulterated amusement—he's more shocked by my new seat than I am.

I'm mortified beyond words—beyond recovery, apparently—while he stares at me, biting his lip against what must be hysterics. "Jesus, Jill. What'd *you* drink tonight?"

I struggle to right myself. "Nothing, thank you very much."

He's snickering, and I want to smack him. "Really? Because that was—"

"You pulled me down! And shut up, would you? You'll wake my dad."

His laughter quiets. "Jake's cool. Remember when we were in middle school and he caught us smoking the cigarettes we stole from

Zoe? All he did was toss the pack and sit us down in front of a documentary about lung cancer."

"Yeah, and neither of us smoked ever again."

"My point is, he didn't freak out. And I did not pull you down."

"I was walking and you grabbed my pants!"

"I didn't want you to leave."

I whack his chest. "I was going to my desk, you moron."

He rubs the spot where I hit him, as if I'm capable of causing him pain. When he's satisfied there will be no bruising, his hand lands on my leg. It's inadvertent, I think. A comfortable resting place, although his other arm is looped behind my back thanks to the way he caught me when I fell.

We must notice the position of his hands, my body, the close contact, at the same time because all the oxygen funnels out of the room. His attention flickers to my mouth, and heat floods my face. What the *hell* am I doing in his lap?

"Yeah . . . ," he says, shifting. Not such a cocky pirate after all.

I muster the little dignity I've managed to retain and prepare to push myself up. "Sorry. You're okay, ri—?"

He tightens his hold.

"I'm okay." He's recovered his swagger—I'm sure the copious amount of beer he consumed earlier is helping—and his voice is low, throaty, familiar. It's his flirty voice, I realize, the one he uses with Becky during their (infrequent) good moments. "Are *you* okay?"

"I'm fine." I try again to leave his lap, but his hand glides up my spine, beneath my ponytail, and cradles the back of my neck. Now he *is* flashing me the grin, the one I was hoping for when I opened my curtains, the one that exudes confidence and promises fun. I want to hate him for teasing me. For using me. For being so freaking enticing.

I could never hate him.

"You don't have to go anywhere," he says.

"Max." It's a warning. It's an invitation. With a smile and a stroke of his fingers along the curve of my shoulder, he's drawn me in, and I'm losing the very fragile grasp I have on this situation. I study the stubble on his jaw to avoid his eyes, but then I want to touch it, feel its coarseness against my fingertips.

I give my head a shake and focus on my hands clasped in my lap. I breathe, in and out, but the beer, the cinnamon, the wintry-clean scent of the soap he's used for as long as I've known him . . . I'm certain he hears my heart's incessant pounding.

Softly, he says, "What were we talking about again?"

"How everything's changed."

"Jilly."

I melt into him as he whispers the nickname that never fails to thaw me. "Yes?"

"If you tell me to go, I will."

His declaration lets me see us from a distance, unencumbered by his scent and his warmth and his gentle touch. I'm a reasonable person. A smart girl. And Max is a mess, letting regret engulf him, anger consume him. Just last week I watched him shove a freshman on the quad because the kid accidentally bumped into him. And tonight he's three sheets and looking for distraction. As much as I'd like to help him, I won't be his no-strings-attached hookup, the other woman to his waning relationship with Becky.

I resolve to tell him as much—that he should, in fact, go home. That he should drink a glass of water and swallow a couple of Motrin before bed. That I'll see him tomorrow at school.

But before I can utter a syllable, he's charging forward, eyes glazed, lips parted. I'm so astonished, so stunned, I let him push his mouth against mine, and even though it's heedless and utterly unexpected, I reciprocate. I can't help myself.

I can't process this frantic, feverish kiss, but it shoots straight through me, a streak of heat and want and, oh my God—it's *good*.

Just like that, I forget all the reasons why kissing Max Holden is an awful idea.

2

E EASES ME OFF HIS LAP, NUDGING me back until I'm stretched out on the rug. He joins me clumsily, adjusting to keep his weight from crushing me. His mouth finds mine again, heat and spice and fervor, and I return his kiss with passion I didn't know I possessed.

Kissing Max doesn't feel strange or forced or immoral.

It feels indulgent, satisfying, *thrilling*.

Until, through my fog of euphoria, I sense a shift of the air, and register the *click* of an opening of a door.

My dad's voice fills the room. "Jillian? Max?! What the *hell* is going on in here?"

Despite my shock, I emerge too slowly from my lusty daze.

Max and I are breathing like we just finished a set of wind sprints. He's stretched out on top of me. My fists grip the waistband of his sweats. My camisole is twisted up around my ribs—he has a hand beneath it!

From his place in my doorway, my father is witness to every dirty detail.

I wait for Max to apologize, to roll off me, to fling himself out the window, but drunken stupor must've robbed him of logic, because he drops his sweaty forehead to my neck and breathes a long, low, "*Fuck.*"

I shove him, simultaneously straightening my top and scrambling to get up off the floor.

"Dad . . ." But that's all I've got. There's no way to justify the literal tangle he's caught me in.

Max hauls himself up to stand beside me—not too close. He's squirming, tugging at his pirate vest, pushing a hand through his wild hair. He looks like a snared animal, alarmed and fretful and desperate to flee, which is pretty congruent with how I'm feeling.

My dad pounds a fist against the doorjamb. "What in God's name is he doing here?"

Max and I share a glance. Limited options churn behind his puffy eyes—*door or window, door or window?* It's glaringly apparent when he comes to terms with the fact that there's nowhere to run.

"Um, visiting?"

My dad scuffs a toe on the carpet, posture inclined, stare lethal, like a bull preparing to charge. I notice his sleepwear: candy corn sprinkled over flannel pants, a googly-eyed jack-o'-lantern grinning gaily from his T-shirt. Meredith's aggressively themed purchases, sported because Dad relinquished his Man Card four years ago, the day he said, "I do."

Hysterical laughter fizzes in my throat. I have no idea what's wrong with me; this is so *not* funny.

Dad takes a step forward.

Max matches it with a step back, as if there's a force field keeping the two of them from getting too close. "Jake, I can explain."

My dad flaunts a deadly smile. "Really? Oh, this should be rich. What possible explanation could you have for sneaking into my house in the middle of the night? What was that thud I heard? Did you trip? Did you *fall on top of my daughter*?"

Max has the sense to bite his tongue, but I can't say I'm thrilled when he glances at me, passing the baton.

"Dad, calm down."

"I will *not* calm down!"

"But it's okay—"

"I can't imagine anything *less* okay!"

"We were just talking."

It's a blatant lie that summons flames from deep within him. "Talking my ass! You were *not* talking. You were . . . you were—"

Meredith materializes behind him. She's sporting the feminine version of his Halloween pajamas, but the jack-o'-lantern on her top is stretched over her newly rounded belly. Her face crinkles with confusion. "Jake?" she says, touching his arm.

"I'll handle this," he snaps, whipping around. Then, in a tone marginally softer, "You should be in bed."

She rests a hand on her stomach. My half sister is growing inside, draining the life from my stepmother. At six months pregnant, Meredith still throws up daily, and she's only just finished a long stint of bed rest. Still, doctor's orders dictate she take it easy, and she complies because even after dozens of cutting-edge, astronomically expensive fertility treatments, it took her years to conceive this baby, who's due in February.

She sighs, glancing from Max to me. She must deduce some version of what my dad walked in on, because she arches her professionally shaped brows, bidding the silent question: How dare we disrupt her baby-cultivating sleep?

She gives my dad's arm a squeeze, swivels on her toes, and shuffles down the hall.

Damn it. As crazy as Meredith's capable of making me, her presence was a welcome—if short-lived—diversion. Now Dad's attention is channeled back at Max and me, and his anger hasn't abated.

"Holden, you're lucky I don't keep a gun in this house, because if I did . . ." He pauses, his lawyer's brain considering the threat he's about to discharge. He must think better of it—possible future legal repercussions or Max's challenging home life, I'm not sure—because he pulls in a breath and comes away with a fraction of composure. "I want you out of here. Now."

"Yes, sir." Max's voice drags when he adds, "I'm sorry, Jake. I didn't—"

"Save it!" Dad barks.

As Max moves to exit my bedroom, I feel a pang of envy, watching his relatively painless escape. There's no way I'll be getting off so easy.

But Dad extends a hand, blocking the doorway before Max can disappear into the hall. "Make no mistake," he says, dripping venom. "You're not welcome in my house again unless you're accompanied by an adult, and you are *never* allowed in Jillian's room. Have I made myself clear?"

Max gives a curt nod. "Yes, sir." And, in a move that can only be described as humiliating, he ducks under my dad's arm and passes swiftly down the hall. I startle when the front door slams.

Dad returns his attention to me, but it seems his ire has followed

Max across the street. His shoulders plummet and his face droops and I feel *awful*.

"Jillian," he says. "I'm so disappointed in you."

In seventeen years, I've never given him occasion to utter such a statement. Tears well in my eyes because, God, this sucks. I'd rather suffer the angry shouts he launched at Max than this quiet but deep-seated displeasure.

"I really am sorry."

He heaves a sigh. "Max Holden? Tell me you didn't invite him here."

"I didn't. He knocked on the window. He's having a really hard time."

Creases line my dad's face. The Holdens and the Eldridges have been a unit since he and I moved in across the street a decade ago. Joint holiday celebrations, backyard cookouts, riverside strolls, family vacations—we used to do everything together. I recall the Super Bowl bash Marcy hosted a few years back. By halftime, Dad and Bill were several beers in, joking about how Max and I would probably end up married, which was perfect, Bill surmised, because we'd breed football prodigies with a talent for baking. Dad cracked up—he was a happy member of Team Max back then.

"Max is not your responsibility," he says now. "That kid's on the fast track to self-destruction. He was drunk, wasn't he?"

My lack of answer is confirmation enough.

Dad sighs. "Scouts are supposed to be at his game Friday night. He's going to throw away his chances at being recruited. And *this*." He waves a hand at me, then the floor—the scene of the crime—his mouth twisted in revulsion. "I won't stand for him taking advantage of you."

"He wasn't taking advantage—"

"Uh, doesn't he have a girlfriend?" It's a rhetorical question.

Becky's been a fixture at the Holdens' for ages, first as Ivy's best friend and now as Max's turbulent love affair. *Everyone* knows he has a girlfriend.

"It wasn't like that," I say, but maybe it was. Now that I'm picturing us tangled on the floor through my dad's agonizingly astute filter, I can't deny that Max's motivations were less than romantic. He used me to cheat on his girlfriend, and I willingly participated.

"I expect better from you," Dad says. "Max is intent on being miserable, and you're not the kind of girl to lose sight of her goals for a screwup."

My goals. They've been set in stone for as long as I can remember: graduate high school on honor roll, earn a Grand Diplôme in Professional Pastry Arts from the International Culinary Institute in New York City, and open my own pâtisserie in a charming town, where I'll spend my days baking and serving adoring customers. Nobody's been more supportive of my goals—my *dreams*—than my dad; he's been funneling money into my culinary education fund since I was ten. I just wish he could see that one weak moment won't derail me. I indulged in a careless kiss with my unavailable childhood playmate; I didn't commit grand theft auto.

I'm suddenly very tired. Tired of listening to Dad bash Max. Tired of looking at his drawn expression and the way it contrasts with the inane jack-o'-lantern on his T-shirt. Tired of defending actions I'm not even proud of.

I fake a yawn. "I've got to be up for school in a few hours."

He glances at the digital clock on my nightstand, then scrubs his hands over his face, as if the motion will erase the memory of Max and me horizontal on the carpet. "I thought we were beyond this, Jill, but I'm going to have to set some boundaries."

"Seriously? I made one mistake—"

"One mistake that traces back to one very unstable person. I love Bill and Marcy, but their son's become a terrible influence, and I won't have him taking you down." He pauses, making sure he has my full attention before saying, "I want you to stay away from Max Holden."

3

AD LEAVES THE HOUSE BEFORE DAWN, AN attempt at beating traffic on his way to a meeting in Seattle, and this morning Meredith has an appointment with her doctor—one she doesn't mention until just before it's time for her to drive me to school.

"Catch a ride with Max," she says, hitching a thumb toward the window where his truck sits in full view, warming up in the driveway across the street.

Meredith is perfectly put together, sitting at the kitchen table with her feet up on the chair across from her, sipping green tea from a travel mug. Meanwhile, I bustle around, wiping down counters, collecting stray mail, dumping my dad's breakfast dishes into the dishwasher. There's been a complete role reversal in the six months she's been pregnant, and I don't love it.

"Dad said to stay away from Max."

"Then ride the bus."

"Never."

"What about Ivy?"

I wrinkle my nose, downing the last of my cooling coffee as I hitch the strap of my bag over my shoulder. Riding with Ivy is to risk a Becky run-in—no, thank you—and anyway, I have nothing in common with Max's big sister. She's crème brûlée: fancy and feminine and double-take gorgeous, with a hard outer shell I've never cared to crack. Besides, her car's already gone.

"Jill, just go with Max," Meredith says wearily, resting a palm on her stomach. She does that a lot now—shields the leech baby with her manicured hand—and it's strange. Not that I relate to most of what Meredith does. She and my dad started dating when I was ten, she moved into our house when I was twelve, and there was a wedding a year later. It's not that I dislike her; I just don't get her. She's so . . . pristine.

She slips her feet into the patent-leather flats beneath her chair. "I have to go if I'm going to get to my appointment on time, and you can't let what happened last night make you late for school. It'll be a ten-minute ride. You'll survive, and your father will, too."

Damn it.

Back when she was on bed rest, Meredith often let me take her Saturn to school, and on the occasions she needed it, my dad would drop me off. But I've had to ride with Max a few times, too, on mornings when Meredith's had errands and Dad was tied up with early meetings, and it sucks. Max's truck is cluttered, he insists that every morning begin with twangy riffs courtesy of the Highwaymen, and he's almost always grumpy. But today the horror that was last night clamors around in my head. . . . Max and I kissed, and my dad walked in on us, and that's seven shades of screwed up.

Begrudgingly, I shoot him a text to let him know he gets to play chauffeur, then hurry across the street, littered with a blend of pine needles and pinecones and fallen leaves, to the Holdens' driveway. I pass the truck, exhaust streaming from its tailpipe, and give the front door two knocks before letting myself in, same as I always have.

I find Marcy and Bill in the kitchen. She's still in her bathrobe, pouring steaming water from a teakettle into an oversize mug. He's in his wheelchair, sporting a royal-blue tracksuit and immaculate sneakers that'll probably never touch pavement.

"Morning, sweetie," Marcy says, wrapping me in a hug. She's warm and soft and homey, like fresh-baked cinnamon rolls. She welcomed me into her family's fold the moment my dad and I moved onto the street. She used to do her fair share of babysitting where I was concerned, and she taught me almost everything I know about baking.

When she releases me to tend to her tea, I stretch my mouth into a big smile and walk to where Bill sits. His eyes are on the small kitchen TV, tuned to ESPN as usual, but they move to follow me as I come closer. I assume the louder, livelier tone that comes inherently when I address him now. "Morning, stranger. How's it going?"

He replies with a wobbly grin and jerky nod. He's too thin, birdlike in his fragility, nothing like the indestructible man I used to know. Still, he's Bill; his eyes gleam with familiar amiability. I squeeze his shoulder and move to where Marcy's washing dishes.

She bumps her hip against mine. "Catching a ride with Max?"

"How'd you know?"

"He may have grumbled something about it while wolfing down his omelet. He's upstairs brushing his teeth, but he should be ready soon. How're Jake and Mer?"

"Busy," I say. "Dad with work. Meredith with baby stuff."

"And you? We hardly see you anymore. Find yourself a nice boy to date?"

I swallow back the snicker that comes with that ridiculous question.

The boys in my circle are hardly datable . . . Jesse's blissfully spoken for, Leo's up front about his love-'em-and-leave-'em attitude, and Kyle's not interested in girls. Max . . . he couldn't be *less* datable.

"Nope," I say, casual. "School and work keep me too busy."

"Good girl," Marcy says, drying her hands on a dish towel. "I wish Max shared your priorities—any idea what's going on with him?"

My face practically ignites. God—is she baiting me? "Uh, no . . . Why?"

"He's in the foulest mood. Almost insufferable. Isn't that right, Bill?"

From his place at the table, Bill nods.

Marcy rubs the gold cross pendant she wears on a fine chain around her neck, as if shining it with her fingertips. She waits, hoping I'll share some nugget of wisdom, some brilliant insight into her son's petulance, I guess. The thing is, I do have a rather foggy idea as to why Max might be especially ill-tempered—less than twelve hours ago, he drank too much, fought with his girlfriend, then kissed me, the very *last* person he should be kissing. There's not a chance in hell I'm going to discuss traitorous, drunken hookups with his mom, though.

"Huh . . . Not sure."

"I wish there was something I could do for him." She lowers her voice, leaning in close. "He's taken Bill's stroke so hard—harder than both my girls. I just don't want him to do anything stupid."

I recall the throwaway comment he made last night, about how he could've hopped behind the wheel of his truck after getting pirate-drunk. "None of us do, Marcy."

With that, Max comes thumping down the stairs. He's wearing his letterman's jacket, and a black knit beanie covers his dark hair. He gives me a cursory nod of acknowledgment, mumbles good-bye to his parents, and saunters out the front door.

I hurry to follow.

By the time I reach the F-150, Max has closed himself inside. The unmistakable strumming of classic country leaks from the cab, and a shudder of annoyance ripples through me. I silently curse the automobile gods, because if I had a car of my own, I wouldn't be forced to endure what's sure to be a torturous ride with the most miserable person in all of McAlder.

Still, Max isn't completely ill-mannered; he throws the truck's passenger door open for me. I'm greeted by a gust of heated air and Willie Nelson's nasal voice wailing nonsense about heartache. As I step onto the running board, he murmurs, "Hey."

My foot slips.

"Shit!" I shriek, fumbling for the door handle, barely managing to catch my balance. I heave myself gracelessly into the truck, glaring at my dew-wetted shoes. Nothing like a narrowly avoided crash landing to foil feigned indifference. Max is watching me, I know he is, but my bruised ego won't let me meet his eyes. I buckle up, my cheeks flaming.

"So," he says, backing down the driveway.

"So," I return.

"Sleep well?"

"Fine. You?"

"Eh . . . Got any tests today?"

"Um," I say, thrown by his attempt at conversation. "In French."

"I've got a quiz in civics. Forgot to study."

Shocking.

He doesn't say anything else, so I don't, either. A decade of friendship, and this is what we're reduced to.

Daunted by the prospect of ten minutes of meaningless staccato chitchat followed by cumbersome silences, I fish earbuds out of my backpack and scroll through the music on my phone, searching for something to drown Willie out. Max drums the steering wheel, effectively ignoring me, and I feel a jolt of frustration. What right does he have to be nonchalant? He was the one who came to my window. He was the one who initiated the kissing. He was the one who cheated on his girlfriend. Why am *I* stressing out?

I make myself a promise: I will stop worrying about the sharp-edged dynamic that is my relationship with Max Holden. He doesn't care. Why should I?

He swings the truck out of our neighborhood and onto one of the two main roads in our tiny town—McAlder is, quite literally, a map dot on the fringes of suburbs that've cropped up under Washington's perpetually overcast sky. We live in the shadow of Mount Rainier, among countless evergreens, between two runoff rivers that swell with melted snow and salmon every spring. McAlder's the sort of town where people move to escape the bustle of city life: quaint, but close enough to civilization for an easy commute, which is why my dad chose it after he and my mother, Beth, split up. Career-driven, she moved halfway around the world to cook fine cuisine. Dad, on the other hand, settled in the most family-friendly community he could find (first in a condo, then in the house where we live now), and hired a secretary to lessen his workload so he could spend time with me.

I chance a peek as Max straightens the steering wheel and guns it. He's in his typical driving posture—slightly slouched, one hand hanging at twelve o'clock—wearing his jacket, plus a hooded sweatshirt and faded jeans. He's probably nursing a hangover, and he's sporting his semipermanent scowl, but still. He looks good.

I smother a sigh as he brakes behind a line of traffic. The corners of his mouth turn up and, lightning fast, he snatches my phone from my lap and turns my music off.

I pull my earbuds out, intent on retaliation, and lunge for the dash.

I spin the volume dial, silencing Willie. "How do you listen to that crap anyway?"

Max shrugs in his annoyingly offhanded way, refocusing on the traffic, which is at a standstill in front of us. "It's better than the emo shit you listen to. And since you're set on a music-free car ride, we can talk."

Talking feels like an enormous undertaking, especially in the aftermath of the slop-tastic kiss that never should've been. "Talk about what?"

He gestures to the line of cars idling in front of us. "Maybe you can tell me why traffic's so backed up."

"I have no idea. Accident? Construction?" I reach for my phone, certain our conversational quota for November's been met.

Without taking his eyes from the road, Max swats my hand—the swift reflexes of an athlete. "I thought we were gonna talk?"

I rub the spot where our skin made contact. Tingles. Undeniable, *unwelcome* tingles. "Fine," I say. "Talk."

"How's Meredith? You know, with the baby?"

Not my favorite topic, but better than a certain alternative.

"Okay, I guess. She still gets sick, and her blood pressure's high. Apparently that's a bad thing when you're pregnant. Her ankles look like gigantic sausages. It's disgusting."

"Zoe's looked like tree trunks before Oli was born." He shifts the truck into park, since we're basically gridlocked. He's wearing the adoring expression that always finds its way onto his face when he talks about Oliver, his two-year-old nephew. "I bet your parents can't wait for the baby to get here."

Meredith can't. She won't quit talking about the pregnancy, the nursery, her miles-long list of possible names. It's my dad who's complicating things. One would think he'd be overcome with joy at having another child, especially after Bill's tragedy, but he's anxious about money and work and Meredith's health—sometimes I hear them arguing late at night. And secretary or not, he's never home anymore, which sucks. I'm starting to think he should erect a cot in the corner of his downtown McAlder office.

"Meredith is thrilled," I tell Max.

He turns a mischievous half smile on me. "How weird is it to have solid confirmation that your parents are doin' it?"

I frown. "Not that I've asked or even care to know, but I'm pretty sure this baby was conceived in a petri dish."

He appears confused, but then a lightbulb flickers behind his eyes. "Oh. Jesus. Sorry."

I cringe at the thought of my dad and Meredith "doin' it." Then I wonder . . . Would I be equally revolted by the thought of Dad with my mother, had they remained married? Beth is a celebrated Parisian chef now, distant, save snail-mailed birthday cards and the occasional e-mail. I have no grounds on which to base this presumption, but I doubt she was a frail, sickly pregnant woman like my stepmother. I imagine her with a big, rounded belly, standing before a stainless-steel stove, stirring a stockpot filled with steaming bisque. The notion makes me wistful.

I turn to Max. In my sternest voice, I say, "Let's never discuss Jake and Meredith's sex life again, okay?"

"Yeah, okay," he says, wearing the shadow of a smile. Then, randomly, he asks, "Hey, you thirsty?"

"I don't know . . . I guess."

"I'll be right back." He opens his door, letting in a gust of damp air as he slips out of the truck. He slams it before I have a chance to question him. With my mouth hanging open, I watch him trot across the street and down the block, toward McAlder's only 7-Eleven.

He's been gone ten seconds when, of course, traffic starts to snake forward. I fidget, embarrassed, as a few horns trumpet. It's not long before there's a block of empty road between the front bumper of Max's truck and the car up ahead. I turn around and give the driver behind me a raise of my shoulders and an apologetic smile. He glares, pointing to his watch.

Damn Max and his impulsivity.

Car horns begin to bellow in earnest, discordant as a flock of tone-deaf geese. I sit, helpless and embarrassed, until I spot Max's keys dangling from the ignition—the truck's still running. I unbuckle my seat belt and slide across the bench, then shift into gear and, gripping the big steering wheel, ease my foot off the brake. I've driven plenty of times, but nothing as burdensome as the F-150. I let it coast slowly down the block, appeasing the impatient drivers behind me while keeping an eye out for Max. I can't very well ditch him in the cold, but that doesn't mean I'm not entertaining the fantasy.

And then I spot him, jogging toward me and his barely rolling truck. He's got a huge lidded cup in one hand and a can of Red Bull in the other. I brake and, to a cacophony of horn blasts, shift into park. He opens the driver's-side door and jumps into the seat I'm frantically scooting out of.

I'm a breath from yelling at him for leaving me stranded when he shoves the enormous cup into my hands. "I brought you a soda."

"Oh. Uh, thank you," I say, flustered by his considerate, if ill-timed gesture. Fountain Coke's my favorite—always has been—and he knows as much. Is this his idea of a peace offering?

He pops the top of his Red Bull and revs the truck's engine. Another horn cuts through the fog, blaring far longer than what might be considered polite. Glancing in the rearview mirror, he mutters, "Keep your pants on, asshole," and then we're off.

4

$\mathcal{E}$VEN AFTER WHAT TURNED OUT TO BE a construction delay, Max gets us to school in plenty of time, yammering about another party at Linebacker Leo's this weekend. I'm not sure if it's the Red Bull he downed in a few noisy gulps, or his once-insatiable need to fill silence reemerging like the sun from behind a cloud, but he doesn't shut up until he pulls into his parking space at McAlder High School.

I catch a glimpse of his letterman-jacket-clad teammates hovering in the traffic lanes. Kyle (a junior like Max, Leah, and me) is tossing a football back and forth with Jesse and Leo even though it's misty and forty degrees. They conduct this ridiculous makeshift parking lot practice most mornings, and their combined sense of oblivious entitlement and affable nonchalance always makes me smile. They're hard not to like.

"Thanks for the Coke," I tell Max, winding the cord of my earbuds.

"No problem." He cuts the truck's engine, then watches while I fish a tie from the back pocket of my jeans and gather my hair into a ponytail.

"Why do you do that?" he asks when I've finished twisting the elastic.

"Do what?"

"Wear ponytails all the time."

I check the side mirror to be sure my hair is smooth and, at the same time, dodge what I suspect might be a too-intense expression on his face. "I don't know. I like it out of my way."

He's quiet, expectant, his attention like a weight atop my shoulders, and it feels rude to continue staring quasi-ignorantly at my reflection. Despite the warning bells clanging in my subconscious, I turn to face him.

Big mistake.

His gaze *is* too intense, and now I'm trapped. His eyes hold mine until time extends long and taut. A voice in my head shouts, *Look away!* But I can't—he's trying to communicate using those expressive eyes of his, and something in me, something rebellious and exasperating, is committed to receiving his message.

He leans forward, reaching out. At first I think he's going to touch my cheek and I suppress an anticipatory shiver, but his fingers extend beyond my face to my hair. He wraps the end of my ponytail around his hand in this deliberate, reverent way that whips up a frenzy of questions, the most urgent of which are: *Why is he touching my hair?* and *What the* hell *is he thinking?*

He moves closer and suddenly we're in a vacuum, Max and me, cocooned in the warmth of his truck, the sounds outside distant and insignificant. This intimacy, this spark of connection, is familiar. Last night . . . there were good parts, sweet parts, tucked among the chaos.

I'm tempted to lean into him, but this isn't me—I don't swoon over boys. I don't swoon over *Max*. And yet my heart thuds so forcefully, the truck's likely shaking. His attention falls to my mouth and for a brief, terrifying second I wonder if he might kiss me. Again. Because that worked out *so* well last time.

Still, my breath catches.

The corners of his mouth lift in a smug smile. And then he levels me with the most awkward question ever: "You're thinking about last night, aren't you?"

Despite the recent strain that's plagued our friendship, he knows me well.

"No!"

"Yeah, you are." He pulls back, giving my ponytail a little tug before releasing it. His distance is a relief, and a disappointment. "You didn't get in trouble with your dad, did you?"

"No," I lie again.

"'Cause it was no big deal, right?"

My shoulders rise, then drop.

"I mean, I know I acted like an ass," he goes on—at least *he* can speak the truth. "But things between us aren't gonna be weird, are they?"

Not weird*er*, I guess.

My palms have gone clammy, and eye contact is nearly impossible. I gather the wee bit of poise I've managed to preserve in the wake of this hellish exchange and use it to strengthen my voice. "Please, Max. Give me a little credit."

"Yeah, okay," he says, sounding uncertain. "Me stopping by, the kissing, all of it . . . It's gonna stay between us, right? I mean, it'd suck if Becky found out because"—he glances at me briefly, uncomfortably—"well, you know."

Becky's the last person I want to talk about. The last person I want to *think* about. She and I aren't friends, but I feel like a jerk for letting Max kiss me while they're together. He may've been drunk, but *I* wasn't, and I'm hardly going to go blabbing about the indiscretion I helped facilitate. It's freaking embarrassing.

"I'm not proud of what happened," I tell him in a chilly tone. "So don't worry. Becky won't find out."

"Hey, don't get all angsty. It's just—"

"I'm not *angsty*, and you don't have to explain. She's your girl-friend—I get it. Besides, it was no big deal. You said so yourself."

"Oh, come on. I didn't mean it like that."

The last few minutes catch up to me in a rush of anger, and I swivel in my seat to face him squarely. "God, Max! Just let it go, okay?"

I'm expecting him to counter, and I'm hoping he'll apologize, but he doesn't respond at all; he just stares out the windshield, unaffected, and I'd like to strangle him. Instead, I follow his gaze. Leo uses a giant hand to snatch Kyle's pass from the foggy air. He's laughing, as usual.

Max checks his watch, then retrieves his bag. "You need a ride home?"

"I'll ask Leah to take me."

He stills, one hand gripping the door handle. "Jilly."

I meet his gaze and his expression, now the opposite of unaffected, startles me. It's identical to the one he wore last night, when our kiss met its abrupt end. Frustrated, contrite, yet not entirely regretful. He holds it—mouth tight, brows drawn, eyes swimming with emotion—ensuring that I bear its full weight. Then he shutters all those feelings inside and graces me with a cool smile. "See you around."

He slams the truck's door and heads toward the guys. Jesse launches a pass in his direction and he leaps, snagging the ball from

33

the air like an NFL all-star, graceful and agile, and I almost forget about his mention of Becky and his insensitive reminder that she remain in the dark. I almost forget about the asshole comment he made regarding my so-called angst. And I *almost* forget about the chills I felt when he twined my hair around his hand, and the warmth that erupted in my chest when I thought he might kiss me.

Almost.

5

I CLIMB DOWN FROM THE TRUCK. I'm shoving thoughts of Max into the darkest recesses of my mind, looping one strap of my bag over my shoulder when, from a good fifty feet away, Leo calls, "Jill! Go wide!"

My bag whacks my hip as I whirl around. A football rockets through the air, a blur of russet leather speeding toward my face. With a gasp and a quickness that surprises me, I dodge it—barely. It whizzes past my ear, bounces on the asphalt, and rolls under the bumper of a nearby Kia.

"Jesus, Leo, watch it!" Max shouts. "You almost took her head off!"

Leo chuckles. "Aw, come on, Jill. You're supposed to catch those!"

I stoop to retrieve the ball. "How about a little warning next time?"

"Seriously," Kyle says. "Bruise my best friend's face and I'll be forced to bruise yours."

Jesse taunts, "You should've had it, Jill!"

Leah, Jesse's faithful girlfriend, strolls over. "Give her a break. None of you guys could've caught that pass."

I throw the ball—a perfectly arced spiral—to Kyle. Sinuous and freakishly accurate, he's one of the best quarterbacks McAlder's seen. He's also blond and lanky and far prettier than me; most presume he's in the closet, but nobody cares one way or the other because he's the nicest person ever, and he wins football games. He's all-American with a twist, like apple strudel.

He catches my pass, flashing an appreciative grin. "Nice, Jelly Bean."

I beam at his silly nickname. "Learned from the best."

I don't allow myself to look at Max, but I suspect he's scowling. After all, he was the one who taught me to throw a football, years ago, in the street between our houses.

The soda I drank in the truck—the soda *he* bought me—fizzes in my throat.

Leah blows Jesse a kiss. She's flawlessly dressed—dark jeans, tall leather boots, fitted jacket. Her air of sophistication enviable but matchless. She grins at the mischievous brow raise her boyfriend sends in return, then links her arm through mine. "Ready to head to the quad?"

Part of me would rather hang in the parking lot, tossing the football around with the guys like I might've a few years ago. But a bigger part of me is looking forward to escaping with Leah, who radiates Zen. After the ride I just suffered, I need some girl talk.

We take off for campus. I listen as she chatters, resisting the urge to peek at the guys until we hit the quad, where I allow myself the tiniest backward glance. Max launches a pass and then, by chance, glances in my direction. Our eyes meet, and his expression is strange, unfamiliar and indecipherable. Our shared gaze holds for no more than a second, but that's all it takes for weirdness to come rushing back, a groundless sensation, like I'm floating on the open sea without a grain of sand in sight.

....

"So," Leah says as we meander down a walkway on the quad during lunch, headed for the bench we claimed at the beginning of the school year. Unless it's really and truly pouring, nobody but freshmen eat in the cafeteria, which means the quad's swarming with upperclassmen every day at noon. "I've been thinking about it, and I've decided that you should run for student council this spring."

I laugh, taking a seat on our bench. "No, thanks."

"Why not? You don't do anything after school."

"Uh, I have a job, remember?"

"But do you really need one?"

I unpack my lunch, stifling a snort because yeah, I do. It's not as if my tasks at True Brew are backbreaking—pouring espresso is kind of fun, especially when I share shifts with Kyle, whose parents own the coffee shop, but I sure wouldn't do it for free. The savings account my dad opened for me will take care of the International Culinary Institute's steep tuition, but living in New York's expensive. I'm saving every penny of every paycheck I earn. Leah has no idea how costly NYC is and anyway, she's planning to follow Jesse to Washington State University, a much more economical choice, which is why she thinks my job's superfluous.

"With the baby coming, there are a lot of extra expenses. . . ." My voice trails off as I start to worry, again, about the unacknowledged strain that's seized the Eldridge household. It's heavy, and I wish I could unload, but I'm pretty sure this kind of stuff's foreign to Leah. Her parents, first-generation Korean immigrants who work nine to five at Boeing and come to every home football game to help her cheer Jesse on, never seem to have worries more pressing than whether it'll rain on their freshly washed BMW.

Tucking a stray lock of hair into my ponytail, I pick at my lunch, contributing minimally to the conversation. When I've eaten all I can stomach, I pull out the bag in which I packed a few homemade cookies.

"They're healthy," I tell Leah, offering her one. "Oats and raisins and dates. And, I used applesauce instead of butter."

She's already nibbling. The scent of nutmeg wafts through the air. "Mmm . . . They're divine."

I smile. There's nothing better than watching my friends enjoy my baking.

"Oh, I just remembered," she says, brushing stray cookie crumbs from her lap. "I saw the most adorable newborn outfit at Macy's the other day. A tiny denim skirt with lace-trimmed leggings and a floral peasant top, *and* it was on sale. Tell Meredith she should check it out."

"Will do," I say blandly. While I'm indifferent about the world of children and parenting, Leah can't wait to be a mom. Her life's goal is to marry Jesse (who will undoubtedly take over his share of Hatz-Holden Logging, which his father and Bill founded almost thirty years ago), teach preschool, have litters of babies, and keep a lovely home. Not so different from Meredith, come to think of it.

"Has she picked out nursery furniture yet?" Leah asks.

"I have no idea. I stay far, far away from Meredith and her Pottery Barn catalogs."

She gives her head a dreamy shake. "You're so lucky to be getting a baby sister. You'll be able to hold her and rock her and dress her. Just think about it!"

My brow crinkles. I *am* thinking about it; I'm thinking of what this fetus has already cost me: a healthy, capable stepmother, the easy-going father I used to know, and a whole lot of free time, now spent helping out around the house, filling in where Meredith can't. It's not like I wish the leech baby out of existence—I'm not a monster—but to say I'm looking forward to meeting her would be a serious over-statement.

"And when she's older," Leah goes on, "you can buy her first Bar-bie. You'll be the one who teaches her about boys and makeup and push-up bras."

"Have you forgotten who you're talking to?" I ask with a laugh. "I was brought up by Jake Eldridge, with very little maternal influence to speak of. I never owned a Barbie. I didn't learn how to put on makeup until a few years ago, thanks to Marcy Holden." I look down at my barely-there chest. "And I'm not exactly an expert in the push-up bra department."

"Ah, but you *should* be," Leah says sagely. "Speaking of—"

Something across the quad has captured her attention. I follow her disdainful look to find Becky McMahon standing among half the boys' basketball team. Skinny with ginger hair and apple-green eyes, she's cocaptain of the dance team, along with Ivy Holden. She's also an enormous flirt, as evidenced by the starry-eyed way she's gazing at Bryan Davenport, point guard extraordinaire.

Leah and I look on as she lays a hand on his arm. He's in my trig class and, frankly, he's not very attractive. He says something pre-sumably witless and she cackles, a sound that carries through the quad like the caw of a hungry crow.

"What the hell?" Leah says, shaking her head. "She's a swine."

"Who's a swine?" Jesse asks, approaching with Leo and Kyle at his heels. He sits down next to Leah and drapes his arm over her shoulders.

"Becky," she says, popping the last bite of her cookie into his mouth. "She's always screwing with Max, not to mention making a scene about it."

He's at Becky's side, suddenly, speaking fiercely into her ear as the five of us watch from a distance. She unearths a tube of lip gloss and applies it like Spackle, ignoring him. Max is far from perfect, but I can't believe how awful she's been to him over the last few months. It's like she's forgotten about what happened to Bill, like she doesn't even care that Max has, for whatever reason, deemed himself responsible for his father's stroke. Instead of trying to build him back up, she's egging him on, letting him believe it's cool to drown his unhappiness in alcohol.

When he stops speaking, Becky rolls her eyes and gestures in Bryan's direction. She's red velvet cake—bold and confident, but with a sharpness that puts people off.

Kyle whistles a few bars of "Tainted Love," the theme song he's assigned to Max's relationship with Becky, then shudders. "Jesus. I've never seen two people make each other so miserable."

On cue, Max swivels around and saunters toward us. His hands are shoved deep into the pockets of his jacket, his shoulders bent against the cold.

Becky trails after him, the spiky heels of her boots clack-clack-clacking against the pavement. As they near us, she cries, "Why are you walking away, Max?!"

Anyone with half a brain can see that their relationship is a vicious cycle of provocation and dysfunction, but both of them continue to lope back for more, as if mind games and manipulation are the foundation on which their alleged romance is built.

"Just forget it," Max mutters, eyes on the ground.

"No! What's your problem?"

He shakes his head and it's so pitiful, I can't help myself—I'm standing up, stepping between them, opening my mouth, inserting myself into a fight that's so *not* mine. "You're the one with the problem, Becky. Bryan Davenport? Even you can do better."

"Jill," Max cautions, but his voice lacks spirit.

Becky's face buckles in a glare aimed straight at me. "What goes on between Max and me is none of your business."

"You've made it everyone's business." Out of the corner of my eye, I see Kyle nodding and I'm spurred on, though I'm aware of how grossly hypocritical my next words will be. "If you don't want outside interference, keep your hands off other guys while you're on the quad."

As if drawn by a silent mean-girl summons, Ivy Holden appears. She shares Max's dark hair and gray-blue eyes, but where his features are sturdy and masculine, hers are delicate and soft. Her voice, though—it's sharp as broken glass, and it cuts deep. "Maybe *you* should let my brother live his life."

There's a retort on the tip of my tongue, but I bite it back. There's no point in arguing with Ivy or Becky or anyone else—not on Max's behalf, not while he's just standing there, staring at the pavement like he wants to dissolve into it.

"Max can take care of himself, Jillian," Ivy tells me, slow and clear, like she's talking to a second grader. This is her modus operandi. She's never outright mean, but she exists in a bubble of pretension, and she can make a person feel tiny with nothing more than a look. She's the very opposite of her mother.

"I *know* that."

"It's time you got your own life," Becky says. "And you can start by bumming rides from someone who's not my boyfriend." She lets her gaze rake Max up and down, then adds, "In case you haven't noticed, he's not your little playmate anymore."

He peers at me, just briefly.

I gathered as much last night, when we were making out, I want to tell Becky—the perfect comeback. But I've become mute, and I'm blushing like nobody's business, silently willing the lunch bell to ring. God, I suck at confrontation.

Kyle slings a supportive arm around me. "You're pathetic, Becky. One of these days, Max is gonna wake up and figure that out."

Ivy rolls her eyes, emitting a wispy know-it-all laugh.

And then Max does wake up. He moves a step forward, and I hope he'll take a stand against his sister, who's acting pompous as usual, or Becky, who's treating him like a slab of meat. I hold my breath as he leans in to say something muddled in his girlfriend's ear. She nods, and for a nanosecond I'm grateful to him for emerging from his fog long enough to defuse the tension. But then Becky pushes up on her toes to kiss him hard on the mouth, and while he doesn't actively reciprocate, he doesn't push her away, either. My meager lunch sloshes in my stomach.

"I'll see you after school," she tells him, sultry, *nauseating*, before turning to strut away.

Like she's connected to Becky by an invisible thread, Ivy turns to follow, but Max grabs her arm. "Hey," he says, low and cross. "Stay out of my shit, would you?"

She brushes her bangs back. "Becky's my best friend."

"So what? She doesn't need you to fight her battles."

She lifts an eyebrow, gives me a hostile look, then glances back at her brother. "And *Jillian* shouldn't be fighting yours."

And then she's gone.

"Wow," Leo says, breaking a precarious silence. "Trouble in paradise."

Max shakes his head. "Paradise my ass."

"Dude, why are you still putting up with her?" Jesse asks. When Leah gives him a swift elbow to the ribs, he adds, "What? Just because I'm the only one with balls enough to voice the question we're all thinking?"

"He puts up with her because she puts out," Leo contributes obligingly.

Max sulks while Leah groans and the guys snicker. I scuff the toe of my shoe against the pavement because I fail to see humor in any of this—not the face-off I just took part in, or the fact that Ivy sides with her friend over her brother, or the thoughtless way Max and Becky treat each other. And I don't think his sorry attempts at keeping this thing with her afloat are funny, either. Ninety-nine percent of the time, he's a kicked puppy greeting his abuser with a wagging tail. And that remaining one percent?

He's in my bedroom, kissing me senseless.

6

NOVEMBER DRAGS ON, A BLUR OF MIDTERMS and True Brew shifts. I stay well clear of the Holdens' house, and when I see Becky sashaying down the hallways at school, I avoid her, too.

I can't avoid Dad and Meredith, though—not when their late-night squabbles filter through the walls of my bedroom. She bugs him about his increasing workload, and he carps about her spending unnecessary money. When it's daylight and I can't give them the wide berth they've come to deserve, they nag me: Why can't I help out around the house more?

It's thanks to my parents that I accept Leah's invitation to watch one of the boys' districts-prep football practices on a rare afternoon off from True Brew. The weather's not atrocious, especially for mid-November, and time with her's infinitely better than time at home. We make camp on the rickety bleachers that line the practice field and catch up to the background clamor of colliding helmets and combative grunts.

More than once, I find my gaze traveling to the field, to number eighty, to Max.

He's always been intense about football, and he's *so* good. He catches everything thrown his way, and he runs the ball like a dolphin cutting complex paths through choppy water: innate, fluid, effortless. Of course, that makes his being benched during last week's final regular-season game (because he lost his shit after a questionable call and got in a referee's face) even harder to swallow. But while he was on the field? Flawless.

Leah's my ride home, so I'm stuck waiting outside the locker room with her after practice because she just *has* to tell Jesse what an extraordinary job he did. I make sure to hang back behind her as the team files out—lugging gym bags and smelling collectively of Irish Spring—hidden, should Max emerge before Jesse. But Kyle beats them both, hooking his arms around Leah and me like it's been weeks rather than hours since he last saw us.

"You came!" he says, tossing his head back theatrically. "And to a mere practice!"

"I've come to plenty of practices," Leah says.

"But Jelly Bean hasn't."

"I come to all the home games—just to watch you call perfectly executed plays and drop neat passes into waiting hands."

He grins. "And that's why you're the best."

But I'm not—not really. Outside of work, I haven't seen as much of Kyle as I'd like. I've been dodging him at school because he's almost always with Max, and I've been keeping an enormous secret from him. Leah, too. Neither of them knows about the Halloween kiss, mostly because I'm too mortified to talk about it, and also because I told Max I'd keep it to myself. Becky'd yank my hair out in tufts if she knew my mouth had been anywhere near her boyfriend's. Besides, like Max said, it wasn't a big deal.

Only, maybe it was *kind of* a big deal. . . . Otherwise, wouldn't I have forgotten about it by now, like he apparently has?

Finally, Jesse comes banging out of the locker room. Leah bails on Kyle and me to disappear around the corner with him, and I'm quietly thankful for their consideration. The thought of watching them get all lovey-dovey makes my heart shrivel. Truth is, sometimes I covet what they have: a relationship that's easy, and natural, and mutually beneficial.

I've never had that. I've never even *cared* about that, until . . .

I pull my ponytail free, letting my hair fall around my face. Then I cross my arms, like it's possible to physically shield myself from these thoughts, these memories of that night.

"What's up?" Kyle asks, dropping his bag, leaning up against the wall.

I join him, propping a foot on the brick. "Nothing of importance."

"Really seems like you've got something on your mind."

I have a lot of somethings on my mind, actually, but none fit for sharing. "Oh, you know," I say noncommittally.

"No, I don't." He gives me a side-eye glance, whistling the chorus of "That's What Friends Are For." I laugh, and he smiles. "Seriously, you can talk to me, Jill."

"I know, it's just that—"

The locker room door opens and Max strides out, shouldering a loaded gym bag. He's clearly surprised to see me. "Oh. Hey."

"Hey," I say, wondering if my voice sounds as high, as *nervous*, as it does echoing in my ears.

"Good practice, dude," Kyle tells him.

"Yeah. Thanks. You, too." A thorny silence passes before he tacks on, "What're you doing here, Jill?"

I clear my throat. "Tagging along with Leah. She wanted to watch

Jesse." *I definitely did* not *want to watch you*, I mentally add, pushing my shoulders back.

He's looking at me; I'm staring at the floor, but I feel his attention like a gust of cold air, and I have a million regrets about agreeing to come to this practice, not to mention hang out after. How is it that this boy's able to burrow so deep under my skin?

But then—who's he to act so chilly? He's the maker of his own destiny, and he's chosen to be with Becky, even though it's dazzlingly obvious to any lucid thinker that they make each other miserable. What's it to him if I'm here or not?

"Well," Kyle says with a clap that makes me jump. "This has been a productive chat, but it's time for me to head out. Jill? You need a ride?"

"I can take her," Max says. "Because, you know, it wouldn't be out of the way."

Kyle blinks at Max, then me, wearing an odd smile. "Or, that could work."

God. I'm supposed to make a choice?

"I've got her," Leah hollers. She rounds the corner with tousled hair and rosy cheeks. Jesse follows reluctantly. I shudder to think about what this talk of my transportation interrupted, but Leah doesn't seem to care. She loops an arm through mine, gives the boys a sweet smile, and tugs me down the hall.

Over her shoulder, she calls out an explanation: "Girl time and all."

· · · ·

Thanksgiving is kind of a nightmare. My dad goes into work early and doesn't return until almost four, an hour past when Meredith asked him to be home for our meal. The turkey is dry, and the mashed potatoes are lumpy. I forget to check my pumpkin pie—my beautiful pumpkin pie, with its creamy, spiced filling. Its crust burns, and I end up dumping the whole thing into the trash. Meredith looks close to tears as she excuses herself from the table. Dad shrugs and gives my hair a ruffle before grabbing his laptop, plus the stack of folders he brought home, and retiring to his study.

Tomorrow will be better, I tell myself later, after burrowing beneath my covers.

When sleep doesn't come, I let myself wonder about the Holdens and their Thanksgiving—their first since Bill's stroke. In the past, we've celebrated together, but this year Marcy opted to break tradition and forgo our joint gathering.

"I just don't feel right celebrating," I heard her tell Meredith and another neighbor, Robin Tate, their friend and McAlder's number one gossip, while the three of them sipped tea in our kitchen last week.

Meredith murmured a response, words too soft to be intelligible, but her tone made her sentiment clear: *I don't, either.*

1

EIRDLY, IT'S THE CHRISTMAS SEASON.

I don't feel all that festive, so after a shift spent pulling espresso shots at True Brew the day after Thanksgiving, I do the one thing sure to make me merry: descend into a baking vortex.

A few of my favorite ingredients: toasted coconut, bittersweet chocolate chips, pecans, overripe bananas, and butter. Every respectable treat involves a stick or two of butter—and not that fake, chemically processed yellow paste. It's got to be the good stuff. Unsalted, full-fat butter. I drop a room-temperature stick into a stainless-steel mixing bowl, add sugar, then blend until light and fluffy.

Time in the kitchen is how I reclaim my center, and it just so happens Meredith has a slew of treat requests for tonight's annual Bunco party. Before she married my dad and became Queen of Conception, she was big on volunteer work, and he's a proud member of the city council. All this McAlder community involvement equals dozens of people showing up at our house the night after Thanksgiving to play the world's most obnoxious dice game while drinking too much.

Far be it from me to deny the masses my delicacies.

I've found my happy place. Flour, eggshells, and butter wrappers are strewn over every inch of counter space, and the smells of chocolate and almond and spice dance in the air. The stove's timer sounds. I open the door and spend a moment admiring my beautiful snow-flake sugar cookies—meticulously cut and light golden brown—before gripping the edge of my favorite Williams-Sonoma baking sheet and lifting them from the oven.

Heat radiates into my fingers, conducted splendidly by a pot holder recently crocheted by my stepmother. My brain registers the pain a second too late and I yelp, dropping the baking sheet onto the countertop. It lands with a metallic clatter that echoes through the house.

I assess my fingers—red and throbbing, damn it—and then the cookies. Five of the dozen confections have fractured into jagged, unrecognizable bits. Clenching my teeth against pain and exasperation, I turn on the faucet and run cold water over my tender skin, cursing Meredith and her stupid Holly Hobbie pot holder.

She wobbles into the kitchen, probably drawn by my silent snark. Her volleyball belly has thrown her petite frame into a constant state of unbalance since it popped (her word, not mine) just after Halloween. She's dressed in coordinating sweats, and when I say "sweats," I mean expensive leisurewear from Nordstrom in a soft shade of pink, the only color she wears lately, because when you're expecting a baby girl, you must constantly dress like a puff of cotton candy. She asks, "Everything okay?"

I turn off the water and hold up her pot holder. "Did you know this is ineffective?"

She blinks. "It's pretty."

My pulse throbs in my fingertips. I hold them up to show her. "Pretty doesn't equal practical. What's the point of a nonfunctioning pot holder?"

She holds a hand to her heart. "Jill, a burn? Let me get some aloe."

The last thing I need is her coddling. Having spent much of my childhood with my walk-it-off dad, not to mention rough-and-tumble Max, I've developed a higher-than-average tolerance for pain. Besides, the cold water helped, and upon second inspection, the burn doesn't seem so bad after all. "I'm fine," I say. "Besides, I've got dozens of sugar cookies to finish before tonight, and then there are the peanut butter bars and pecan sandies, plus the pumpkin spice snickerdoodles I want to make for fun."

She gives me an awed smile. Meredith doesn't cook anything for fun. She's the prepackaged angel food cake of housewives: light and airy, easily influenced by bolder flavors.

"Will you still be able to make the brownies?"

There's a sigh building in my chest, but I swallow it. Sliding one of the salvageable cookies from the baking sheet with a spatula, I deposit it on a wire cooling rack. "As long as I start melting the chocolate soon."

She attempts to straighten a cluster of glass magnets on the fridge. Her hands flutter and flit, shuffling them into a jumble as she says, "You saw the list your father left before he went into work, right? He put it on the dining room table this morning so you wouldn't miss it."

Because I spend loads of time in the formal dining room. *Good thinking, Dad.*

Meredith bustles out of the room, presumably to recover the list that's so important my dad left it in a room nobody sets foot in. I sneak a nibble of the crumbled cookie rejects, then dump them into a

Tupperware container in case I need a snack later—they look awful, but taste amazing. Then I retrieve another mound of cookie dough from the fridge. I'm rolling it across a dusting of flour when Meredith returns, waving a sheet of yellow legal paper.

"Okay, here it is," she says, skimming the list. She hesitates. "I can help."

I fight an eye roll. "You shouldn't even be off the couch. Just read it."

"So . . . the tree needs to be decorated, the winter village needs to be set up, the mistletoe needs to be hung, coolers need to be moved down to the basement, and when you get done with all that . . ." She pauses until I look up from my dough, then smiles in the way that's sometimes helpful in exploiting my dad, but has little impact on me. "Maybe you can take care of the hors d'oeuvres?"

I set my rolling pin on the counter—*gently*. "Meredith!"

She's already got a hand in the air. "I know it's a lot. But the tree's up and the hors d'oeuvres just need to be heated and set out—I can definitely help with that."

She *should* be helping—this is her party. She talks my dad into it year after year. *We should know our community, Jake. It's good for networking, Jake. People expect it, Jake.* And this year: *Who cares if I'm pregnant, Jake? Jillian can help!*

I pick up my rolling pin and resume my work with an urgency I lacked before, because I can do this—I can help my parents maintain tradition, a night of normalcy in a year that's been anything but. Besides, this party's as important to Dad as it is to Meredith. He never misses out on a chance to make business connections, hobnob with the neighbors, and put his party basement to use. I'm more than willing to surrender an afternoon to helping out if the result is his satisfaction.

"I'll ask Kyle to come over," I tell Meredith. Football season's over (the boys lost their third-round play-off game—a heartbreaker) and I'm sure he'll be willing to help out.

She grins. "I knew I could count on you."

. . . .

Kyle breezes in shortly after I call, a cloud of cologne and lively chatter. He leaps into the role of sous-chef, and when the peanut butter bars are cooling, the last batch of cookies is iced, and the brownies are baking at three hundred twenty-five degrees, we tackle decorating.

He's putting the finishing touches on the winter village—miniature people, smiles frozen and ceramic—and I'm teetering on a chair, trying to fasten a sprig of mistletoe to the archway between the living room and the front hall, when Meredith appears, belly first, flushed and breathless. "Jillian, I'm in crisis mode!"

My thoughts soar to the baby and I nearly fall off my chair. "What's wrong?!"

"I need you to play Bunco tonight."

I prop a hand on my hip. "Jeez, Meredith! I thought you were in labor!"

She touches her stomach, confused. "Of course not—the baby's months from ready. The Robertsons just canceled because Jackie has the flu. I've got to have you to fill the table."

Only in Meredith's world would uneven Bunco tables equate crisis. "Uh, no thanks."

She gives me a pouty face. "Please! You're my only hope."

"Meredith, no way." Bunco's mindless, all about luck and a shot at winning a few bucks, and tonight's guest list averages well beyond my age bracket. "The game will go on, even without the Robertsons."

"But there should be four people playing at each table," she says. "Otherwise everything will be thrown off."

This is technically true. Though players are forever moving seats and changing partners, the game flows best with quartets. That's why Meredith invited thirty-two people to come over tonight. But that doesn't mean the game's going to fall apart if only thirty show up.

"It is sort of annoying to play with empty seats," Kyle remarks unhelpfully.

I shoot him a dark look. "Even if I play, we're still short a person."

"I'd fill in," he says, "but there's this root canal I've gotta get. . . ."

"Ha-ha," I deadpan.

"It's okay," Meredith says, waving off our banter. "I talked to Marcy. Max'll play."

Incredulity voids my mind of suitable responses.

Kyle's eyes are wide. "Max? Really? Becky's cool with that?"

I manage to find my voice. "Uh . . . is *Dad* cool with that?"

"Jill, your father knows how important this party is. And Max told Marcy he's fine with filling in, but only if you play, too."

Wait—what? Why would Max care if I play? We've said perhaps twelve words to each other since our post-football-practice encounter a few weeks ago. I tilt my head, considering.

"Oh, just play, Jill," Kyle says, sprinkling fake snow crystals over his winter scene.

"Please?" Meredith says. "I *really* need you."

I toy with the sprig of mistletoe I'm still clutching. . . . If Max is getting in on Bunco Night, and if my joining the game means a tally on the Get Back on Dad's Good Side scorecard I started after Halloween, well . . . "Fine," I say, jabbing a thumbtack through ribbon and drywall. "I'll play."

Meredith smiles victoriously before toddling back to the kitchen. I hop off the chair and sink onto the couch with a sigh.

Kyle flops down beside me. "What's with the attitude? It's just Bunco."

"Bunco sucks."

"I bet you and Max'll have fun."

"Yeah, he's a barrel of laughs," I say, and then, like I've stepped through a magical portal, I'm transported to the night of The Kiss. I experience it all over again—the fluttering in my chest, the tingles on my skin, the heat coursing through my blood. How *right* it felt to be in his arms, despite all the reasons it was wrong. I recall the morning after: the fountain soda, Max's joke about his sister's tree-trunk ankles, the way he touched my hair like it was spun silk.

Why can't I let it go?

"Jelly Bean," Kyle says, bumping my knee. "Something's bugging you. What's up?"

I wish I could tell him, then absorb his insight and soak up his guidance. Keeping secrets from him makes me feel ill, but admitting that I was the trite other woman is freaking shameful. More than that, though, I can't find the words necessary for expressing the weirdness I feel when I think about Max now. It's like this door—a door I didn't even know existed—has swung open, giving me a fleeting glimpse of a remote possibility.

Nope.

Not a possibility.

An *im*possibility.

"It's nothing," I tell Kyle, throwing off a blanket of longing. "We should get back to work, don't you think?"

We do, and when we're finished, he kisses my cheek and takes off, probably worried he'll end up roped into Bunco, too.

I drag myself down the hall to shower, then consider my closet's offerings. I pick my best jeans, dark denim that hugs my butt, and the shimmery sleeveless top Meredith gave me for my last birthday. It's unsuitable for the November chill, but hey, Max is apparently playing Bunco because I am. Why not be a sparklier version of myself while taking part in a game I hate with a boy I'm suddenly hot-and-cold for?

When I'm dressed, I blow my hair out and curl it into soft waves. Then I tackle my makeup, finishing with gloss that leaves my lips with an objectionable sticky feeling.

Anti-kissing gloss.

Tucking the tube into the pocket of my jeans, I take a deep breath and attempt to get my shit together before Max and his family arrive.

8

I'M SURPRISED TO FIND MY DAD ON A kitchen bar stool when I descend the stairs. He's not on time for Bunco; he's *early*. He's using a toothpick to spear a Swedish meatball from the Crock-Pot, but he pauses to let out a low whistle as I walk into the room. "Dressed up for Bunco, I see."

"Don't start," I say, but there's no denying I'm pleased. Over the last several months—since Meredith announced her pregnancy and Bill suffered his stroke—our once indestructible bond has weakened. Since he's barely spared me a glance since that horrible Halloween lecture, a compliment aimed my way feels special.

He pops a steaming meatball in his mouth. He's a foodie, but he's cool with bar snacks, too, so long as they fit the occasion. "These aren't bad."

"One of Meredith's specialties," I say, taking stock of the kitchen. All of the counter space is occupied by warming hors d'oeuvres, and the air is heavy with the scents of sourdough bread, melted cheese, and caramelized onions. "Frozen meatballs that've spent hours marinating in their own grease."

"In other words, *gourmet*," he says with a wink.

Dad met my mother at a chef's tasting just as he was beginning to practice real estate law. They married, Beth further cultivated his love of fancy cuisine, I was born, and then she had an existential crisis and flew the coop, leaving them bitterly estranged. Even after she left, though, Dad hung on to his passion for fine fare. Once I was old enough to behave myself, he and I started spending Saturday evenings dining at the best restaurants in Western Washington, critiquing flavor and texture and presentation. I've never shied away from trying new foods with unique ingredients, though dessert's always been my favorite course. Dad's partial to expensive cuts of steak and stoutly brewed beer.

Saturday night dinners ceased when Meredith pranced into our lives.

Dad tweaks one of my curls. "I hope you didn't get gussied up for the Holden kid."

My cheeks warm. Tonight'll be the first time he and Max share space since Dad caught the two of us groping each other. "He's only playing because Meredith asked him to," I say. "Same reason I'm playing."

"Hopefully he'll be able to keep his hands to himself."

I become very involved adjusting cookies on their platter. "Dad, Halloween—what you saw—that was a one-time thing. A mistake. Remember? Max has a girlfriend."

"I could give a damn. That kid can have a whole harem of girls waiting to fulfill his every need, so long as none of them is my daughter. Understood?"

"Yeah. Understood." I'll acquiesce to pretty much anything if he'll shut up about harems and hands and *fulfilling needs*.

He's watching me, his expression serious. "Try to remember, Jill. You deserve better."

The compulsion to defend Max is strong—we've got too significant a history for me to tolerate his name being dragged through muck—but contesting my dad is pointless; he argues for a living. I roll my neck to ease the tightness this exchange has caused.

Dad points the end of his toothpick at me. "I don't want him in your room—not tonight, not ever. Got it?"

"Got it."

I watch as he pops another meatball into his mouth. His hair's chestnut like mine, though his is beginning to gray at the temples, and his eyes are deep brown, a reflection of my own. He's like whole wheat bread, sturdy and steadfast, and I try not to hold his dislike of Max against him. I know he's got my best interests in mind. At the moment, though, a change in topic seems like a brilliant idea.

"I baked a veritable banquet of desserts for tonight," I tell him, and then I go on to list the confections I spent all afternoon perfecting.

"Doesn't surprise me," Dad says. "You're already making a name for yourself in McAlder. You know, I actually heard someone refer to you as Master of All Things Delectable the other day?"

"You did not."

"I absolutely did. And I thought, 'That's my girl!'"

I smile. "Just wait until I learn all there is to know from the International Culinary Institute. I'll blow this town away with my treats."

Meredith breezes into the kitchen. She's wearing a coral sweater-dress, and her flaxen hair, freshly trimmed, grazes her shoulders. Her eyes are bigger than a Disney princess's. "The International Culinary Institute?" she says. "I thought that wasn't happening."

I laugh, a terse sound. "Of course it's happening."

"But . . . the money."

"What about the money?"

My dad gives the front of his hair a nervous tug. "I, uh—"

"Dad, what's she talking about?"

Meredith smooths her dress, plainly apprehensive. "Oh, Jake. You haven't told her?"

"Told me what?"

My dad discharges a heavy sigh, sending his wife a reproachful look before settling his gaze on me. "Jill, I've been meaning to talk to you about this." If his tone was solemn when he was warning me about Max, it's downright grim now. "I didn't want to tell you *tonight*, but . . ."

My heart thuds in anticipation of what's obviously bad news. "God, Dad. But *what*?"

"Your culinary school fund . . . It's become unavailable."

"Unavailable?"

Meredith winces as he amends, "It's gone, Jill. The money is gone."

It feels like there's a lump of yeasty dough expanding in my throat. "Gone? *How?*"

My parents exchange a glance doused in guilt. "It went toward Meredith's medical expenses. Our health insurance doesn't cover fertility treatments, and Mer's been through years of them. The costs became a mountain of debt, and that money was sitting in an account, collecting pennies of interest. It only made sense to use it."

My mind's racing, and I feel, suddenly, like I'm going to be sick.

"Otherwise," Dad's saying, his voice far away, "we'd be so far in the hole, we'd never climb out. That's no way for a family to live. I know you were counting on that money, but using it to help cover Mer's infertility treatments was the most responsible choice."

Gone.

Thousands and thousands of dollars, saved for years and years.

Money earmarked for me. For the International Culinary Institute. For my Grand Diplôme. Now funneled toward my stepmother and the leech baby who's holed up in her belly.

My eyes burn. I can't believe my education wasn't a priority. A *consideration*. I can't believe they emptied the account without a word about it to me.

"Jill, I'm so sorry," Meredith says quietly.

"I know this is a surprise," Dad says, "but you have more than a year to make the money back. We'll do everything we can to help."

Make the money back? Laughable. I've got a savings account of my own funded by my True Brew paychecks. It might get me a *plane ticket* to New York.

"I'm sorry," Dad says. "I really am."

The compulsion to run, to bury myself in my bed and stay there through the weekend, weeping until I'm emptied of tears, is nearly unbearable. This is a blow, a dream-shattering, destiny-crushing blow. My breath comes shallow, like I've been punched in the gut.

"You understand, don't you?" my dad says.

I don't understand—not even a little bit, and not even when I try to view his news objectively, through my most altruistic filter. My emotions boil over, riotous and wrathful. "No, I don't understand! You've ruined everything—my whole future!"

Meredith moves to touch my hand, but I snatch it out of her reach. This is her fault just as much as it's his.

"Jill, it'll work out," my dad says.

"You don't know that. You don't know anything! God, Dad, how could you do this? How could you not tell me?!"

He flounders and I wait, my hands balled into fists, desperate to hear how he'll justify his actions, this secret he's been keeping for who knows how long.

He's opening his mouth to respond when the doorbell rings, sparing him an explanation. The relief that washes over his face is infuriating.

"Probably the Holdens," Meredith says, eyeing Dad. She looks like she's seconds from laying into him—because he didn't tell me about the money, or because her party's in danger of being ruined? "Marcy said they'd come a few minutes early. Would you let them in, Jill?"

I balk, huffing out a petulant breath.

"*Please*," Meredith says.

I only do as she asks because I can't stand to look at her or my father another second.

I march toward the foyer in a daze of dashed aspirations. I'm tempted to veer off course, to detour to my room, to blow this stupid party off completely—it's not like commitments mean anything in this household—but then it occurs to me that Max is likely standing on the front porch, and the prospect of seeing him keeps my feet moving in the direction of the foyer. If anyone can distract me from what just happened in the kitchen, it's him. I swallow past the brick of disappointment lodged in my throat and swing the front door open.

Most of the Holden clan stands before me. Marcy's all smiles; she hired a nurse to sit with Bill while she spends the evening at our house, a rare reprieve from her husband's care. Ivy's filling in as her date, and it's entirely possible Marcy bribed her for the privilege of her company. The oldest Holden offspring, Zoe, who acts fifty-six instead of twenty-six and lives an hour north, stands with her husband, Brett, whose parents are watching Oliver while they get their Bunco on. And then there's Max.

"Hey," I whisper, feeling raw and exposed.

There's a weird moment of silence during which they all just stand there, staring at me, and I wonder if they can see, somehow, my life's goals lying in fragments at my feet.

Marcy passes Ivy the bottle of wine she's holding and reaches out to hug me. "Jill! You look lovely, sweetie."

I return her hug, savoring its momentary comfort, then greet the others in turn, forcing a wooden smile. Brett, carrying a casserole dish with pot holders, bends to kiss my cheek and says, "I hope you were in charge of desserts." Zoe, in a buttoned-up gray cardigan, sweeps my hair over my shoulder and says, "You really do look nice." Ivy, wearing a ruby-red bustier and skinny jeans, dark hair mirror-shiny, gives me a quick once-over before saying, "Who're you trying to impress?"

I lift my chin indignantly. "No one."

She glances at Max, then back to me. "Whatever."

I'm glad when she brushes by, taking her superiority with her, but now Max and I are on our own. He hangs back, dressed in jeans and a blue cotton button-down. Hatless, with a five o'clock shadow, he looks . . . good. His mouth bobs open, like he has something to say but can't retrieve the words. He closes it after all, letting his eyes travel over me—my made-up face, my loose hair, my cuter-than-average outfit—and my heart loses its footing.

When I'm sure I can't survive his scrutiny another second, he says, "Your dad's not hiding around the corner, waiting to kick my ass, is he?"

My dad. *God.*

I shake it off—the loss, the hurt, the anger, the confusion. I'll deal with it, think about it, *feel* it tomorrow, when I'm alone, but tonight maybe I don't have to—not if I'm with Max.

He leans closer and whispers, "Really, is he cool with me being here?"

"It's fine. Meredith wouldn't have invited you if it wasn't. Still, it might be best if we steer clear of him."

"Oh, believe me," he says, stepping into the house, "I plan to."

Bunches of neighbors roll in shortly after the Holdens, until the kitchen and the living room are packed with people. Max and I hang back, hugging a wall. He takes a surprising stab at chitchat, but it's halted and uncomfortable, probably because of me, and I'm pretty sure this is going to be the longest night ever.

"How was Thanksgiving at the Eldridge house?" he asks, clearly grasping at straws.

"Lame. How was Thanksgiving at the Holden house?"

"Shitty. My mom bought a soggy, precooked turkey, then insisted we sit at the table and express our gratitude even though no one was feeling all that thankful. After dinner, Ivy sulked in her room, and Zoe bitched at Brett for sharing whisky with me while we watched football. My dad just sat there, staring at us like he barely knew us— like he didn't *want* to know us."

A moment of clarity forces my perspective to shift; lost college money is very, very bad, but Max's dad almost *died*, and even though he didn't, he's forever changed—all of the Holdens are. "God, Max. I'm sorry."

"Life blows," he says with a shrug. "Anyway, think I could snag a beer?"

I arch a brow. "Is that a good idea?"

"Yes, *Mom*, it is. It's Bunco Night—we're gonna liven things up." He grins and I'm wavering. It must be obvious, because he adds, "Come on, Jill. You and me."

It's not like he has to get behind the wheel later, and tonight of all nights, I could use something to dull the ache of my drained account.

Besides, my dad said to keep Max out of my room. Never once did he say to keep him away from the booze.

"Coolers are downstairs," I say. "I'll show you."

He follows me to the basement. Back when my dad was working with an architect on the plans for our house, he'd been all about the party basement, a room that could accommodate his pool table and a fully stocked bar and the biggest TV on the market. Before Bill's stroke, he and Dad used to spend *College GameDay* Saturdays and *Monday Night Football* evenings down here, drinking and shouting obscenities at the refs. It's been a while since this room has been used for its intended purpose—socializing—but tonight it's crowded with people, card tables, and folding chairs. The lights are low, and flickering candles that smell of vanilla and spruce are scattered across the bar. Dad and Meredith mill around, faking it, I assume, making sure newcomers have drinks and are clear on the oh-so-complicated rules of Bunco.

They avoid eye contact with me. I oblige.

I lead Max to the row of coolers Kyle and I lined up earlier. I keep watch while he stoops and paws around in the ice until he finds the brand he prefers—cheap and light—then pulls a red plastic cup from the stack teetering on the bar. He tilts it and pours expertly.

"What about you?" he asks, dropping the empty bottle into the recycling bin.

"Um . . ."

"Oh, come on, Jilly," he says, eyes gleaming with mischief. "Let's get crazy."

My knees nearly buckle as I imagine a series of *very* crazy scenarios.

Dad's voice echoes in my head: *I expect better from you.* But guess what—*I expected better from him.*

Besides, what's so wrong with getting a little crazy?

"Fine," I tell Max, "but I don't like beer."

"How 'bout I mix you a drink?"

I scan the room again. Marcy's chatting with Ivy, Meredith's wrapped up in a conversation with Zoe and Brett, and Dad's talking with Meredith's friend, Mrs. Tate. She's got him good and occupied, sharing all sorts of juicy dirt, I bet.

I nod at Max, who quickly and surreptitiously grabs another cup and fills it with ice, a generous splash of rum, and Coke. I take the cup from his outstretched hand and sample. The rum burns my throat, but combined with the sugary soda, it's not bad.

He flashes me a smile, *the* smile, the one that makes me feel far less inhibited than I should. "Well?"

"Yum," I say after a second sip.

Meredith calls my name from the other side of the basement, and I pick my way through the crowd. She's all lit up, entrenched in her role as sparkling hostess, but once I'm standing in front of her, she drops the act. Softly, she says, "Jill, I really am sorry. Your dad . . . I had no idea he hadn't—"

"I don't want to talk about it," I say brusquely. I take a swig of my drink, practically daring her to ask if it's spiked. She doesn't.

Instead, defeated, she asks, "Will you go over the rules with Max? We'll start soon."

I turn away to retrieve him from a football-centric conversation and sit him down at the head table. I give him an overview of the game, the four rounds, the luck necessary in rolling three dice for specified numbers, the point system for which he'll use his own scorecard, and the number of chances he'll have to roll. I keep my attention on our tutorial, but I feel his fixed stare, as if the ins and outs of Bunco aren't mind-numbingly boring.

When I'm done, he takes a long drink of his beer, watching me over the rim of his cup, then says, "I like your hair that way."

Before I can give what will almost certainly be an awkward response, I spot Ivy on the other side of the room. She's standing with Zoe and Brett, but she's not paying attention to what they're saying. She's watching Max and me, her eyes darkened with suspicion. Because I'm sitting with her brother—her best friend's boyfriend.

I scoot my chair away from Max's as my dad holds up a hand to quiet the room. "Let's get started," he says when the buzz of voices has faded. "Refresh your drinks and find a seat."

I remain at the head table. Max doesn't make any effort to move either, and it's not long before Meredith and Marcy join us, rounding out our quartet. Meredith seems to have recovered from our non-conversation; she shines like a lightbulb while Marcy quizzes her on baby names. Max takes another gulp from his cup. I fidget in my chair like a kindergartner who needs a bathroom break. What a delightful picture the four of us must make.

"Jill," Meredith murmurs as we wait for stragglers to find seats. "Really. Are you okay?"

"I'm fine."

"But you look flushed."

"Well, I feel *great*." I sip from my cup and inspect my scorecard, hoping she'll shut up. Easily sidetracked, she begins to discuss nursery colors with Marcy, paint names like Rosy Cheeks, Sassy Lilac, and Lush Meadow.

Max plucks a mini candy cane from the dish in the center of our table and tears the cellophane. He snaps the peppermint in half and passes me the curved piece. "You *do* look flushed," he whispers with fake concern and a shit-eating grin.

I slip the candy into my mouth as Meredith rings a bell to begin the game.

As the first round gets under way, my age-old theory about Max Holden being incredibly lucky is confirmed. On his first turn, he racks up eight points. Alternatively, my first turn earns two. He catches my eye often as we roll and pass, roll and pass. For a moment, I entertain the notion that he's watching me, which is absurd. Sure, I'm a polished version of my usual self, and generationally we're outnumbered, but Max has little reason to pay me attention.

He has Becky.

Bunco moves quickly; it's a game without strategy, which makes it perfect for socializing. The first round's over before I know it. Max takes my cup and mixes me a refill while I switch seats for the second round. I've found my spot by the time he returns with my cup. He has to lean over me to place it on the table, and as he does, his arm brushes my bare shoulder. I'm almost positive it's intentional, and my skin erupts in a flurry of goose bumps.

"Thanks," I say, tipping my head to look at him. His eyes are dark as rain clouds; the word *brooding* pops into my head. "How're you doing?"

"I've won four of six. I think that's pretty good." He peeks at my card, sees my one measly win, then laughs, dropping a hand to my shoulder. "Bunco's not your thing, huh?"

The warmth of his palm seeps into my skin and wit fails me. I scan the basement for my dad and find him at the bar with Marcy and Mrs. Rolon, the bottle blond who lives down the street. He's refilling their wineglasses, laughing at something Marcy's just said, oblivious to the fact that the neighbor kid is giving his daughter heart palpitations with a shoulder squeeze.

"It's cool," Max tells me. "I'm doing well enough for the both of us."

I try to recall the last time he and I were *us*.

Dad's voice carries over the clamor of conversation: "Tables, everyone!"

I turn to find him staring at me. He doesn't look happy. Maybe because of our earlier discussion, or maybe because I'm with the very boy he expressly told me to stay away from. I don't care either way, but apparently Max does.

He snatches his hand away. "I should, uh, find my seat."

"Okay," I say, sorry to see him go.

I try to appear useful and collected, not flustered and tipsy. I rearrange the dice. I reposition the snack bowl. I make needless marks on my scorecard. My pulse resumes a seminormal pace as the three empty seats at my table fill.

Time for round two.

9

THE EVENING PASSES, DICE ARE ROLLED, DRINKS are downed. At halftime, I escape up the stairs, buzzed and oddly buoyant. Behind the locked door of the powder room, I assess my reflection in the mirror. My hair holds the curl I coaxed into it, but I'm critical of my scarlet cheeks and the longing that shines too bright in my eyes. There's no denying that Max's attention makes me feel good, but it makes me edgy, too. He's going through a rocky time and as of tonight, I am, too. Plus there's his girlfriend, who'd explode in a ball of fiery rage if she caught her boyfriend and me flirting.

I take a long swallow of my drink, then a few deep breaths, trying to break up the knot of worry that's landed in my stomach. The girl in the mirror stares at me, wild-eyed and wanting.

There's a knock on the bathroom door, and I remember: there's a party in full swing downstairs. I wash my hands, comb my fingers through my hair, and smooth on a fresh layer of lip gloss. As I'm slipping the tube back into my pocket, the door clatters with another knock. I yank it open, ready to give whoever so obviously lacks patience a piece of my mind, but it's Max who stands in the hall. He gives me a discomfited smile and steps aside so I can join him.

"Took you long enough," he says. "What the hell were you doing in there?"

I give a cryptic raise of my eyebrows.

He chuckles and lifts his hands in surrender. "Okay, never mind."

"What are you doing up here?"

"I'm ready for another," he says, showing me his empty cup. "Your dad gave me a look last time I went near the coolers. There's beer in the kitchen, right?"

"Yep. Come on."

He follows me into the empty kitchen, where I take a beer from the fridge and hand it to him. He twists the top and takes a long pull. I watch with interest as he swallows, his throat bobbing in a way that's far sexier than anything I've seen in my seventeen years.

He sets his bottle on the counter. "Headed back down?"

"In a few minutes."

"Avoiding the crowd?"

"Something like that."

He hoists himself up to sit on the countertop, the spot where Kyle and I mixed brownie batter this afternoon. "Mind if I hang out till the break's over?"

My heart, the mutinous thing, dances a two-step. "Yeah. Okay."

He takes another swig of beer, then asks, "So? You having fun?"

For a nanosecond, I consider telling him about my lost money, the pastry-chef piece of my heart that's been ripped out and stomped on. But then, "Uh, I guess."

"I am. I always have fun when you're around, Jilly."

I guzzle my drink, his breathy words replaying in my head. My face is so hot. Because of him? The rum?

"We should hang out more often," he says. "You and me. It's never just you and me anymore."

"Yeah, well, your friends keep you busy. So does your girlfriend."

He shrugs. I try to get a handle on his expression, which is a lot like attempting to read hieroglyphics. "Still," he says. "I miss you."

My stomach takes a nosedive, landing somewhere in the vicinity of my toes. "What am I supposed to say to that, Max?"

"Nothing. It's cool."

Clearly it isn't. I don't know whether to celebrate or cry.

He saves me from the probable humiliation of jamming my foot into my mouth. "So, Bunco . . . I had no idea this game was so cutthroat."

"Right?" I say, glad for the change of subject. "You'd think we were playing for blood instead of cash."

He hops down from the counter and gestures for my cup. I pass it to him and he fills it three-quarters with ice and Coke. "I'll fix this for you downstairs," he says. "You ready?"

I nod, then trail behind him, through the kitchen and into the living room. But he stops suddenly, just short of the stairs, and I almost crash into him as he pivots to face me. "Listen," he says, pushing a hand through his hair. "What happened on the quad a few weeks ago, Becky being Becky, treating you like shit . . ."

"Max, I've forgotten all about that."

"Yeah, well, I haven't."

"You don't—"

He holds up a hand. "Just let me, okay? I'm not excusing her, but she has her reasons for acting the way she does, which mostly have to do with me. Ivy's not helping, either, but none of that matters because my point is, I was a dick for not stepping in. I should've told her to shut up." He runs a palm over his face; he looks supremely uncomfortable—a lot like how I feel. "Anyway, I just . . . I wish it hadn't gone down like that, and I'm sorry."

His admission of fault is stunning—I can't remember the last time he accepted culpability for anything. But I don't want to talk about Becky. Not tonight. Not ever. "It's fine," I manage.

"You sure?"

"Of course. I've let it go." I mean it—I'm going to forget my frustrations concerning him and Becky. Him and *me*.

He's standing, motionless, in the warm glow of the living room lamps, gazing down at me. His enormous ego appears to have withered; he's almost reticent. "Jill," he says, low and tentative, "do you ever think about what happened on Halloween?"

"Um . . . ?" The conversation? The kiss? The revulsion splashed across my dad's face when he discovered us?

"Because I do, sometimes." He smiles, adorably sheepish. "Is that weird?"

My eyes find the floor, to which I say, "No. I think about it. Occasionally."

"I know I was a mess. And I know your dad was pissed—hell, he's probably still pissed. But . . ." He hooks his fingers with mine, a charming, innocent gesture. "It wasn't *so* bad, was it?"

"It wasn't bad. It was—"

From the basement, my dad's jolly voice: "One minute until game time! Tables, people!"

Max yanks his fingers back. His gaze darts around the living room. We're alone. I'm relieved, but sour, too, because I think what we were about to have was a moment—a moment we need to figure out what's going on between us—and it was interrupted. Again.

"Jillian? Max!" Dad, not so jolly anymore.

"Come on," Max says. "Jake'll strangle me if he catches us together, and we still need to top off your drink."

I have the presence of mind to keep a respectable distance from Max as we descend the stairs, but my dad still slaps me with a look of irritation, which I ignore. I take my seat and sneak peeks at Max as he wanders with practiced nonchalance to the bar. He pours the beer he's kept tucked behind his back into a more discreet cup, then doctors my Coke with a splash of liquor. There's a lucky disturbance in the corner of the basement—it seems Mrs. Rolon has knocked her glass of red wine onto the alabaster carpet; Meredith's comforting her while Dad sops up the mess—and Max is able to return my full cup without half the town watching.

The game begins again, more uproarious than before, and it isn't long before Max and I find ourselves back at the same table. He weasels his way into the chair to my left while busybody Mrs. Tate and her husband, Officer Tate, round out our foursome. Officer Tate gives Max's cup a curious look but must think better of raising concern. This is a party, after all, and he's off duty. Besides, the Tates don't have kids—her job as a hospice nurse and his commitment to law enforcement are their life's purpose. Maybe Officer Tate assumes Max isn't stupid enough to drink in a roomful of adults.

Max *isn't* stupid; he's fearless. He used to use pieces of scrap lumber to build bike jumps in the street. He used to climb out of his second-story window, then launch himself off the roof, landing on the trampoline below. He used to wade into the river with nothing but an inner tube and a heap of gumption, and let the current carry him a mile downstream. After, he'd hoof it back up the bank for another run.

I love his courage, and sometimes I really hate it.

When the round begins, Mrs. Tate rolls the dice with a focus that makes me want to laugh out loud. I swallow my drink in an effort to suppress my giggles, while Max gapes at her antics. Her face is bright red, clashing with her strawberry-blond hair—and her movements are sloppy, like she's had one glass of chardonnay too many. Still, she's racked up some points by the time she's finished. "Your turn, Jill," she laments, passing me the dice.

I sweep them up and roll. Two fours and a three, a near Bunco. Officer Tate claps politely. I roll again and watch as the dice tumble to the table. Two more fours. Huh . . . Is it possible I've found a groove?

There's a bump against my ankle as I pick the dice up for another turn. I ignore it, but it happens again. Subtly, I glance to my left. Max is waiting for me to roll. His mouth quirks into a smile as he nudges my calf, gently but deliberately. I curb the impulse to gawp, but I'm floored that even *he* has the balls to play footsie within spitting distance of my dad.

"Jillian, it's still your turn," Mrs. Tate prods.

I dump the dice. They hit the tabletop with a clatter: two fives and a one. So much for my groove.

The game continues in a blur. My mind hops back and forth, agonizing over my dad's mandates regarding Max and my compulsion to let loose—with Max.

I ask myself, *Why not raise some hell?*

My cup seems to possess a bafflingly bottomless quality. How many times has Max refilled it? I've lost count, but that's mostly because I've been so busy marveling at him. Against all odds, he's become the life of the party, cheering with neighbors, fist-bumping people three times his age, and laughing, loud and jovial. His liveliness fills me with affection so acute, my mouth stretches into an irrepressible grin.

When the final round of the game comes to a close, my lips are pleasantly numb, my shoulders are loose, and my mind is free of worry. . . . Bunco *is* fun!

I spot Max drifting toward me. In a feeble attempt to look occupied, I count the wins on my scorecard, a task that takes all of a half second because I've only won three of sixteen games.

He sidles up next to me and counts aloud, ". . . eleven, twelve, thirteen, fourteen. Plus a couple of Buncos. Pretty good, right?"

"Uh, yeah," I say with a disbelieving shake of my head.

He takes my card and turns it and his own in to Meredith, who's tallying scores and divvying prize money. Our fellow Bunco players swarm the bar, waiting for the announcement of winners. Max returns to my side, standing brazenly close, his warmth running the length of my arm. "If I win," he murmurs, "I'm gonna use the cash to take you to dinner."

I'm unquestionably drunk, but even so, that strikes me as a terrible idea. The specific reasons why are scattered around in my head, and I work hard to sort them out. Dad and Becky are obvious roadblocks, but even if I momentarily discount them, there's still a problem. . . .

What if Max and I give dating a shot, and it doesn't work out? Our families are already cracking under the weight of inescapable change; we hardly need to toss the drama of a failed romance into the mix.

I look up to speak of reason and responsibility, but I become distracted by the shape of his jaw, angular and unyielding, as if carved from stone. His eyes flicker and flash in the candlelight. A flirtatious voice—my voice?—says, "Dinner? I'm going to hold you to that."

Somewhere, someone taps a glass, and I seek out the sound. My dad, holding a pilsner and a spoon, watching us with unconcealed exasperation. Max shifts away as Dad's gaze zeros in on me—*Watch it!*—before he transitions into his host persona. "First, the booby prize," he says. Low laughter rumbles through the room. Everyone knows it's the lowest scorer who receives the booby. "This year, the booby goes to . . . our very own Jillian!"

I make my way toward him amid a smattering of applause, face flaming, feet clumsy. He gives a phony grin while Meredith hands me an envelope in which two ten-dollar bills are tucked—hardly a prize worth listening to my father use my name and the word *booby* in the same sentence.

I pass the better part of Max's family on my way back through the crowd; Marcy squeezes my hand in congratulations, Zoe and Brett give me twin thumbs-up, and Ivy points her nose in the air. Typical. I let her snub roll off my shoulders, listening as the prize for third place is announced: Mrs. Tate, who pumps her fists in the air like she's just completed a marathon. She hugs Meredith, then my dad, nearly knocking him into the wall as she throws her arms around his neck.

Max muffles a snicker and slides behind me. The crowd hides our closeness, his solid chest pressed flush against my back. He's gravity, binding my feet to the floor. Lucky, because I'm perilously close to floating into the stars.

"Are we almost done here?" he whispers.

My heart beats loud as thunder. "Mm-hmm." And then, because I've lost my inhibitions and apparently my mind, I say, "Want to hang out after?"

A split second of torturous silence passes before he answers, "Definitely."

10

THE SIGNIFICANCE OF HIS CONSENT SLAMS INTO ME.
Dad's still talking, announcing the prize for second place, a faceless neighbor I take no notice of. I'm too consumed by what's to come when this godforsaken ceremony is over.

Max is presented with first prize, and Meredith hands him an envelope stuffed with money. He grins and bows to a round of applause, confident and gracious all at once. My dad looks on, irked.

The party dies down after the cash is distributed. Guests trickle up the stairs and out the front door. Officer Tate hauls Mrs. Tate to the foyer, because she's apparently too sauced to walk on her own, and Brett has his arm draped around Zoe as if she's a human crutch— she looks annoyed as she drags him across the street to where their minivan's parked in the Holdens' driveway. Meredith makes a pot of coffee and distributes mugs to Dad, Marcy, and Ivy, who are milling around with almost-empty platters of food, Bunco supplies, and trash bags full of greasy paper plates and sticky cups.

I'm exhausted and dreading my early shift at True Brew, but I linger with Max in the kitchen, sitting beside him at the breakfast bar, watching him drain his beer and devour leftovers like he hasn't eaten in weeks. Meredith buzzes around like a housefly, cleaning single-mindedly: scraping trays, sweeping crumbs from the stove, clanking empty bottles into the recycling bin, anything that doesn't require heavy lifting.

Max gives her a dubious look, then shovels an entire brownie into his mouth. He chews discerningly, then asks me, "Did you make these?"

"Obviously." As if Meredith is capable of such delicacies. "Kyle helped."

"They're incredible." He grabs another before she pulls the plate out from under him. I roll my eyes at her back.

"The secret is to add a little coffee to the batter," I tell him. "And for the chocolate chunks, I buy the best bars I can find. Belgian, usually. And cocoa powder—the darker the better. It makes the brownies much richer." I'm rambling, I realize, about baked goods. I snap my mouth shut.

Max licks a bit of chocolate from his finger. Drunk Jillian has the almost overwhelming urge to point out that if he's trying to be provocative, he's succeeding.

"Oh, go on," he teases. "I could listen to you talk desserts all night."

Meredith glances at us, amused, and says, "Basement cleanup is going to take a while. I'd better go supervise." She totters down the stairs and starts giving instructions to Dad, Marcy, and Ivy, who was surely coerced into helping by her mother.

Max looks my way. "Well?"

We can't hang out in the open. I wouldn't mind disappearing behind the closed door of my bedroom, but Dad's voice echoes in my head: *I don't want him in your room—not tonight, not ever.* While I don't care much about pleasing my father tonight, I don't want him to slaughter Max.

An idea strikes, and I smile at my brilliance. "Come on."

In an attempt to lead him down the hall, I stagger and shoulder the wall. He catches my hand and pulls me to a stop. Laughing, he says, "Who put that there?"

"Right? Stupid wall."

He tucks a lock of hair behind my ear. "You really committed to getting crazy."

"Thanks mostly to your mixology."

"Yeah, well, it was cool having you as my partner in crime." He glances at the ceiling and his face changes. He takes a slight step to the right, eyes alight. He gives a nod, indicating I should shift too. I do, confused but intrigued. He looks up again, meaningfully. I follow his gaze.

A sprig of green with waxy white berries, attached to the archway with a festive red bow.

"You know what this means?" Max asks slyly.

I give a laugh that comes out sounding more like a bark. "Mistletoe is a parasitic shrub," I say, because that's a fact he needs to know *right now.* "It's also poisonous—eating it can make you really sick."

"I'm not offering you a taste, Jillian." And then, incredibly, "You don't want to kiss me?"

I prop a hand on my hip. "How drunk are you, Holden?"

He gives my question a moment's consideration before saying, "Not nearly as drunk as I was last time we kissed." He rubs his hands together, like he's prepping to discuss plays in a midfield huddle. "Let's do this before someone comes upstairs."

God, he's serious. "What about Becky?"

He snorts. "Since when do you care about Becky?"

I don't *care* about her, but when I think about what Max and I did on Halloween, I feel guilty, and ashamed, and I wonder why he's pegged me a willing collaborator in his two-timing.

Partner in crime, he said. Is that who I want to be?

Just as I'm remembering my morals, deciding to put a stop to whatever the hell this is, I make the mistake of looking up. Max is sort of gorgeous with his hair all spiky, his lips turned up in a hopeful grin. All kinds of alluring. All kinds of kissable.

I've had a lot of rum.

I shut out the siren in my head, the one that's wailing, *Bad idea! Bad idea!*, and take a tiny step forward. Mistletoe—it's tradition. Besides, tonight's about letting loose, right?

Oh, Max smells good, very good, a clean, woodsy scent that reminds me of pine needles and hiking and moonlight. His eyes are smoky like always, but there's something different about them, too, something inviting. He blinks languidly and everything—my knees, my pulse, what's left of my resolve—goes weak.

"Jesus, Jilly, you look terrified. We don't have to."

"No, I'm fine." And I think, maybe, I am.

He rests his hands on my shoulders. "You're sure?"

I nod.

I close my eyes.

I wait an immeasurable moment.

Max's lips touch mine.

He kisses me—*really* kisses me—warm and soft and leisurely, and I kiss him back, leaning into his chest. I feel him smile. He skates his hands across my shoulders, under my hair, along my neck, until his calloused palms cradle my face. I shiver, delighting in his tenderness.

He pulls back, and for one horrible second I think it's over. But then the softest groan escapes him and he walks me backward, presses me against the wall, and opens his mouth over mine. He tastes like chocolate and beer and I wonder: Will I ever get to kiss him when he's sober?

I shove that musing out of my head, content to focus on the here and now.

Max Holden is kissing me like it means something.

Like he wants to keep kissing me, forever.

MY ARMS ARE WOUND AROUND HIS NECK. His hands are knotted in my hair. His kisses are gentle and sweet, but thorough. My skin burns from the stubble on his chin, and I'm losing myself in him. This fierce, fiery longing has got to be the most exhilarating, most confusing emotion I've ever experienced.

He puts the barest of space between us, a slow smile spreading across his face. "Holy shit. That was . . . wow."

I'm amazed I've kissed him into near speechlessness.

We're not safe, though. A witness could wander up the stairs at any moment, and now that it's started in earnest, I'm nowhere near ready for our time to end. This reckless, voracious desire for more . . . It's the best kind of intoxicating.

I take his hand and pull him down the hall to my dad's study. Pushing the door open, I step inside. Dad's black cherry desk sits in the center of the room, his closed laptop and a smattering of pens atop it. There's a small desk lamp, too, but I leave it off. The darkness ups the forbidden factor. It makes me brave.

Max loiters in the doorway, leaning on the jamb. I'm wondering to what extent he's feeling the beer when he says, "Well, this is the worst idea ever."

"Are you kidding? It's perfect."

"How do you figure?"

"Max, I'm sorry to tell you this, but you're not allowed in my bedroom anymore."

He laughs. "I'm pretty sure you and me aren't allowed to be *any-where* alone."

"My dad's not coming in here—not tonight. Besides, do you have a better idea?"

His brow lifts as he considers. "No. Guess I don't."

I don't so much sit as fall onto the leather sofa. I have the fuzzy notion that I should be embarrassed by my clumsiness, by my drunkenness, but whatever. Pulling my feet onto the cushion, I rest my chin on my knees and gaze at Max. "Are you going to join me?"

With a resigned sigh, he pushes the door closed, finds his way to the sofa, and sinks down beside me. Sneaking a hand under the hem of my jeans, he lets his fingers dance around my ankle and then, very slowly, up my shin. His tiptoe-touch tickles in the most amazing way, and I have a moment of astonishment regarding this new reality.

His hand stills and he leans forward, right into my bubble. "Jillian, what are we doing?"

I'm not sure. I'm not sure of anything anymore, except that he's leaving what happens next up to me. I can end this now and save myself inevitable heartache. I can do the right thing concerning Becky. I can save Max from another round of emotional ups and downs.

If I ask him to leave, he will.

Gazing into his eyes, I think of our first kiss—not the Halloween kiss, but the one that happened years ago, during a trip we all took to Disneyland just after Dad and Meredith were married. When our parents set us free in the Happiest Place on Earth, Ivy and Zoe paired off, refusing to go on rides with their thirteen-year-old brother and the tomboy from across the street, which was fine with Max and me. Things were easy back then; we goofed around to a soundtrack of endless laughter. We spent hours riding Splash Mountain and Space Mountain and Matterhorn Mountain until our necks were stiff and our stomachs were inside out. On the final day of our trip, we discovered Pirates of the Caribbean and its partially air-conditioned queue. Though it was never acknowledged in the light of day, on that ride, dark and damp, amid beer-guzzling, animatronic pirates, Max and I shared a tentative kiss.

Tonight feels equally exciting, but different, too. Easy and natural. Like it's meant to be.

"Jilly," he says softly. "Quit thinking so much. Tell me what you want."

I take a deep breath. His hypnotizing boy scent washes over me, and then I do know what I want. I know *exactly* what I want.

"I want you to kiss me again."

He does, a sweeping, sizzling, breath-stealing kiss that sends prickles like want racing across my skin.

When it's over, he stays close, resting his forehead against mine, letting our inhales and exhales fall into sync. Our fingers are twined together and his eyes are closed, his expression vulnerable, unguarded. It hits me, how intimate this moment is—so much more intimate than the kiss it followed—which makes my mind whirl. What we're doing doesn't feel casual or blithe. It feels deeply personal, like something couples do.

Max and me . . . we're not a couple.

I draw back, at the same time pushing him away. He must think I'm being playful, because he flops against the back of the couch. He whispers my name, reaching for me again, but freezes when a wedge of light slices across the study.

I blink, disoriented. Ivy Holden stands backlit in the study's doorway.

As usual, she pays me little attention. "What the hell, Max?"

"What the hell, Ivy?" he parrots. "You know how to knock?"

"I didn't think I'd need to. Mom's looking for you." She folds her arms across her bustier, snooty. "What are you two doing in here?"

God, how bad does this look? Max and I are sitting on the same couch, but there's a chasm of open air between us. The room's dark, but it's late. We're alone, but for all Ivy knows, we were hiding out until the cleaning's done.

I open my mouth, but Max beats me with a grumbled, "None of your business."

"Oh, yeah? It might be Becky's."

"Leave her out of it."

"She'd be crushed. You, with *Jillian*?" She says my name like I'm a lesser species, a cretin, like her brother's probable philandering would be more acceptable if it were with anyone but me. "You've got to be the world's worst boyfriend."

"Fuck off, Ivy."

Her eyes spark. "Why, so you can drink yourself stupid? Cheat on my best friend with the neighbor girl? You're such a loser, Max, and after everything that's happened with Dad. He'd be so disappointed."

He shoots off the couch, taking a confrontational step toward his sister. I'm so horrified, so *mortified*, I can't bring myself to intervene. I sit, frozen, watching the two of them with a briskly whisked stomach.

"Get out," he says.

"Gladly. But just so you know, Jake's on his way up. You two might want to wrap your party up before he finds you." With that, she pivots and disappears down the hall.

My dad. I've just engaged in a booze-soaked hookup in his study, with the only boy he's ever objected to. A surge of shame slams into me.

Max crosses the room to open the door. Light floods in; it's jarring. His voice, however, is gentle. "Jill."

I'm too thrown by his inexplicable calm to respond.

"Jilly. Your dad."

I struggle to my feet, then trudge across the room as if through deep sand. I follow Max into the hallway and to the front door like I'm tethered to him. It's frigid on the porch, and very quiet. The air smells metallic, wintry, and the sky is clear, filled with tiny pinprick stars. I get woozy looking up at them, but not the pleasurable, drunken woozy of earlier. This is a confused, rueful sort of woozy, one that leaves me nauseated.

Max leans against the rail. "You're freaking out."

I chafe my hands against my arms and nod.

"Don't, okay? Ivy didn't see anything, and even if she did, she'll forget by morning 'cause she'll be back to thinking about herself."

"She hates me."

"She doesn't hate you. She's jealous."

Gorgeous, confident Ivy, jealous of *me*? "You're nuts," I scoff.

He gives me a solemn smile. "You and your dad. Think about it."

"But I—"

"Hey, I'm not saying her bullshit makes sense, but it is what it is. Ivy's a daddy's girl. Things are different now, and she's messed up because of it." He pauses, looking up at the star-speckled sky. "We all are."

Ivy never used to care about me one way or the other, but since

Bill's stroke, she *has* been catty and mean. My brain is sloshy, and it's taking a century to draw a simple conclusion, but maybe Max is right. Even though things are rough between my dad and me, a debilitating health condition on his part would change my temperament. Nasty or not, I feel bad for Ivy.

Still, she could be inside, telling Dad what she just walked in on.

I'm bubbling over with regret, but admitting as much to Max feels wrong, like I'm trivializing what happened between us. Though maybe I should be trivializing it. I mean, we made out. Big deal. He has a girlfriend, one he has no apparent plan to break up with. A few drinks, a few laughs, a few kisses. It *is* trivial, all of it.

I cross my arms and slide a step away, letting distance cement the idea in my head. His posture turns rigid and his eyes go shifty, like my protective stance makes him unsure of where to look. The cold air is a thick, solid thing.

"Anyway," he says. "Thanks for, uh, hanging out."

"Yeah. It was fun." Lame. So lame.

He moves to the steps, his shoes shuffling across the wooden planks of the porch. He pauses, giving me a long once-over. "Jill . . . You okay?"

I force a smile. "Don't worry about me. You've got enough going on as it is." There's a sharpness to my voice I didn't intend, a serration I wish I'd smoothed.

He doesn't say anything else—no *see you later*, no hug or peck on the cheek—though that's undoubtedly for the best, because the magic of the evening is wrecked. He lopes down the walkway, and I watch until he disappears behind the Holdens' front door.

My entrance into my own house is far less graceful. Too bad, because my dad's standing in the foyer, witness to my unfortunate stumble. His fists are glued to his hips. His face . . . Oh God.

"You're drunk," he spits.

I imagine a thread attached to the top of my head. It pulls me upright, tall. I push my shoulders back, too, and swallow, though thickly. All of this feels very necessary, but takes far too long. At last, I respond. "No, I'm not."

"Don't lie to me." His voice is quiet and scary-calm. "This is Max's influence, isn't it? You were outside with him just now, and alone with him while we cleaned up the basement."

I put a hand on the door to keep from swaying. "I was . . . walking him out."

"I knew it was a bad idea to have him here. Drinking under my roof, and with Officer Tate in the house. Drinking with *you*."

"Don't blame Max, Dad. I knew exactly what I was doing." Staging a mutiny, basically, because a few hours ago, my world was turned upside down. Did he honestly expect me to grin and bear the loss of culinary school and New York?

The hurt I spent all night trying to drown rushes to the surface, and I blink back tears.

"Look at yourself," my dad says. "You're barely on your feet. You can hardly maintain eye contact. You *reek* of rum." He tugs at his hair, heaving a sigh. "I know you're upset about the money, and I don't blame you. I'm sorry—you have no idea how sorry I am. But no amount of bad news excuses drinking at seventeen. You're grounded, Jillian. With the exception of school and work, you're not to leave this house."

I don't trust my voice to remain steady, so I shrug, a move my dad must read as disrespectful, because he becomes a volcano, red and dangerous and ready to erupt.

"I never thought I'd see you make such irresponsible decisions," he says, his voice roughened with anger. "I don't like the person you're becoming. Not at all."

His declaration strikes me in the gut. I close my eyes against a bout of dizziness.

"Go to bed," he says. He shakes his head, disgusted, as I turn for the hall.

I will not stagger.

I will not stumble.

I will *not* cry.

It's on occasions like this that I wish for a mother—not faraway Beth, and not preoccupied Meredith. A *real* mother, who might take my side, who might step in to temper my father's rashness.

Just before I close my bedroom door, he calls, "I hope Max is worth it, Jillian."

Is he?

I collapse on my bed, unnervingly drunk and thoroughly confused.

He's just a guy, I remind myself. *He's the boy across the street. He's a friend.*

He's just a guy.

But I don't think he is. Not anymore.

12

AFTER A NIGHT OF FITFUL SLEEP, I get to endure ten minutes in the car with my still-furious father. He's on his way to the office, where he'll probably spend the better part of the weekend. His overtime works out well, though, since he's insisted on shuttling me to work—I might still have alcohol in my system, he speculates, which means I'm not driving myself anywhere. And besides, I *can't be trusted*.

Kyle's beaten me to True Brew, as usual. He's whistling a cheerful rendition of "Jingle Bells" and running shots of espresso through the machine, seasoning it, when I stagger through the door. His well-rested grin and a gust of toasty, coffee-scented air greet me.

Kyle's parents opened True Brew ages ago, and it's the only independently owned coffee shop in our Starbucks-saturated county to survive the highs and lows of being a small business. There's almost always a line of cars in the drive-through, and the shop is usually busy with some combination of grocery-getter moms, khaki-pantsed businessmen, students lugging armloads of textbooks, couples on quiet dates, and passionate Bible study groups.

This morning, customers of any sort strike me as daunting.

I tie on my apron and go about writing today's special (*Frosty's Favorite: Cool Mint Mocha*) on each of two display chalkboards. When I've finished, I stock the pastry case with this morning's bakery delivery. The yeasty-sweet aromas of muffins and coffee cake and bagels turn my stomach. Kyle checks the tills, mumbling quietly as he counts bills and coins. When our preopening tasks are complete, we have a little time before we need to unlock the glass-paneled door. I take advantage by propping my elbows on the counter and dropping my heavy head into my hands.

"Aren't we bright-eyed?" Kyle says.

"Long night." I've been rehashing it, fuming over my dad's assertions, dissecting Max's behavior, excusing mine away. And then there's the matter of my New York money, gone forever. My stomach cramps; I need to spill before I give myself an ulcer.

Kyle fills two cups with drip coffee and slides one to me. "So? Bunco treated you well?"

"Bunco sucked," I say, tearing open a sugar packet. I dump it into my coffee and add a splash of half-and-half, stirring until my drink's a deep caramel color.

Kyle smiles. He has a sneaky way of advancing conversation with a flash of his golden-boy grin. "Game got a little too wild for ya?"

I sip my coffee, avoiding his eyes. "Actually, yes."

"Well? Let's hear it."

I debate which secret to divulge. I'm not cool with telling Kyle about my spent culinary school fund—at least, not until I come to terms with the sad fact that my life's aspirations have gone up in fertility flames. And then there's Max, who's Kyle's friend, too, and disclosing what happened last night would just be way too weird. But then my stomach does that gross cramping thing again, and I let the words fly fast, before I have a chance to overthink them. "Max and I kissed."

He blanches. "Uh, okay. Wait—*what?*"

"We kissed," I repeat. "Please don't make me say it again."

"Wow. Really?"

"Kyle! Why would I make something like that up?"

He's quiet for a moment, like he's considering my question. Then he says, "Is this . . . a good thing?"

I frown. "What do you think?"

"I think you look exhausted, which means you lost sleep, which means you're torn, which means your feelings aren't clear, which means this *could* be a good thing . . . maybe? If you're into Max, just tell him."

"I never said I was into Max."

His brows ascend his forehead. "Then forget about it."

"Easier said than done."

"Because part of you liked that kissy-kissing." He grins. "Maybe *all* of you liked it."

"You're an ass," I say, shaking my head. Kyle abides by the assumed don't-ask-don't-tell policy of our peers, but he's up front about his sexuality with Leah and the guys and me; he has been since last summer, when I walked into True Brew to begin a shared closing shift and witnessed him accepting the phone number of a very cute, very male chai tea drinker. "You being an ass goes against all logic," I tell him after another swallow of coffee. "You're supposed to be sensitive and intuitive, full of answers."

"Oh, please. Stereotype much? I carry a Y chromosome, which gives me the right to act like a Neanderthal anytime I please."

"Kyle, come on," I whine, slumping against the counter. "Help me!"

"Hell, Jill, if you and Max decide you wanna be together, cool."

"But we *can't* be together."

"Why not?"

"There are plenty of reasons. Let's start with Becky McMahon."

He shudders. "Ew."

I laugh—I can't help it. Kyle's disliked Becky and her dramatics since we were in middle school, but when she started goading Max into drinking to the point of irresponsibility, he decided he hated her.

"Seriously," he says. "Becky's awful. The way she's always guilting Max, bitching at him until she gets her way . . . It's underhanded, and it's shitty. I can say with certainty that you'd never treat him that way."

"Doesn't matter. He's with her and he shows no signs of ending it. God, Kyle. I think he played me, and he's definitely playing her. How did I let this happen?"

"You didn't *let* it happen," he says, dropping a hand onto my back. "It just did, because you're human and so is he. But you're both good, otherwise I wouldn't give either of you the time of day. It'll work out, Jelly Bean." He smacks a kiss on my cheek before stepping away to flip the OPEN sign and unlock the door.

True Brew comes alive with activity. Kyle mans the counter, serving the customers who've wandered in for hot drinks. I work the drive-through, mostly because the pace is faster and less conversation is required. The morning flies by as we sling coffee and croissants, tea and toasted bagels, making small talk in the lulls between customers.

Midmorning, a familiar crimson Civic appears in the drive-through—Natalie Samson, my dad's secretary. I wonder if she's headed to work on this fine Saturday, and whether Dad asked her to stop here first, just to check up on me. I wipe my hands on my espresso-spattered apron, slide the window open, and greet her with false cheer. "Hey, Natalie. What can I get for you this morning?"

She's dressed like a sorority girl gone corporate: tight sweater, dark makeup, vampy manicure, honey-colored hair coiled into a loose twist. She's in her early twenties, working her way toward an AA at the local community college. My dad hired her last year, when his first secretary—sweet Mrs. Silver, who always kept a bowl of butterscotch candies on her desk—retired. "I'll try the special," she says, "and can I get a double cappuccino, dry, with two Equals?"

Dad's drink—he asks for it whenever he visits True Brew—which means Natalie's likely here on a recon mission. I bite my lip, pull espresso from the grinder, and vow to be professional. After all, it's not her fault Dad's using her as a spy. "Early morning for you," I say, working to keep my tone conversational.

"I'm headed to the office. Your dad's a busy man, Jillian."

I drown the milk wand in a pitcher of nonfat. The hiss of steam isn't enough to impede chitchat, and I feel compelled to respond. "It's nice of you help him out on a Saturday."

She smiles. "He pays time and a half on the weekends."

She goes on, prattling about the case Dad's working on, and how he's starting to teach her the ins and outs of real estate law, but I'm tuning out. Talk of my dad's busyness coming from Natalie, dolled up in her best one-size-too-small business-casual, bothers me for reasons I can't quite pin down. It's not just that Dad's been working long hours. He's been distracted and moody at home, too. My default is to blame Meredith—she pushed for a baby no matter what the sacrifice—but rationally, I know her pregnancy isn't the sole source of his distance. There's his increased caseload, worries about money, and Bill's health, too, which I suspect has forced him to face all sorts of issues regarding his own impermanence.

But it's not like he's the only one who's stressed—I'm drowning in schoolwork, killing myself trying to help out around the house, and now I get to agonize over how to pay for the only school I've ever wanted to attend.

I miss normalcy.

I miss my *dad*.

. . . .

A steady stream of business eats up the morning, which is perfect because without the fast-paced distraction of work, my mind would somersault into overdrive. When things finally settle down, Kyle pours me another cup of coffee, adds my requisite splash of cream and heap of sugar, and says, "So, what're you gonna do about Max?"

"Nothing," I say with resolve I don't feel. Last night's flight through the unfamiliar has become today's terrifying free fall. "He can ride off into the sunset with Becky."

"I think you should at least talk to him."

"Kyle. I suck at talking."

"Yeah, but Max is our friend. Your neighbor. It's not like you can hide from him."

"I can try."

"Sure," he says gently, "but do you want to?"

He may be onto something—something I'm currently unwilling to explore—but what am I supposed to do? Max and I can't continue whatever last night was, though the thought of telling him to stay away makes my skin itch. But then, who am I to assume *he* wants to continue hanging out with *me*? He's been drunk the two times we've been together, and he has a girlfriend who, like it or not, sticks to him like cake to an ungreased Bundt pan.

Besides, he's Max and I'm Jillian, and we're friends—if that.

Through the shop's front window, I spot a white truck pulling into the parking lot, the emblem of a smiling cow adorning its side. "I'm going to let the milkman in. You good here?"

Kyle swipes a sprinkling of coffee grounds from the counter. "Yep, got it."

I open the back door that leads into the storage room and watch as the milkman hauls in crates of nonfat, 2 percent, half-and-half, whipped cream, and newly seasonal eggnog. I sign his invoice and pay him with a purchase order, then go about loading the big stock fridge with dairy products. The cold air clears my head, and the filtered melody of Kyle's whistling—he's moved on to "Joy to the World"—eases my nerves.

Then the rumble of another truck muffles Kyle's tune. The gritty crooning of Johnny Cash's "Cry, Cry, Cry" carries into the back room, and I freeze with a gallon of milk in each hand.

Max hardly ever comes by True Brew; he doesn't even drink coffee.

I can't make out the details of his exchange with Kyle over the Man in Black's guitar riffs, but I can tell it's taking place through the window, and I can discern their grave tones. At last I hear Kyle say, loudly, "See you later, dude."

The F-150's engine revs, then fades.

I plunk the remaining milk into the fridge, wondering why he came and what he said, and mostly, why he left without a word to me. Then I slam the fridge's door and make my way into the shop to interrogate Kyle.

He's waiting for me, hands on his hips, a look of reproach peeking out from beneath his shaggy hair. "You're going to talk to him," he says. "Right now."

"I heard his truck pull away."

"Nice try. He's in the parking lot, and—fair warning—he's wrecked."

I swallow. "Wrecked?"

"You'll see when you get out there."

"I'm not going out there. I can't."

"You can." He strides across our work space, plucks my jacket from its hook, and holds it out for me. With a resigned sigh, I untie my apron and trade up. Kyle zips me to my chin and pats my shoulder. "There we are. You're gonna feel better once you guys work this out."

On autopilot, I make my way out of True Brew. I trudge across the foggy parking lot, my feet crunching wet gravel as I approach Max's truck. Exhaust spills from its tailpipe, and a slow, steady bass beat vibrates the cab. I step up to the driver's-side door.

God, he *does* look wrecked.

He lowers the window. "Come sit with me?"

I nod and round the truck to the passenger side. I get in, settling myself on the seat without looking at him. Johnny Cash has been turned down to less than earsplitting, but I can still make out "Peace in the Valley," a song that couldn't be more depressing if it tried. It's warm in the truck, and it still smells the way it did when Bill drove it during his logging days: crisp and organic, like the woods after a rain shower.

"I brought you a Coke," Max says, nodding toward the huge lidded cup in the holder.

"Wow." I pick it up and take a sip. "This must be, like, sixty ounces of soda."

"Yeah, I figured you might need a boost. How are you?"

"Tired, I guess. You?"

"I'm good." He traces his finger around the blue Ford logo on the steering wheel, and I can tell he's gearing up to say something heavy. "Listen, Jill, I feel like shit about last night. There are rules about this stuff. It shouldn't have happened the way it did."

It shouldn't have happened. . . .

I climbed into the truck intent on telling him some version of the same thing, but hearing my words fall from his mouth bruises my heart.

"You're right," I say, my voice as insubstantial as meringue. I sit up straighter, attempting to gather the shattered bits of my dignity. It *shouldn't* have happened, as evident by Kyle's confusion and my dad's displeasure. I say, "There *are* rules. You have a girlfriend."

"I know." He scrubs a hand over his face, mumbling, "I'm such an asshole."

"It didn't even matter, Max, okay? We'll forget it happened."

He shakes his head, clenching his hands into fists. "Like that's possible."

Silence stretches out between us, and not the comfortable kind. The truck's cab is like the inside of a teakettle. The water's boiling. The pressure's building. There's nowhere for it to go.

I whisper, "I'm sorry," to break the silence, and because I truly am. Despite the obstacles standing between Max and me, I hate to see him hurting. He cheated on his girlfriend—he's obviously shredded—and here I am, a freaking consolation prize, spewing pointless apologies the morning after. I feel like Cinderella after the ball: unremarkable and defeated.

"You shouldn't be sorry," he says, hard and cold.

"Well, I am."

"You didn't do anything."

"Maybe, but—"

"Jillian! Just don't, okay?"

I stare at him and he stares back, so abruptly hostile I'm at a loss for words. *He* was the one who showed up at my house on Halloween.

He was the one who suggested drinking last night, who initiated the flirting, who pointed out the mistletoe. He nudged me into a zillion bad decisions, and then he showed up here to rub my nose in them.

If anyone has reason to be bitter, it's me. At least he has Becky to fall back on.

"You don't have to be a jerk," I say, harsh.

He looks at me with wide eyes, like he's been lost, wandering for ages and just stumbled upon the compass he didn't know he was missing. "I'm not trying to be a jerk," he says, suddenly repentant. "It's just . . ."

My chest squeezes as his unfinished thought fades into the music, but I push the feeling down, away. Self-preservation says Max doesn't deserve my compassion—not today.

I reach for the door handle. "I've got to get back to work."

He cuts the ignition. "I'll walk you."

I want to be away from him, far, far away, but I'm too rattled to protest.

It's a quiet twenty-yard trip across the parking lot. When we reach the shop door, I toe the pavement with my shoe, frustratingly reluctant to tell him good-bye. He stands very still, watching me, ratcheting my pulse up, up, up. Then, before I have a chance to deflect him, he steps forward and folds me into his arms.

It's startling, yet immediately comforting, like *home*.

I bury my face in the softness of his sweatshirt and his arms tighten around me, the heat of his body sheltering me from the frosty air. He sighs deeply, contentedly, and an idea arrives so suddenly and with such precision, I can't force it away. . . .

My body fits perfectly against Max Holden's.

His lips touch my hair, and even though it's the middle of the day and we're both sober, it feels strangely, wonderfully right.

He whispers, "You smell like coffee."

I pull away and stagger backward, before I fall too far into him. "I've got to go," I say, shoving the shop door open. I hurry into the building, leaving Max outside in the cold.

It's not until later, after Kyle's talked himself hoarse trying to console me, that I realize I left my Coke in the truck.

13

THE DAY AFTER SCHOOL LETS OUT FOR winter break, I work an opening shift at True Brew with Kyle and then, when I get home, I get comfortable with my laptop so I can research scholarships that might help me attend the International Culinary Institute after all. While the ferocity of my initial anger has dulled, my craving for New York's as strong as ever. Empty account or not, I'm not ready to give up.

The school itself offers a few options, and there are private scholarships, too, but the choices aren't as plentiful as I'd hoped. Two thousand dollars here, five thousand there . . . discouraging. Tuition for the nine month Professional Pastry Arts program is close to thirty-five grand, and that doesn't include housing and other living expenses. Still, I bookmark the money I might qualify for, to be more carefully considered this summer, after school's out, after the leech baby's born, after things at home have calmed down.

Hopefully.

While I'm poking around online, I hear Dad return from another morning at the office. Meredith requests his help with changing table assembly in the nursery, but apparently an unexpected errand comes up, because not ten minutes after they get started, he calls down the hall to my room, "Jillian, get your coat. We're going out."

We're still not talking much, Dad and me, but there's been no more yelling. It seems he's let the whole drunk-at-Bunco thing go, aside from my ongoing grounding, and I'm done hurling accusations because, yeah, Meredith and the baby are important, and debt sucks, and who am I to dictate how my father spends money?

Hesitantly optimistic, I head down the hall to see where he needs to go, and find him standing by the front door in a pair of pressed jeans and a heavy jacket, holding his key ring.

"What's up?" I ask, eyeing the beat-up boots he's chosen, the ones he wears when he's doing yard work.

"Marcy called. The Holdens don't have a Christmas tree yet, and she's worried about how they'll get one." He looks at the floor, giving his keys a restless jingle. "That was Bill's job, of course, so . . ."

"So you offered to pick one up?"

He nods. "I thought you could help."

"Sure," I say, willing to do just about anything to improve the Holdens' first Christmas since Bill's stroke. "Let me grab some shoes."

I meet him in the driveway a few minutes later, my feet in a pair of lined boots, my hands burrowed in the pockets of my fleece, feeling hopeful about this one-on-one time with my dad. It might be what we need to start correcting what's gone awry.

As soon as I'm buckled up, he backs into the street. He's shifting his Durango into drive when Marcy Holden comes flying out her front door, waving a hand in the air. Dad brakes as she hustles down the slope of her driveway and over to his window. He lowers it.

"Jake," she says, slightly out of breath. "I can't thank you enough for doing this. I'm sure the tree farm is the last place you feel like spending your afternoon."

"Don't worry about it," Dad says, reaching through the window to squeeze her shoulder. "I've told you—don't hesitate to ask anytime you need something."

Marcy smiles. "In that case, I need something—in addition to the Christmas tree."

"Anything."

She hesitates. "Take Max with you?"

A deafening silence engulfs the Durango.

"Please?" Marcy says after a beat. "He's been impossible. He's always helped Bill with the tree, plus he's been fighting with his girlfriend. He needs to get out of the house. Would you mind terribly if he tags along?"

Dad heaves a sigh, but I have a sinking feeling he'll let Max join us. He's known Marcy too long to deny such a desperate request, and besides, it's not like she hasn't helped him with me over the years. Still, I will my dad to decline.

He says, "Send him out."

God. This is happening. . . . Dad, Max, and me, on a merry trip to the tree farm. I've half a mind to leap from the Durango, but preservation of my dad's sanity and Max's life sway me into staying put.

Marcy hurries into her house to retrieve Max, and then, sure enough, he's ambling through the door in a sweatshirt, puffy vest, and knit cap.

"Max," Dad says as he climbs into the backseat, a stiff greeting.

"Jake," Max returns. Excruciating pause . . . "Hey, Jilly."

An incredibly disturbing impulse to cry overtakes me, hearing him use my nickname smooth as melted chocolate. We haven't spoken since that awful morning at True Brew, mostly because I've gone to great lengths to avoid him, even while Kyle rolls his eyes at what he calls my *refusal to face reality*. I blink, swallowing the sadness that's ascending my throat.

What is wrong *with me?*

A dark cloud—literal and metaphorical—hovers over the Durango all the way to the tree farm. Dad leaves the radio off, probably so Max and I can stew in our failures as teenagers and human beings more effectively, and by the time we pull into the muddy parking lot, my nerves are overwrought. The cold air, scented like earth and sap, is a welcome alternative to the stifling tension of the Durango.

Before Meredith moved in and insisted we invest in an artificial tree (no fallen pine needles!), Dad and I bought a Christmas tree at this farm annually. It's one with two options: pick the tree you like best and hack that sucker down, or pick the tree you like best and have a trained professional do the actual sawing. My dad favored option two—he's not really a kneel-in-the-mud kind of guy—but it seems Max has other ideas. He's secured a handsaw and a large cart for tree transporting before Dad's tucked the ends of his scarf into his coat. He shakes his head in Max's direction, as if initiative and a sense of adventure are synonymous with foolhardiness.

Max leads the way down packed-dirt lanes of firs and cedars and pines. His tree-shopping style is quiet and contemplative, and involves a lot of senseless branch poking and head tilting. Apparently, he has no need for outside opinions. After twenty minutes of perusing, Dad pulls his phone from his pocket, stepping around branches and wheel ruts while answering e-mails.

When Max has at last picked a tree—a colossal, beautifully symmetrical Douglas fir—his inner lumberjack emerges. He drops to his knees and begins to saw at the trunk, breaking a sweat and tossing me his hat halfway through. My dad couldn't be less interested, though it looks like Max could use a little help holding the tree steady—surely Marcy had a reason for sending us all out here together. I'm tempted to volunteer my services because I feel useless standing around with my hands literally in my pockets, but this outing has the ring of a solo mission. If cutting down the Holden family Christmas tree used to be Bill and Max's thing, to intrude without request would be to steal from tradition.

When the tree at last hits the ground, Max straightens, wiping his brow with the dirt-streaked sleeve of his sweatshirt. My dad's attention drops from his phone to the tree, then rests on Max. "Your mother will be happy with that one," he says before returning to his messages.

Max rolls his eyes and hauls the tree onto the cart.

Our trip to the checkout stand is slow thanks to the heavy tree and the unwieldy cart. I carry the handsaw, the only contribution Max'll let me make. My dad leads the charge, obviously eager to get home.

He acquires a long length of twine from a farm employee and pulls the tag from the tree Max selected. "I'll pay. Try to get that thing on top of the Durango without scratching the paint," he says, handing Max the twine and his keys.

"Yes, sir," Max says, saluting his back as he walks away. He grabs the cart and shoves it toward the parking lot, muttering, "Bastard."

I frown, but choose to follow him, preferring his solemn presence to my dad's abruptly pissy mood. "How're things?" I ask as we walk.

"Fantastic," he says drily, trudging on.

The sky is full of churning clouds, like a storm's gathering fury, waiting for the perfect moment to unleash its wrath. It must be throwing the ions in the air out of whack—that's the only excuse I have for following up with the most impolite, most *intrusive* comment in the history of despairing teenagers: "Your mom said you and Becky have been fighting."

He grunts, a disbelieving sound. "So?"

I can't help myself. . . . "What about?"

"Are you kidding?"

"I'm trying to make conversation. Friends should talk."

"Well, *friend*, you've never given a shit about Becky and me before."

"I've given a shit about you for the last decade, Max."

"Then let it go. This is not a conversation I'm cool with."

"Fine." I lower my voice, mumbling into the fog, "Though I don't get it."

He spins around, nearly tipping the cart. "You don't get it? You don't get why it'd be fucked up for *me* to talk to *you* about problems I'm having with my *girlfriend*?"

"I'm only trying to help," I tell the mud, though that's not true. I'm fishing. I have no idea what's going on with him and Becky because when I see the two of them at school, I scamper away like a bunny from a pair of wolves. I remind Kyle constantly that he should keep his thoughts on McAlder's most toxic pair to himself, and when Leah, who still doesn't have a clue about what went on between Max and me a few weeks ago, brings up the damaged duo, I change the subject right up. But the truth is . . . I'm dying to know.

"I don't need help," he tells me, steering the cart around a pothole. "Not from you or my mother or my sisters."

His unhappiness is like a boulder standing between us, heavy and impenetrable. God, he frustrates the hell out of me. "How long are you going to keep up this suffer-in-silence act?"

He expels an exasperated breath. "Okay. Fine. You wanna know about me and Becky? Things have been shitty for months, but our most recent fights—last night specifically—are about you." My stomach winds into a knot as he continues, "I don't feel good about screwing around behind her back, so I put it out there. She was upset. Can you blame her?"

I hunker down in my fleece so he won't catch the horror splattered like paint across my face. "You shouldn't have told her. We said it didn't matter."

"No, *you* said it didn't matter."

"We agreed to forget."

"Have you, Jill?" he asks. "Have you forgotten?"

I haven't. I relive those stolen kisses Max and I shared all the time. I can't quit thinking about his hands in my hair, his breath on my skin, the adoring way he treated me under the mistletoe, like I was special. Like *we* were special. I can't stop thinking about kissing him—I can't stop thinking about *him*—and even though I'm too scared to confront what that might mean, I can't bring myself to lie outright.

He laughs through my silence, dull and dismal. "Yeah. That's what I thought."

He turns, shoving the tree-laden cart toward the Durango. I trail him and, without a word, do my best to help lift the tree onto the roof. He knots and double-knots the twine, and when my dad still hasn't returned, we take our respective seats to wait within the relative warmth of the car.

The quiet is agonizing.

"So," I say, facing the windshield, twisting and untwisting my hands. "Are you and Becky, like, done?"

"No. I don't . . . I don't know what we are. She's humiliated—she made that very clear, right after she burst into tears and slapped me.

Ivy's pissed, too. I betrayed her best friend; she knew I was cheating; how can I even live with myself? That's a direct quote."

"God, Max."

"Yeah. Tell me about it."

I want to tell him a lot of things: I'm sorry he's having a tough time, it sucks that his sister's upset with him, he can do better than Becky—he's *worthy* of better than Becky—but my dad picks that moment to open the driver's-side door. He collapses into his seat, like he's the one who just toppled a seven-foot fir.

"Everything okay in here?" he says, eyeing Max, then me.

"Great," the two of us say in unison.

14

MARCY INVITES DAD, MEREDITH, AND ME OVER for dessert two days before Christmas.

In the past, we've spent Christmas Eve at the Holdens', playing board games and devouring a feast of prime rib, twice-baked potatoes, roasted asparagus, and Victorian Christmas pudding (brown sugar and almonds and currants and spices, among other flavorsome things). Until last year, Bill dressed up in a Santa costume and handed out gifts to his kids, me, and, more recently, Zoe and Brett's son. Before my family walked back across the street for the night, Dad would produce his childhood copy of "The Night Before Christmas" as if by magic, then read it aloud, his deep voice reciting the verses with perfect, rhythmic cadence.

This year, we'll miss Christmas Eve with the Holdens. Meredith has suggested we travel a few hours south to Portland, where we'll spend the holiday with her too-old-to-travel parents. Dad protested because lately, that's what Dad does, but Meredith won the battle—she is pregnant, after all.

Today in the kitchen, I dip a sampling spoon into the nearly done sweet-potato filling I've spent half the afternoon working on. Soon, it'll fill the flaky, from-scratch pie crust that's chilling in the fridge. The filling tastes smooth and rich and sweet; I added a couple of tablespoons of bourbon pilfered from my dad's liquor cabinet in hopes of intensifying the flavor, and it's perfect.

Any pastry chef worthy of her rolling pin knows how important it is to check for taste and texture and doneness. Baking is a science: measuring and mixing, a series of actions and reactions, separate parts of an aspiring whole. Heat is almost always involved because heat forces change, melds the ingredients into something different. Something better.

Meredith appears in the doorway, assessing the kitchen with her hands on her bloated waistline, back arched, the way I've only ever seen pregnant women do. She frowns at the mess I've made but, to her credit, refrains from complaining. "How's it going?" she asks instead, brushing a few spilled sugar crystals into the sink.

"Okay. The pie's almost ready for the oven, the cranberry tartlets are nearly done, and the peppermint sugar cookies are already in Tupperware."

"Do you think you'll be ready to head to the Holdens' in a few hours?"

"Should be. When will Dad be home?"

She glances at the microwave clock. "Hopefully by five. I told Marcy we'd be over at six, and I don't want to be late."

I pour the sweet potato filling into its chilled pie shell and ask a loaded question. "What's he doing at the office again anyway?"

"Your guess is as good as mine," Meredith says with annoyance that makes my ears ring. Sighing, she lifts the lid of the Tupperware housing the peppermint sugar cookies and inhales their cool scent. "May I?"

I nod, using an offset spatula to smooth the pie filling.

She snags two cookies before toddling out of the kitchen.

I slide my favorite ruffled pie pan, loaded with sweet potato goodness, into the oven, trying not to stress about Dad and Meredith and tonight, our first attempt at a Holden-Eldridge gathering in the wake of Bill's stroke, and the first time I'll see Max since our awful outing to the tree farm.

. . . .

Dad walks through the front door at six fifteen. Meredith leaps down his throat, lecturing him about punctuality and consideration and good manners. He takes it in stride until she mentions the strict meal/medicine/rest/therapy regimen Bill is on. That's when he demands that she "Lay the hell off!"

They're not speaking when, at six thirty, we step into a sad drizzle and cross the street.

All's forgotten when Marcy opens the front door. She hugs Meredith, then Dad, and everyone's smiling and schmoozing like my parents weren't just bickering like stray cats over a discarded can of tuna.

It's mind-blowing, how well they hide the truth.

Marcy leads us past the living room, where the Douglas fir we picked up the other day sits in a corner, trimmed and twinkling with white lights, to the kitchen, where most of the Holdens have gathered. Zoe sits at one end of the big kitchen table, surrounded by an array of coloring books and crayons. Brett and raven-haired, innocent-eyed Oliver, a two-year-old facsimile of his uncle Max, sit across from her.

Bill's at the table, too, his wheelchair parked below its surface, wearing a mask of contentment and a collared shirt that fits too loose on his once robust frame. He's studying his grandson in this introspective way that's contrary to the rousing ambiance he used to lend to gatherings. I watch as Zoe leans over to pat her dad's arm.

Ivy, who I've spoken to exactly zero times since she interrupted Max and me in my dad's study, stands at the stove. She's stirring a copper-bottomed pot of hot cocoa in a striped dress and knee-high boots, her long hair blown out straight and sleek. I recall what Max said about her being jealous and mentally roll my eyes. Confidence wafts off Ivy Holden like heat from an open flame.

I turn away before she notices me—I don't have the energy for spitefulness—and begin laying out the treats I brought. Marcy's confections are already displayed on the counter, buffet-style. She's made a caramel apple torte cake, a pecan pie, and an apple pie with a gorgeous honeycomb crust. The kitchen smells amazing, and the selection is worthy of the finest pâtisserie, and I'm in heaven—until I spot Ivy closing in.

"Jillian," she says briskly.

"Ivy," I reply, glancing over my shoulder to be sure there are witnesses. I have a feeling she's going to confront me about what Max told Becky—the kiss, the betrayal, my involvement—and it's probably going to get ugly. But Marcy, Dad, and Meredith have crowded around the table, and no one's paying any attention to the two of us.

Great.

Ivy smooths her bangs and says, quietly, "Have you heard from my brother today?"

There's a good chance this is an attempt at entrapment—some scheme she and Becky cooked up to nail Max for a crime he's yet to commit. I unwrap my platter of cranberry tartlets and reply impassively, "He's not here?"

"We don't know where he is. Mom told him to be home before you and your parents came over, but he hasn't even called."

I place my sweet potato pie atop a stand, my heart faltering. . . . Max is missing? "Have you talked to the guys?"

Ivy nods. "He's not with Jesse or Kyle or Leo. My mom's going crazy worrying about him. I can't get ahold of Becky, so . . . Maybe they're together?"

"Probably," I say, feeling some relief. The thought of Max and Becky hanging out in an unreachable den of sin makes my mouth taste bitter, but I'd rather know he's with her than know nothing at all. "He probably just lost track of time. I bet he'll be home in a few minutes." Even as I say this, though, I'm not sure it'll prove true. Chances are, Max is fine, but that doesn't mean he'll be moseying through the door for pie anytime soon.

I leave Ivy to help Marcy and Meredith serve hot cocoa. After passing a steaming drink to everyone at the table, I squish into an empty space, far from Oliver and his sticky toddler hands. Brett slides a tray of add-ins—mini marshmallows, crushed candy cane, cinnamon sticks, and orange twists among other tasty things—our way. I add a dollop of whipped cream and a few chocolate chips to my mug, then watch as Ivy sneaks a handful of mini marshmallows to her nephew, who appears to be on his way to a sugar overdose.

Across from me, Marcy's helping Bill sip cocoa from a straw. She must be stressing about Max's whereabouts, seeing as how her son's propensity for responsible decision making has gone down the toilet.

God, I hope he shows up soon.

No one mentions his absence as the clock journeys toward seven and then beyond, but it becomes obvious that we're waiting on him. The implicit question builds and hovers over the untouched desserts, thickening like tapioca.

When Oliver at last rubs his eyes and rests his chocolaty chin on the tabletop, Marcy stands, clasps her hands together, and says, "Goodness, Oli, I'm ready for a treat. Should I serve the desserts now?"

Oliver perks right up. "Tweat! Tweat, pwease!"

Zoe runs a hand over Oliver's head. "I don't know, kiddo. It's getting late."

"God, Zoe, lighten up," Ivy says. "Let him have some pie."

Zoe flings a glare at her sister. "Why don't you stay out—"

Brett drops a hand onto Zoe's shoulder and nods in Bill's direction. She glances quickly, guiltily, at her father, then snaps her mouth shut.

"What?" Ivy needles. "Stay out of your perfect parenting?"

Zoe pulls in a breath, but Brett jumps up before she has a chance to retort. "I'll help you with the plates, Marcy," he says. He looks pointedly at his wife. "Zoe, why don't you and Oli keep your dad company?"

As if Bill's a charity case. This time last year, he would have told Ivy and Zoe to quit bickering while at the same time reviewing the standings of whatever football teams happened to be playing on TV, and passing my dad a beer. Now he stares with dismay at his daughters. Zoe, chagrined, picks up a turquoise crayon and begins filling in one of the shapes on Oliver's coloring page. Ivy takes her phone out of her pocket and taps away at its screen.

Meredith nudges my dad. "Jake, tell Bill about the case you're working on. The one with that broker out of Tacoma? The dilapidated hotel?"

When Bill was healthy, he and Dad never discussed work. They stuck to football and families, lagers and stouts, because the worlds of logging and law have very little overlap. I'm sure the last thing my dad feels like rehashing is some tedious hotel case, but Bill can't help fill this silence that's becoming stifling.

Their friendship's so strained now, nothing like the easy camaraderie they used to share. The transformation makes me sad, and nostalgic for the past.

Once, on a cloudless day when Max and I were twelve—Dad and Meredith had just announced their engagement—we attempted to chalk a rendering of the solar system in the middle of the street. Bill, who'd been busy trimming his junipers, set his clippers aside so he could plop down on the pavement with us. He talked about rocket launches and moon walks as he rifled through our bucket of chalk, helping us pick out colors for the planets. My dad joined us when he got home from work, armed with a reference book and a tape measure for accuracy's sake, and by the time the lamps came on, the street had become a galaxy, and all four of us were dusted head to toe in chalk. Marcy joked about hosing us off before letting us inside for Cokes.

Now Dad launches into a dry monologue about misconduct and faulty documentation that would have me yawning under different circumstances. I feel sorry for him, and Bill. I wonder if they miss chalk drawings in the street as much as I do.

Marcy and Brett are nearly done loading dessert plates with gluttonous portions of pie, cookies, torte, and tartlets when the doorbell chimes. Zoe rises, but sinks back onto the bench as Marcy darts out of the kitchen ahead of her. Beside me, Ivy's gone stiff. We sit in silence, waiting.

Marcy's saccharine voice carries into the kitchen. "Officer Tate!"

Officer Tate serves on the police force of the town adjacent to McAlder, so this visit shouldn't be in any sort of professional capacity, but why else would he show up unannounced?

A cold sweat breaks out across the back of my neck—*Max*.

He was hurt during a football game a few months ago, after being taken down by a tackle so violent it was startlingly audible from the grandstand. He made it off the field, arm dangling awkwardly, but the second he crossed the sideline, he hit his knees. I swear to God my heart stopped beating. It was all I could do to keep my butt on the cold aluminum bench, gripping Leah's hand while coaches and trainers swarmed him. The injury turned out to be a stinger—a harmless but painful charge of electricity that shot through the nerves of his arm after the hit. They were brief but terrible, those moments I had to consider what life would be like if Max wasn't okay.

He's fine, I tell myself now. *He* has *to be fine.*

Officer Tate's ramblings are indistinct, but I pick up a few key words: *driving, beer, serious, illegal.* The muted explanation carries on, peppered with fretful-sounding *Yes, sir*s and *I understand*s from Marcy. The tension in the kitchen is almost unbearable; even Oliver—who was presented with dessert before the doorbell rang and has made a mess of pecan pie on the table—has fallen victim to the grave atmosphere.

"I should have taken him to the station, Marcy," we hear Officer Tate say. "Frankly, I put my job at risk by bringing him here. He's underage, which means zero tolerance. He could have hurt himself. He could have *killed* himself, or someone else."

Zoe drops the crayon she's been clutching, and Meredith makes a little choking sound. Bill's face has drained of color, and my dad's tugging on his hair. I feel dizzy, light-headed, a little sick, like I just stepped off a roller coaster.

"I know," Marcy says, her voice wavering. Max screwed up big-time—irrevocably. I can't even look at my dad, who predicted a mishap like this weeks ago.

"You're lucky it was me who stopped him," Officer Tate says, "not another officer who doesn't understand your . . . situation."

The foyer, the kitchen, the house . . . So, so quiet.

And then, haltingly, Dad says, "Bill?"

Bill's rigid in his chair. His hands form fists so tight the tendons in his knuckles strain.

"I don't want to intrude," Dad murmurs, using the slower speech pattern we all fall into when addressing him now, "but do you want me to . . . Should I go out there?"

Bill gives a jerk of his head—*No!*—before letting his chin drop to his chest. There's worry in the hunch of his shoulders, helplessness in his slackening fists.

"Okay," Dad says. "Okay." I feel marginally better as I watch him make eye contact with the Holden girls: Zoe, who's pulled Oliver onto her lap, and Ivy, whose quivering lip makes my throat tighten.

"I'm grateful to you for bringing him home, Officer Tate," Marcy says. "Bill will be, too. We'll talk to him. We'll be sure nothing like this happens again."

The front door slams. A moment later, Max storms into the kitchen, followed closely by his mother. "I was fine to drive!" he shouts, whipping around to face her. "I had a couple of beers at Becky's. That's it!"

"You had a *case* in your truck! You're *seventeen*! I cannot believe, after everything we've been through this year, that you would climb behind the wheel of that truck half-drunk!"

Max yanks at the collar of his sweatshirt as if it's choking him. "Tate's a pompous ass. He had no reason to pull me over."

Marcy grasps the gold cross hanging from her neck. "He said you rolled through a stop sign! Thank goodness there were no other cars around. Thank goodness it was *him* who stopped you. Thank goodness he chose to pour the beer out. You heard what he said: You could have ended up in jail!"

"Oh, Jesus," Max says, snotty and sluggish. "Let's not blow a little beer out of proportion."

It's disgusting, the way he's acting. I so want to wake him up to how he's hurting his mother and devastating his father, but I'm frozen in my seat, a lot like Bill. I steal a glance at my dad; he's glaring at Max, mouth set in a grim line. He catches my eye. *I told you*, his stare boasts.

"Out of proportion?" Marcy says. She points to the table where we sit, family and friends present to witness the train wreck Max's life is becoming. "We have company. Company I had to abandon so I could speak to the police officer who would have been well within the limits of the law to throw you in a cell. How would a record affect your hopes of playing college football? Your scholarship chances?"

"College is a long way off," Max says flatly. He glances at Bill, who's staring at the opposing wall as if the people arguing around him are someone else's family. Ivy slides closer to him, like her nearness might protect him from the hurt Max's crappy choices inflict.

He swipes a cookie from the buffet and takes a big bite. Crumbs cascade to the floor in a display that's horrifying in its irreverence. Still, I can't look away. None of us can, which is terrible and unfair and absolutely ironic. I suspect this is exactly what he was drinking to avoid: forced togetherness, a less-than-joyful holiday gathering, families trying too hard to restore a normal that's irreparably shattered.

Marcy holds out her hand. "Give me your keys."

Max's anger flares. "What?"

"Your keys," Marcy says. "I want them."

"*Why?*"

"Because your father and I trusted you to use that truck responsibly. You're doing the opposite."

"How the hell am I supposed to get around?"

"Figure it out. I refuse to watch you risk your future—your *life*.

This household does not have the financial security to gamble on your poor choices. We can't afford legal fees if you're arrested, and we can't afford additional medical costs if you cause an accident."

Her open hand is steady and still in Max's agitated face.

He yanks his keys, adorned with a leather football key chain, from his pocket. He fumbles momentarily before crushing them into his mother's palm. Then he stalks toward the stairs, breathing heavily and grumbling faintly, so swollen with emotion I worry he'll burst.

It hits me hard, the irresistible, idiotic urge to follow him, talk to him, hug him—*something*. Plaguing what-ifs have made his sweetness, his enviable zest for life, go rancid, but he's still *Max*.

I shoot up from my place on the bench.

"Jill!" my dad barks.

Max already has a foot on the stairs, but he pivots slowly to look at me, question marks blinking behind his eyes. He's not inviting my company, but he's not discouraging it.

"Sit down, Jillian," Dad says.

The kitchen falls silent but for the sound of Oliver's wheezy winter breath and the hum of the furnace. Nine pairs of eyes are trained on me, watching to see what I'll do.

Max lingers, motionless, while I stand on legs that wobble with uncertainty. I want to go to him because, more than anything in the world, I want him to tell me he's willing to try to get his life back on track. But I don't think he is, and I won't enable him—not like Becky. I won't tell him it's okay to drink and drive, to hurt his parents, to risk his future. I won't let him use me as a diversion from everything that's wrong in his world. I will not—*cannot*—trade my priorities, my values, my sense of worth, to be his second best.

I sit back down.

Max shakes his head, his gaze pinning me to my place on the bench.

He looks disgruntled.

He looks unmoored.

He looks *broken*.

He releases a hefty sigh, and then he throws his fist through the wall.

15

I'M MISERABLE, SO TIME PASSES LIKE MOLASSES from a chilled jar.

Portland for Christmas: endless, tax-free shopping trips for baby clothes, baby gear, baby products. The long drive home: Dad and Meredith, silent but on edge, the aftermath of an argument I missed. The lull between Christmas and the new year: work at True Brew, work on my original chocolate chip cookie recipe, work on my English lit reading list. The highlight? Dad's officially forgiven my Bunco binge. I'm no longer grounded, and I celebrate with an evening at the movies with Leah.

I spend the afternoon of New Year's Eve working on my butter nut brittle recipe. Dad's not home, but Meredith sits, uninvited, on a kitchen stool through several slightly flawed variations of the candy, taste testing and offering her candid opinions ("How about a tiny bit more vanilla extract?" or "Finely chopped pecans *with* the peanuts might be yummy!"). Her criticisms are mildly irritating, but it seems the leech baby has refined her palate; I hate to admit it, but her input proves more helpful than it has in the past.

We're interrupted when Marcy calls and begs me to come over. She needs me to keep an eye on Oliver. I'm a breath from telling her I can't (because little kids are frightening) when she launches into an explanation about how she's watching him for Zoe and Brett, but she's got to run to the pharmacy to pick up one of Bill's refilled prescriptions, which can't wait. "Max is on his way," she adds. "If you could just sit with Oli until he gets here."

Max. I haven't seen him since he clobbered the wall just before Christmas. The distance we've been keeping feels all wrong, particularly today, because for as long as my dad and I have known the Holdens, Bill and Marcy have hosted a New Year's Eve party that rivals my parents' Bunco Night. When we were younger, Max, Ivy, and I spent the evening hanging out in the upstairs bonus room while our parents and the better part of McAlder celebrated a floor below. Just before twelve, we'd sneak down to sit on the staircase, eager to spy on the midnight kissing. Ivy got all giddy and sentimental, while I pretended to gag along with her brother, though even back then, a gangly preteen with braces, I wondered when I'd have my first New Year's kiss.

"I'll be right over," I tell Marcy, because the likelihood of seeing Max somehow supersedes my child phobia.

I hang my checkered apron on its hook and head to my room to exchange my sweats for jeans. I catch Meredith swiping a third piece of brittle as I hurry past the kitchen.

"Have fun!" she calls through a mouthful.

There's nothing fun about two-year-olds. Oliver's undeniably adorable, but he might as well be a Martian—that's how little I relate to him. And I can tell he doesn't care much for me, either, probably because I don't kneel down and assume a Minnie Mouse falsetto when speaking to him. I'm wondering how desperate Marcy must be to have called me, Repeller of Children, as I dash across the street. By the time I ring the Holdens' bell, a fine mist is clinging to my fleece and I'm agonizing over all the ways I'll likely fail at babysitting.

Marcy flings the door open. "Bill's sleeping," she says, ushering me into the house. "His doctors are worried about him getting sick thanks to cold and flu season, so I've convinced him to nap every afternoon. We're hoping the extra rest will help keep his strength up."

Poor Bill.

"Ivy's out with Becky," Marcy continues, zipping her jacket. Her mouth pinches as she says that second name, probably because she's still pissed about the night Officer Tate brought Max home—as she should be. I can't for the life of me figure out what Becky was thinking, letting him get behind the wheel. "Max went to the gym with his friends, but Leo's bringing him home now. Oli's watching TV. I doubt he'll even notice I've left, but if you need anything, call me." She gives me a quick hug, grabs her purse, and scurries out the door.

I make my way to the living room where, sure enough, Oliver is engrossed in an episode of *Barney*. His little head, covered in dark, spiky hair like Max's, bobs along to music.

"Hi, Oliver," I say.

He doesn't look away from the dancing dinosaur. I'm not offended; I don't really want to talk to him, either.

I sink down onto the couch beside him, feeling oddly displaced in this house that's almost as familiar as my own. It's obvious the living room's been recently cleaned. It's devoid of anything Christmas, like the holiday never happened at all. I wonder how long it took Marcy to box up the ornaments and dump the tree Max so carefully picked out, erasing all evidence of holiday merriment—not that there's been a whole lot of that this year.

On the TV, Barney finishes a vivacious song about taking turns. Oliver, apparently sensing a break in the fun, turns to me and says, "Juice."

"You want a drink?"

He blinks huge eyes rimmed in long lashes, caricature cute. "Juice, *pwease*."

"Okay, sure. Let's go see what we can find."

He follows me to the kitchen, where I try and fail to ignore the wall just off the staircase, the one Max put his fist through. The damaged area has been patched and painted over; it's barely discernible. My dad brought the incident up a zillion times while we were in Portland, as if I could forget the look on my oldest friend's face as I effectively rejected him. I wonder if Brett took care of the repair, or if Max manned up and cleaned his own mess.

Oliver tugs on the hem of my fleece, and I tear my attention from the wall to dig a spouted cup from a cabinet. I fill it to the brim with apple juice.

The second the lid's secure, he grabs it and sucks the juice down.

"More," he says, holding the cup out again.

"Really? I think that's enough."

"More!" he screeches. Fat crocodile tears fill his eyes.

"Oh, okay, don't cry! I'll get you more." I take his cup and refill it quickly, motivated by the threat of a tantrum. I don't want him to disturb Bill, and I don't want Max to roll in and find that I'm incapable of handling this person who can't even tie his own shoes. "Let's go see if *Barney*'s still on, okay?"

I dangle the cup in front of his face and, predictably, he follows like a greyhound chasing a rabbit. When he's back on the couch, juice in hand, I congratulate myself on handling his near meltdown like a pro. Maybe it won't be so hard to have a baby around our house after all.

Oliver tosses a stuffed turtle onto my lap while Barney drones on about kindness to a group of children far too old to fall for his shtick.

I pick up the shabby toy. "Is this your friend?"

He nods. "Turtle."

"Yep, he is a turtle. What's his name?"

"Turtle."

"But what's his name?"

"Turtle!" Oliver shouts, his face flushed with outrage. He snatches his stuffed animal back and glares like I'm completely obtuse.

"A turtle named Turtle? Very clever, Oliver."

He smiles an impish smile that reminds me of his uncle Max, then fires Turtle across the room, knocking down one of the potted plants Marcy has lined along the windowsill. The terra cotta doesn't break, but dirt fans out across the floor.

"Oliver! That wasn't nice!" I brush loose soil back into the pot with my flattened palm, thinking, *Brat, brat, brat*. The plant appears jostled but unharmed, so I fit it back into its container and then, out in the foyer, I hear the front door slam.

Perfect. Max, home just in time to catch things falling apart. I'm wiping my hands on my jeans so evidence of my incompetence isn't obvious as he comes sauntering into the room, wearing workout clothes, a backward baseball hat, and a scowl.

Just like that, I forget all about Oliver and what a babysitting hack I am.

"What's going on?" he says.

I stare, transfixed by the shadows under his eyes and the scruffiness of his jaw and the bruising, faintly yellow, on the knuckles of his right hand. A wave of longing crashes into me, and I inhale a tremulous breath.

He has to repeat his question before I remember myself. "Oh, um, Oliver made a mess."

"*You* made a mess," Oliver says, pointing at me. I want to disagree, but I'm sort of tongue-tied. Also, it might be juvenile to argue with a toddler.

Max rounds the couch and sinks down next to his nephew. He musses Oliver's hair in this sweet, devoted way that makes my heart turn over. "Oli, be nice to Jill," he says, and as my name leaves his mouth, he looks at me. His perusal holds for a second—my naked face, my sloppy ponytail, my baggy fleece—before he gives his head a little shake and props his feet on the coffee table. He focuses on Barney and his gaggle of dancing kinder-friends, as if I'm not standing five feet away.

When I can't tolerate the silence any longer, I fill it with mindless prattle. "So, um, your mom'll be home soon. In a few minutes, probably. You know, in case you were wondering."

"I wasn't." He turns to Oliver. "Whatcha drinking, buddy?"

"Juice," Oliver says.

Max regards me. "Did you dilute it?"

"Dilute it with what?"

"Water. Zoe's a freak about Oliver and juice. He can only have it if it's diluted, and then only, like, half a cup."

"Oh. Sorry." I feel a twinge of guilt, which is stupid. It's just juice.

"Two," Oliver tells Max, displaying two chubby fingers.

"Two what, buddy?"

Oli holds out his empty cup. "Two juice."

Max chuckles. "Oh, man. You better not tell your mommy."

With that, Oliver groans, clutches his stomach, and throws up all over the floor.

I gasp. Max hollers, "Shit!" and yanks his feet out of the line of fire. Oliver starts to cry.

Max recovers with impressive speed. He runs to the kitchen while I sit next to a sobbing Oliver, my hand pressed over my nose and mouth to block the pungent stench of toddler puke. I should probably comfort him or something, but I cannot bring myself to move closer to the vomit. My eyes are watering as it is.

Max returns with paper towels and all-purpose cleaner. He blasts me with an incensed glare before kneeling to wipe the hardwood.

"I'm sorry," I say, my apology muffled by my hand.

He scrubs, grumbling, "Dilute the juice next time."

When the mess has been handled—with zero help from me—Max carries Oliver out of the room to clean him up. I sit stiffly, trying to get a grip on my gag reflex.

They return a few minutes later, Oliver in a fresh outfit, sitting atop his uncle's broad shoulders. I catch a welcome whiff of soap as Max lumbers past, dumping his giggling cargo on the couch.

"I'm sorry," I say again. "I really didn't know."

"It's my mom's fault. You don't like kids; she shouldn't have left him with you." *Because you're heartless, not to mention hopelessly inept*, he might as well tack on. He plops down next to Oliver, giving his bony back a thump. "You gonna be okay, buddy?"

Oliver nods. He's still a little pale, but he's looking at his uncle with fascinated admiration. The uninformed would never guess he just spewed apple juice—a good thing, since Marcy won't be long.

"Thanks for cleaning up," I say. "I don't know what I would've done if you hadn't been here."

Max is gazing absentmindedly at Barney, who's moved on to warbling about farm animals. "You'd be sitting in puke."

I smile. "Well, then, thank God for you."

"Yeah, thank God." He glances at me, and there's a glimmer of warmth behind his eyes when he says, "How was Oregon?"

"Okay. My dad worked remotely, Meredith obsessed over the baby, and we hung out with her parents. A lot." And then I ask a question I want to gobble right back up: "How was your Christmas?"

He stares at me, his face falling like a soufflé. His Christmas was awful—it must have been. It fell only two days after he was nearly arrested for drunk driving, and it was the first since his dad's stroke. He likely spent the holiday staving off his parents' crestfallen looks while icing his bruised hand.

He leans in a little, like he has a secret, and my heart gallops in anticipation. Very quietly, very coolly, he says, "Christmas fucking sucked."

Max, forever an asshole when he's upset.

I recall, suddenly, the beach vacation of three years ago, when I paddled out too far and lost control in an undertow. Max swam to me like an Olympic freestyler, plucked me from the ocean's frothy waves, and paddled for the beach like he performed water rescues daily. Coughing and sputtering salt water, I expected him to fawn over me, but after dumping me unceremoniously on the sand, he tossed up his hands and yelled, "Damn it, Jillian! Do you have a death wish?"

Later, when I'd tearfully recounted the rescue and subsequent shouting to Marcy, she explained that some boys are afraid of their emotions, her son especially, and watching me thrash among the whitecaps had probably scared him. Instead of owning up to it, he yelled. That was hard to swallow at the time, one of those things mothers say to make kids feel better, so I convinced myself that Max was just a jerk. I shadowed Ivy for the next two days, until Max hunted me down and convinced me to walk to town with him. There, he bought me coconut ice cream on a waffle cone, his stunted-boy version of an apology.

I don't foresee any ice cream apologies in my future.

He closes his eyes. The half-moon shadows beneath them are prominent. "I've got Oli," he says. "You can go home."

I rise from the couch, shocked by his dismissal. I'm too hurt to muster genuine anger, but a frustrated sense of helplessness sloshes around in the pit of my stomach. This was a stupid idea, coming here. I should've known I wouldn't be able to fix things with a single impromptu visit. I should be in my kitchen, baking, or in my room, cataloging scholarships. I should be far, far away from Max Holden.

I shuffle out of the living room and into the foyer. I've got a hand on the front doorknob when traitorous tears begin to fall.

I can't go home—I don't want Meredith to know I'm upset—so I duck into the Holdens' powder room to pull myself together.

God. I can't believe I let him get to me. I'm crying over a boy who won't dump his shitty girlfriend, who'd rather sulk than grow a pair and get his life together. I look at myself in the mirror and find my face blotchy and tearstained—pitiful. I don't like the Jillian who looks back at me. She's changed alongside her parents and her neighbors, and not for the better. She's a glimmer of the savvy, determined girl she was last spring.

So what if her college funds disappeared? So what if her parents argue almost as often as they breathe? So what if she's about to become the world's most reluctant big sister?

So what if the boy I care about most in the world has become intolerable?

What sucks is that I don't even know what I want from Max. My feelings are jumbled. Ever-altering. Infuriating. I wish, not for the first time, that I could forget all about him.

I whirl away from the wimp in the mirror and blot my face with a bit of toilet paper. I straighten my spine and lift my chin, then march out of the bathroom, straight to the front door.

I don't allow myself to look back, but I know Max is sprawled across the couch as sure as I know my shadow trails behind me. I know he's tuned into preschool programming with the nephew he adores. I know today's crossness is a product of last week's rebuff.

And I know, somehow, that he can be the old Max, the *good* Max, again.

. . . .

On New Year's Day, True Brew cuts back its hours of business, which means Kyle and I get to open *and* close.

Leah comes in midafternoon to hang out, which is perfect because the holiday's making for a slow shift. She stands opposite the pastry case, sipping the Honey Lavender Latte (today's special) I made for her.

"My new favorite," she says, licking a bit of foam from her lip. "So? How'd we all ring in the New Year?"

Kyle whistles a cartoony downslide. "I played Parcheesi with my parents. Hopefully last night's not an indicator of how this year's gonna pan out."

"I baked," I say, omitting the part about *why* I baked: to pull myself out of another case of Max-inflicted doldrums.

Leah smiles dreamily. "Jesse and I had dinner and saw a movie, and then we went back to his house. I hope he'll always be my New Year's kiss."

Kyle rolls his eyes. "That comment *so* deserves to be mocked, and yet I kind of hope so, too." He turns to me. "You didn't see Max last night?"

"No. Why would I?"

"'Cause your parents hang out? I figured you two might end up getting together."

"Nope, though I did have a brief encounter with him yesterday afternoon."

"A brief encounter?" Leah says. "Sounds like you're talking about a wild animal."

"I mean, basically. I just . . ." The hurt of yesterday's spurn finds me all over again, and I drop my elbows to the counter, letting my chin fall to my hands. "I feel so helpless. We've been friends for so long. . . . I should be able to make it easier for him to deal with what happened to his dad. Instead, I'm just standing by, watching him fall apart."

"That's not what you're doing," Leah says, reaching out to squeeze my hand.

But, yeah, I kind of am. Yesterday's visit was a complete fail, and I abandoned him the night Officer Tate brought him home, the night he needed someone in his corner more than any other. I haven't stopped regretting it.

"You can't keep him from acting like an idiot," Kyle says. "None of us can."

Leah nods. "But that doesn't mean he doesn't need his friends."

"He still hangs out with his friends," I mumble, looking at Kyle. "He sees you and Jesse and Leo all the time. He sees Becky."

"Becky's *not* his friend," Leah says.

Kyle nudges me. "You are. We all are. Max'll come around, but for now, we're gonna have to ride it out. We'll be there for him in the best ways we know how."

I nod. I can do that. I can exist in Max's world the way I used to. . . .

As a friend.

16

THE MONDAY AFTER WINTER BREAK, I CATCH a ride home from school with Leah, then wait in the living room, watching out the window for Leo's Tahoe to pull into the Holdens' driveway. Max's truck hasn't moved since his clash with Officer Tate, but Ivy's car is gone and so is Marcy's, which means Bill's not home, either. This is a good thing . . . I think.

Meredith wanders in and out of the living room, biding time, I guess, trying to engage me in conversation. While I'm putting extra effort into being kind as her pregnancy winds down—the leech baby is siphoning her energy like nobody's business—I'm too anxious for mindless chitchat.

Finally, Leo's SUV veers into the Holdens' driveway. I can hear the heavy thump of his music's bass even from inside the house. Max climbs out, lifts his hand in a wave, then makes his way to the front door. Even though my heart's doing nervous pirouettes, I allow him five minutes—who knows what boys do when they get home from school?—then give Meredith a bogus excuse about needing to borrow a recipe from Marcy and jog across the street.

I have to ring the bell twice before Max opens the door. To say he's confused when he sees me standing on the porch would be a major understatement.

"Uh, hey," he says, running a hand through his hair.

His lack of enthusiastic welcome isn't a surprise, but it makes me even more nervous. Doesn't matter, though—I'm not going to botch this. I'm going to say what I came to say, and then I'm going to let him make the next move.

I breeze past him, right into the house, which smells of fresh baking, like ginger and nutmeg. He trails me to the kitchen, eyeing me like my intrusion is possibly perilous. I open the fridge and root around inside, mentally reviewing my Be Max's Friend plan until I find two cans of Coke. I pull them out and hold one out to him. "Thirsty?"

"I guess." He takes the can, pops the top, then hands it back to me.

"Thanks," I say, trading. I like this about him—his instinctual chivalry—and I find myself smiling as I watch him open the second soda for himself.

He takes a swig, then leans back against the countertop. "What're you doing here, Jill?"

"I came to see how your first day back to school was." I say this like it's nothing—like I drop by to check in on him all the time.

He shrugs. "Predictable."

"And your New Year?"

"I stayed home, a choice that wasn't well-received by . . . some."

Becky. I'm intrigued by this knowledge that he bowed out despite her disapproval. Kind of makes me want to raise my arms in victory.

"I stayed home, too," I tell him. "I baked soft pretzels. Meredith ate four, positively drenched in mustard."

He gives me a tentative smile. "Sounds like a good time. What about your dad?"

"He was out of town. A work thing." Dad and I are still up and down, but that didn't keep me from feeling for him, all alone in some stark hotel room as the clock struck midnight. Made me sad.

Still makes me sad.

"Jill," Max says, sliding a step closer. "You okay?"

I nod because, yeah, of course I'm okay. My dad went away on business. He's back now, and everything's fine.

Except, Max is standing right beside me, and we're in his empty house, and my hands are shaking even as they clutch my Coke can. How on God's green earth did I think this was a good idea? How can Max and I be friends when I'm hyperaware of the energy crackling between us? When I know how his kisses make my skin sing?

I hate this panicky, quivering thing my stomach does in his proximity now.

Heat inches up my neck as he watches me, concerned, and I know—I've got to let him in on the truth about why I'm here. I take a deep breath. "Anyway, I just wanted to tell you that the other day when I was watching Oliver . . . Well, things got weird and that sucks, and I think it might've been my fault because I made your nephew puke." At this, I get a genuine grin. Encouraged, I press on. "Then there was that night with the desserts, when Officer Tate . . . Yeah. I shouldn't have left you hanging the way I did. We've been friends too long, and that was so uncool of me."

He blinks and for a second, I worry I've splashed lighter fluid on the embers of his frustration. Then his eyes go soft. He puts his soda down and touches my arm. "You're not apologizing, are you?"

"I'm—"

"Because you've been nothing but good to me, so don't, okay?"

I smooth my ponytail and will myself to stop blushing. "Okay."

The muffled sound of his phone's ringtone comes from the pocket of his jeans. He ignores it and says, "I think we should talk. Like, for real."

"Your phone's ringing."

"It can wait."

"Is it Becky?"

He quirks an eyebrow. "Does it matter?"

I step away because, *hello, reality check*, but Max reaches for me, his fingers wrapping around my wrist assertively enough to still me. His warmth, his presence, surround me like a cocoon. His phone rings, and rings again.

"Max," I caution. "You have a girlfriend."

"I'll end it."

I sputter a few false starts before asking, "You'd do that?"

"Why wouldn't I?"

"Why *haven't* you?"

He must be out of retorts, because he bites down on his bottom lip. His phone finally shuts up; Becky's probably pulling on her fiery locks, exasperated by her boyfriend's unavailability.

"Jill, we're friends, right?"

I nod and shake my head at the same time, spastic.

"Friends hear each other out, right?"

He's still holding my wrist and the contact's making pudding of my thoughts. I'm hazy with his evergreen scent, the sincerity of his tone, and I take an involuntary step back, until the marble countertop presses into the small of my back. He lets me go, and I can breathe easier now that there's distance between us. "Yes," I say. "Friends hear each other out."

His gaze is intense, trained right on me. "After Bunco, the mistletoe, you said it didn't matter, that we should forget about it."

"And you were on the same page. You said it shouldn't have happened."

"Jesus. I said it shouldn't have happened *the way it did*." I'm having a hard time processing his words, their implications, and I can't believe it when he steps closer. He reaches out to thread an errant lock of hair behind my ear. "Do you really believe it didn't matter?" he asks, and in this moment, he's so very *Max*. "'Cause it mattered to me. I came to the coffee shop to tell you, but the whole thing went to hell and . . ."

He leans forward, tilting his head, and I realize—holy crap—he's going to kiss me. This is not a part of the plan *at all*, but I want him to, and I don't want him to, and my mind's twirling in circles, like he and I used to do when we were kids. Only, we're not going to fall to the ground, laughing while the world whirls above us. We're going to kiss, *again*, and even though I know it's the absolute wrong thing to do, I'm not sure I have the willpower to stop it.

I put my palm on his chest with the intention of pushing him away because, *yes, I can do the right thing*, but he misreads the gesture and covers my hand with his. The tiny bit of conviction I found melts like butter as his other hand finds my cheek. I tip my chin up—*say it, Jillian, tell him to back off*. His cinnamon breath sweeps across my skin, and my eyes fall closed.

His phone begins to ring again, like an alarm—like a freaking air horn—and that's it. I push him away.

My face is sizzling. *Becky, Becky, Becky* . . . God, I wish she'd disappear.

Max silences his phone, vexed, and I wonder: Is she his fallback? Am *I*?

"Jilly," he says, his voice low, abraded, like he's nearly used it up.

I shake my head. "I can't. Not like this."

A shadow falls over his face, but he says, "Yeah. Okay."

There's an elephant tromping around the kitchen, a resentful, ginger-haired elephant who wears Becky's face and swings its trunk with wrathful intention. "Look," I start, because I can't ignore it—*her*—anymore. "I don't understand why, but you've stayed with Becky through thick and thin and all the bullshit in between. Even though you cheated on her, she still wants to be with you. Honestly, I think you guys are terrible for each other, but for whatever reason, you're hanging on. At the risk of sounding like a shrink, I feel like you need to do some serious thinking about what you want from her. It's not fair otherwise."

"Un-fucking-believable," he mutters, staring at his shoes. "You're on her side?"

"Hardly. I just don't want to be the reason you do or don't stay with her. While you guys are whatever you are, you and I . . . can't."

He looks up, his eyes wide and earnest. "But you said we were friends."

"Friends don't kiss, Max."

His mouth turns up, a hint of a smile. "They don't?"

"Nope. Friends hang out. Friends talk. Friends are there for each other." I offer him my hand, cheesy but appropriately platonic. "I want that for us. I really do."

He nods, shaking my hand. "I want that, too."

17

MAX AND I DON'T SEE MUCH OF each other at school in the following few weeks, but we make plans to hang out after: coffee (for me) and soda (for him), long drives in the truck he recently earned back, and homework sessions spent at the library (because I'm laying the groundwork for future scholarship applications and he's playing catch-up). We don't talk so much as absorb each other's company, but that feels okay because it's not a strain on our fledgling friendship. Also, I meant what I said about him and Becky: He should think about what he wants without my influence serving as a distraction.

Things haven't been great between them, according to gossip courtesy of Leah and Kyle. Becky decided Max should quit hanging out with the guys so much, and Max decided Becky didn't get to dictate his social calendar. Other tidbits I've heard: Her parents hate him (a legit possibility), his mother hates her (despite Becky's friendship with Ivy, that's likely now true), and recently, after a particularly ferocious fight on the quad, the two of them had make-up sex in an empty biology classroom (God—*gross*).

When I'm not hanging out with Max, busting my ass in class, or tacking extra hours onto my shifts at work, I'm helping Meredith with baby preparations; she can't lift anything heavier than a grocery bag, which means I get to assemble the crib when it's delivered on a rainy Saturday morning, the last day of January. In the nursery, she sits in this special chair she bought—she calls it a glider—and tries to make sense of the multiple pages of instructions, pointing out pieces of whitewashed wood that need to be fitted together.

Later, after the leech baby's crib is standing straight and sturdy and Meredith's shown me an app she recently downloaded—a contraction timer, of all things—Max rescues me with a text: *Movie at my house tonight?*

Somehow, this proposed activity strikes me as more intimate than anything else we've done lately. I mean, it's not sex in a biology classroom, but me plus Max plus a movie viewed in a dark space seems more like an equation equaling trouble than two friends hanging out.

I call Kyle for his opinion.

"But Max told me he was going out tonight," he says. "Couple of guys on the basketball team are having a rager, and Becky's dragging him along."

"Not anymore," I say, wondering at the catalyst for his change in plans. "He just texted me. . . . Do you think I should watch a movie with him? I mean, it could potentially get . . . weird."

"Jelly Bean, surely you two can sit through a ninety-minute film without your libidos getting the best of you."

I roll my eyes. "You should come."

"Third wheel? Hard pass. Unless . . ."

And that's how Leah ends up invited to the Holdens'. She insists on bringing Jesse, and he calls Leo and tells him to stop by, and before I know it, the evening has turned into an official Movie Night.

My friends and I used to gather in the Holdens' big bonus room often, vegging in front of comedies we'd seen dozens of times. Even Ivy joined us when she wasn't in the midst of social calls and dance team obligations. Last year she came pretty regularly, in fact, and then she started inviting Becky. Seemingly all of a sudden, Becky and Max were a couple. That was right around the time I began to dread the get-togethers. Then Bill had his stroke and the Holden household became a place of sickness and sadness, and Max and Ivy stopped asking friends over.

I've got mixed emotions about this whole Movie Night thing—the notion carries a lot of baggage, and tonight will be Max's and my first attempt at our newly resumed friendship in the company of others. I do my best to relax by making a treat, lemon coconut truffles, which I have to wrestle from my freakishly strong, delicacy-demanding stepmother before heading out the door.

With every step across the dark street, my nerves multiply. Kyle's car has replaced Ivy's in the Holdens' driveway, and Jesse's and Leo's are bumper-to-bumper on the street. Seems I'm the last to arrive.

Normally, I'd give my double knock, then walk right in, but tonight feels formal. I was invited, after all, and I've brought a dessert. So I knock three times, and wait.

Max answers the door. He's smiling, and then I am, too.

I gather my wits, sort of, and after saying a quick hello to Marcy and Bill, who are watching *Wheel of Fortune* in the living room, I follow Max up to the bonus room, where our friends are waiting. Leah has dressed up for our night in because that's the sort of girl she is—an ostentatious chocolate sculpture, showy but sweet—and the guys are lounging in jeans and sweatshirts with various sports logos plastered on them. I give a general wave and place my platter of truffles on the ottoman. While Kyle, Jesse, and Leo descend on them with alarming zeal, I allow myself a two-second peek at Max, who's loitering to my left. He's wearing a University of Washington hoodie, and his hair's sticking up in unruly spikes, and I'm pretty sure he couldn't look better if he tried.

He catches me checking him out—of course he does—and I turn away to assess the viable seating options, instantly regretting my leisurely mosey across the street. Kyle, Leah, and Jesse are lined up on the couch, Leo's taken over the recliner, and Max . . . He crosses the room to the oversize beanbag chair, prime real estate, and flops down, taking up well over half the surface area. Before Bunco—before Halloween—I might've shoved him over and made him share. Tonight, I stay on my feet, unsure of what to do and where to go.

"Jilly," he says, patting the barely there space beside him. "Come sit."

I glance at Kyle, who hitches a *hubba-hubba* eyebrow. I head for the beanbag with the sole purpose of proving his silent but ridiculous assumption wrong. "Scoot over," I tell Max.

He does, but when I sit down, we both sort of sink into the center, until our shoulders-hips-thighs bump up against each other. I'm tempted to rocket right back up, but Max doesn't bat an eye, and honestly, what's the big deal? We've been sitting side by side at True Brew and the library, not to mention within the confines of the truck, and it's been fine. Because we're friends—we agreed—and so far neither of us has done anything to upset the balance we found when we shook hands.

Jesse hops up to dim the lights and Max uses the remote to start the movie. It's one I've seen before, a shame because I could use something other than the many points of contact between my body and

Max's to focus on. But alas, I spend much of the film alternately wondering at and freaking out about his apparent lack of distress.

Halfway through the movie, Marcy appears with three bowls of popcorn. She gives one to Kyle, Leah, and Jesse, one to Leo (because his size dictates an individual serving), and one to Max and me. She smiles when she notices us together, yet she doesn't look all that surprised. After letting us know that she and Bill are turning in for the night, she heads back downstairs.

Max shifts, planting the bowl of popcorn between us. He angles his head toward mine and whispers, "Comfortable?"

I nod. "You?"

"I'm good."

I wiggle deeper into my spot, bending my knees to bring my feet up. The movie's nearing its climax and it's funny—it really is—but I'm struggling to pay attention. I'm struggling to get comfortable, too, because I feel like I can't move, lest I rock our beanbag boat.

"Jill," Max says, hooking an arm around my legs, "I can't see." He tugs my knees down until they're resting against his thighs, then leaves his arm flung across, effectively pinning them there—not that I have a superstrong urge to move away.

Even in the meager light, I catch Kyle smirking.

And then, over the theatrics onscreen, I hear car doors slamming in the driveway, followed by commotion downstairs. Max sits up a little, cocking his head. Not five seconds later, the bonus room door bangs open and the lights blaze on. Becky stands in the doorway, and judging by her disheveled appearance, she's having a wild night. Her ringlets are frizzy, her face is patchy with redness, and her mouth is a tight line. She's in a minidress and tall, tall boots, with pale swaths of bare thigh glowing in the lamplight.

I jerk away from Max, but it's too late. She sees us—how close we're sitting, Max's arm draped across my legs, the way I've sub-consciously inclined myself toward him.

"*This* is why you skipped out on the party?" she accuses, thrusting a finger at me.

"I was just—"

"Becky." Ivy comes into view behind her, also dressed for a night out—though not as outrageously. "He wasn't feeling well, I told you."

"He looks fine!" She's wasted—it's so obvious. Her eyes are blood-shot, and she keeps rocking back on her heels. She looks careless and cutthroat—practically possessed.

Max rises from the beanbag, standing at his full height. "I *am* fine," he declares in the same frank tone he might use to say *the sky's blue*. "I just didn't feel like partying."

If I'm taken aback by his admission, Becky's flabbergasted. Her eyes dart from him to me, drilling holes straight through my soul. She's questioning what Max sees in me, as a friend or otherwise, and her expression is so anguished, so bitter, my cheeks become circles of heat. I sink into the beanbag, wishing myself anywhere but here.

Becky turns her glare on Max. "How could you do this to me?!"

"We were watching a movie." He waves a hand toward Leo, Jesse, Kyle, and Leah, looking on with assorted expressions of discomfort. "It's not like this is a private party."

"Isn't it? Because you two looked pretty fucking cozy!"

I expect Max to go all humble, to waver under her allegations like he has in the past. But instead of trying to wheedle his way back into her good graces, he says, "Becky, if I'd wanted to see you, I would've gone with you to the party. If I'd wanted you to stop by, I would've invited you."

Her eyes are bright with tears. God, this is awful.

Ivy drops a sympathetic hand onto her shoulder. To her brother, she says, "You don't have to be a dick."

"And you didn't have to bring her here."

"What would you have had me do? Let her leave by herself?" Ivy scoffs. "You of all people should know what can happen if the cops catch you driving drunk."

Max's hands curl into fists. "I wish you'd mind your own business."

"I wish you'd quit screwing up!"

He ignores his sister and takes a purposeful step toward Becky. "It's time for you to go," he says, though not unkindly. "I'll drive you home."

"I'm not going anywhere with you!" She lunges, planting her palms on his chest and shoving hard. He doesn't move—doesn't even sway—but I'm done. I can't watch her put her hands on him, and I can't watch him try to tend to her, even though I know it's exactly what he should be doing. She's in shambles, and Ivy's not doing her any favors; where usually I've got nothing but ill will when it comes to Becky, now all I feel is pity.

She's crying, sloppy sobs that serve as a perfect diversion. I stand, catching Kyle's eye. He gets up, too, and we're nearly clear of the bonus room when Max says, "Jill, wait."

"It's okay," I tell him, waving a hand like, *deal with your shit*. I want him and Becky to be over more than I want my next breath, but I'm not interested in standing around, waiting to see if he'll make a clean break.

"I'll walk Jill across the street," Kyle tells him.

Max nods, and that's it—Movie Night's over.

Leah, Jesse, and Leo are up as well, gathering their things and slinging on their jackets. Ivy's comforting Becky, wearing a look of utter helplessness, and I feel an unexpected pang of sympathy. It's not like she expected a scene like this, and I know a little something about trying to push logical decisions on someone who's determined to dig their hole as deep as possible.

Kyle loops his arm through mine. We head for the door together, listening to Becky snivel as we make our escape. I look back one last time to see her cross-legged on the floor, her head resting on Ivy's shoulder. Max is hunched over the two of them. He's murmuring something, his voice tight with consternation, with commiseration, and it doesn't take a scholar to figure out that this was Becky's intention—she's trying to win his attention, his affection, by acting all bat-shit.

I wonder if it'll work.

Once we've waved Leah, Jesse, and Leo off, Kyle and I cross the street to my house, tomblike in its tranquil darkness. He walks me all the way to the porch, quiet until he's not. "So, what's going on with you two?"

"Who?" I ask dumbly.

He flashes his patent *don't bullshit me* scowl. "You and Max."

"Nothing."

"That wasn't nothing. I know we talked about being there for him, but did we mean *be there* for him?"

"I'm not in the mood for riddles, Kyle. Just say what you want to say."

"Okay," he says in this smart-alecky way that makes me steady myself against the porch railing even before he gets started. "I think you like Max more than you're letting on, and I think he likes you. I think he's relaxed when he's with you—content when he's with you. I think Becky's a spoiled fuckup. And I think you're standing in your own way."

"There are a lot of things standing in my way."

"*Her?* No competition."

"Kyle. On the off chance Max and I one day got together, she'd make hell of my life at school. Ivy would, too. Besides, it's not just Becky. My dad hates Max."

"Because he's been acting like a dipshit. But he won't always." Kyle squeezes my hand, gazing down at me like a sage old owl. "Your dad loves Max's family, and he loves you. If you guys got together one day, he'd get over it—I'm certain. He wants you to be happy, Jelly Bean, just like me."

18

Y DAD WANTS ME TO BE HAPPY, so he buys me a brand-new KitchenAid Artisan Stand Mixer. It's beautiful—metallic silver, with all sorts of attachments, like a gourmet pasta press and an ice cream maker. He gives it to me the day following the disaster that was Movie Night, and I've got it out of the box and running in a matter of minutes. I'm thankful, *so* thankful, but even as I'm measuring flour and spooning yeast, I'm recalling the expression my dad wore as I accepted the mixer: reminiscent and proud, a little regretful.

I read his gift for all the things it says: *I'm sorry I'm not around more*, and *For the love of God behave*, and *I'm trying to be a cool dad again.*

I make homemade pizza crust, and even though savory foods aren't really my thing, I add some marinara and mozzarella and zesty pepperoni.

"I'll set the table," Dad says fifteen minutes later, as I'm pulling dinner out of the oven.

Meredith fills glasses with water and ice and I divide the pizza into slices, pondering this shift in the paradigm; other than holidays, the three of us haven't sat down to dinner together in months.

We're quiet at first, a lot of chewing and swallowing because we're tragically out of practice when it comes to this sort of togetherness, until my dad asks, "How was your day, Jill?"

"With the exception of my new mixer, pretty *eh*. I worked and caught up on homework."

"You should've come shopping with Marcy and me," Meredith says. "We got a swing for the baby, battery powered, pink-and-brown plaid. Darling."

I nod blandly, and Dad does, too. He and I are in agreement about the overwhelming lameness of baby stuff.

"Maybe next time," Meredith adds.

Dad frowns and I know what he's thinking: How many more shopping trips will need to be made before the baby's stocked up? He refocuses on me. "How's the new semester going?"

"Okay," I say, looking down at my plate. He's trying, but his questions make me jittery. The last few weeks have been chaotic—I've barely had a minute to breathe—and the next few months won't be much better, what with the baby coming. And then there's my yo-yo relationship with Max. I wonder, for the billionth time, what he's doing—*how* he's doing. I think of the often-quoted definition of insanity: carrying out the same behavior over and over while expecting different results.

Is that me?

Have I completely lost it where Max Holden is concerned?

I pick at my crust, feeling like a can of soda, all shaken up. I wish I could unload the stress that's peaked in mountains around me, but Meredith's never really been a confidante, and Dad'll lose his shit if he finds out my funk stems, in large part, from my non-romance with the bad-influence neighbor kid.

I set my half-eaten pizza slice on my plate. "I think I'm going to head to my room," I say, pushing my chair back.

Meredith looks at me, worried. "Not feeling well?"

"I'm fine. Just not in the mood for pizza after all. Plus, I've got a lot to do before school tomorrow."

She smiles sympathetically. "We'll save you a few slices in case you get hungry later."

Dad clears his throat, and I turn to face him. "Jill, I know the last several months have been a challenge. I know I came down hard, grounding you the way I did, and I know you're still disappointed about your International Culinary Institute money, but I think you've handled yourself well lately."

Only because I've been faking it, hiding my worries, not to mention my time with Max. I nod, unsure of where he's headed.

He continues, "Maybe we don't say it enough, but Meredith and I appreciate your help. We're proud of you."

I sense that he wants me to reply with something eloquent, something forthcoming, a response to merit the ceasefire he's initiating, but tonight I've got nothing more than, "Thanks again for the mixer."

· · · ·

Much later, after Dad and Meredith have gone to bed, I sneak outside to meet Max for a walk through the neighborhood. The outing was his idea, but once we get moving, he falls quiet, going through the motions without really engaging.

"What's up with you?" I ask, after our first trip around the block.

He shrugs, melancholy, and adjusts the beanie he's wearing.

Rather than poke at him by asking about how Becky's surprise appearance at Movie Night played out, I tell him about my new mixer: its make and model, its various attachments, its quiet hum. I tell him about how perfectly the dough hook mixed the beginnings of my pizza crust, and how beautiful it looks on the kitchen counter. "It's, like, the Rolls-Royce of small appliances," I say.

He glances at me. "What is?"

"Uh, my new mixer?"

"Oh."

I resist the urge to roll my eyes at his inattentiveness. Realizing it's up to me to keep the conversation flowing, I ask, "What'd you do today?"

"Went out."

My skin prickles, and I immediately want to ask, *With who?*

"Leo and I went for a long run," he supplies unprompted.

I'm not proud of the relief I feel at knowing he wasn't with Becky. I don't want to be jealous of something I don't understand. This—our friendship—should be enough.

"How was it?"

"Fine. Boring . . . I had other stuff on my mind." He nudges me with his elbow. "But tell me more about your mixer. What're you gonna bake next?"

I consider. "Maybe a cake? Something delicious and supersweet, like coconut cloud cake, or hummingbird cake. Yeah, hummingbird cake, I think. It's full of crushed pineapple and mashed banana and pecans and other delectable things. Have you ever had it?"

He gives me a blank look. "Had what?"

"Hummingbird cake! God, Max, are you even listening?"

"Yeah, I'm listening." He drags a hand over his face. The night's so cold, his breath creates a cloud of condensation. "Sorry, Jill. I'm just tired."

We head for home.

19

HE NEXT AFTERNOON, THE QUAD IS FOR once drenched in sunshine, crammed with people soaking up vitamin D even though the day's cool.

The final bell's just rung, and I'm weaving through the crowd, hoping to talk to Kyle and Leah for a few minutes before I head for home. They're missing from our regular spot, but Becky's nearby, talking to her old standby Bryan Davenport, plus a bunch of his basketball buddies. When she sees me, she puts on an aggrieved mask that almost makes me feel sorry for her—until she leaves Bryan to strut toward me.

I become a statue on the walkway, watching, waiting as she makes her approach. The last I saw of her, she was sobbing on the Holdens' bonus room floor. What could she possibly have to say to me now, and where the hell are my friends when I need them?

She's advancing, her eyes locked on mine, and my pulse pounds in my ears. Frantically, I sift through a flurry of possible salutations, but my efforts are in vain because when she reaches me, she doesn't stop like I expect. There are no loathsome words. No guilt-inducing tears. She doesn't acknowledge me at all, except to freaking body-check me, ramming the barbed bone of her shoulder into mine as she pushes past.

I am *shocked*.

I know she's pissed about Max bailing on their Saturday night plans, and I know the sight of him and me together on the beanbag chair mutated her into a monster, but—*oh my God*—I can't believe she's resorting to this sort of barbarity.

She'd make hell of my life at school, I'd told Kyle, and yeah, sure enough.

I'm still standing on the path, reeling, when I spot Kyle, football in hand, sauntering toward me to the whistled tune of "Walking on Sunshine." "Jelly Bean," he says, a greeting so cheerful I feel certain he missed what Becky did moments ago. When I don't respond, he stoops down to scrutinize my expression. His smile falls. "Whoa. You okay?"

Pain radiates through my shoulder. My confidence must've been jolted, too, because my response is scarcely a whisper. "I'm fine."

He gives a skeptical raise of his eyebrows but doesn't push. "Have you seen Max?"

"Nope." Thank God, because if he would've been around to witness Becky's clip, I'd be a bazillion times more humiliated than I already am.

He slings an arm around me. "You sure you're okay?"

"I'm sure," I say, shrugging him off. Feeling like the world's biggest jerk, brushing away his concern like I am, I let a lie loose. "I've got to go. I've got Meredith's car and she's waiting for me, and just—I'll call you later, okay?"

He shouts after me, but I pretend I don't hear him as I make a rushed trip through the quad to the parking lot, where Meredith's Saturn waits. I dump my bag into the backseat before sliding into the driver's seat, thankful to be alone with my busted ego. With a shaky breath, I prod my shoulder; it's tender where Becky rammed it, and holy shit, I *loathe* her.

I'm shifting the Saturn into gear when I notice Max climbing into his truck several parking spaces away. I leave my foot on the brake so I can watch him pull his favorite knit cap over his head, crank the truck's ignition, and jab a button on the stereo. My heart beats a quick, hard rhythm because, God, he looks dejected.

He glances up, through our respective windshields, and his sad-puppy eyes find mine. His posture inclines toward me, as if impatient words tread on his tongue, stomping their hooves, waiting for the gate to open. He raises his shoulders in a slight, despondent shrug.

Damn it if my insides don't go all warm and trembly. I want to climb out of the Saturn. I want to hurry toward him. I want to hop into the truck and hug him until his hurt goes away—until *my* hurt goes away.

Because this is torture, the wanting and the not having.

My breath comes shallow as, for the first time in all the weeks we've been hanging out, I envision my life with Max in it—as *more* than a friend. Traversing high school and family and the future in tandem. Maybe we could be good together, Max and me.

Maybe, *just maybe*, we could work.

I give him a nod of acknowledgment before wrenching my attention away, terrified by my sudden, unforeseen attitude shift. I leave tire marks as I peel out of the parking lot.

. . . .

He calls an hour later.

I'm driving aimlessly through McAlder, too worked up to go home. I pull onto the shoulder, not far from the tree farm we visited with my dad, and answer with a wary, "Hello?"

"Jilly, hey. You busy?"

"Not really," I say, guarded after our silent parking lot exchange. I turn on the Saturn's hazard lights so no one barrels into its rear and say, "What's up?"

"I, uh, need a favor." His tempo's off; he sounds exceptionally lethargic.

"What kind of favor?"

"A ride."

"What's wrong with your truck?"

"It's . . . undrivable." He releases the word slowly, with a chuckle and a slur, and I then know exactly why he sounds strange, and why the F-150 is undrivable. He's been drinking.

"Call your girlfriend, Max," I say with an agitated sigh.

"I can't."

"No? Already tried her?"

"You don't know anything," he says, muddy and disjointed.

"No, *you* don't know anything—except for how to be an asshole."

Through the phone line, I hear liquid slosh against glass, followed by a heavy swallow. He must've fought with Becky again. It's the best explanation for the way she treated me on the quad, and for his unhappiness in the parking lot—not to mention his current state of inebriation.

I can't believe I was considering the possibility of *us* all of an hour ago. Max isn't fixable. He might never come around. And for whatever reason, he thinks it's cool to come running to me anytime he needs to be comforted. Or bailed out.

"Call someone else," I tell him. I'm done with his preferred method of coping.

"Forget it. I'll drive myself home."

A wall of anger knocks into me. I've been confused by his behavior for ages, and disappointed in him more times than I can count, but this tremendous animosity I'm feeling is new. I want to hurl my phone through the windshield. I want to hurt him as badly as he's hurting me.

"You are *such* a jerk, Max. I hate you—did you know that? I *hate* you."

"Jesus, Jill—"

"Don't. There's nothing you can say that'll change the way I feel." It's the truth, but no matter how completely this latest setback pisses me off, I can't leave him stranded. I drop my head against the rest behind me. "Where are you?"

A moment of silence passes before he says, "The river."

I close my eyes, sad beyond description because I know the spot. A long, rarely driven road running parallel to the river, once a favorite bike-riding route for Max and me. I still cruise it from time to time, for nostalgia's sake.

Apparently he does, too.

I drive fast, imagining the very worst: Officer Tate and a fleet of squad cars, Max stuck in a cinder-block cell.

When I arrive, I'm relieved to see that the F-150 is the only other vehicle on the road. I park behind it. The rush of river water rages in my ears as I walk to the driver's-side door and throw it open. There's Max, clutching a nearly empty bottle of Maker's Mark by its red, waxy neck.

"Jilly!"

I shake my head, sickened by the slovenly sight of him. I point to the whisky. "Where did you get that?"

"My dad's liquor cabinet." He swirls the contents of the bottle before taking a gulp, swallowing noisily. "I don't think he'll miss it."

I flinch at his derisiveness. I hold out my hand. "Give it to me."

He looks at the bottle, then back at me. A challenge.

"Give it to me, right now, or I swear to God I'll leave. With your keys."

He shoves the booze at me. I dump what's left on the side of the road, then hurl the empty bottle toward the river. It arcs like a football, landing with a barely audible splash.

I turn back to Max; he's unquestionably irate, and I don't care. "Do you have more?"

"I wish."

"Lock your truck. You can come back for it tomorrow. I'm taking you home."

"But I'd rather go to Leo's."

"Too bad. I'm not a freaking shuttle service. Let's go."

I march to my car, rolling my eyes at the pitiful scuffle of his feet as he trails behind me. It's maddening that he's backslid so far. Maddening that I have to play designated driver on a Monday afternoon because he makes the world's most moronic choices.

"Put your seat belt on," I say after he's collapsed into the passenger seat.

"Don't treat me like a fucking child," he retorts with a glare.

I've half a mind to shove him out of the car. "Don't act like a fucking child!"

He buckles his seat belt, then yanks the lever that reclines his seat. He falls backward until he lands, horizontal, with a thud. "Get going," he says, closing his eyes.

My anger simmers all the way to our neighborhood. I meant what I said: Today, I really and truly hate him. Still, I can't fault him for calling for a ride—at least a responsible decision followed the careless footsteps before it. But he shouldn't have called *me*. Becky would've been a more suitable choice. Ivy would've come for him. Kyle, or Leo, or Jesse would've picked his ass up.

Why me?

Why today?

Why the river?

Why, why, why?

When we reach his house, I have to shake him awake. "Go to your room and lie down," I instruct as he groggily straightens his hat. Marcy's car isn't in the driveway, and then I remember: "Meredith told me your parents are visiting a specialist in Seattle. You're off the hook, but for God's sake, don't talk to anyone until you sober up."

He stares at me, vacant and unmoving.

"Max?"

Still . . . nothing.

His withdrawal into hollowness dashes my anger away, replacing it with a heap of fear. And just like that, the ingrained and unrelenting desire to take his pain away returns.

Will I always feel this torturous ache of concern when it comes to Max Holden?

I rest my palm on his cheek. "Max? Are you hearing me?"

He blinks, leaning into my touch. "Yeah. I'm hearing you."

"Are you okay?"

"Fuck no." He looks dazed and doleful, so very out of it. He's definitely still drunk—I see it in the sleepiness of his eyes, the sluggishness of his movements—but he's no longer cross. Now he's just *sad*.

"Things will get better," I say, hoping it's the truth.

He shakes his head. "Dick move back there, right? Verbally assaulting the girl who's saving my ass? You're right to hate me. You should've left me on the side of the road, Jilly."

Jilly. God. He knows exactly how to play me. I pull my hand away. What was I thinking, touching him? Too impulsive, too intimate, totally inappropriate.

"I would never leave you on the side of the road. You know I wouldn't."

"Yeah . . . I'm sorry I keep screwing up." To his credit, he sounds sincere.

"What happened? Why the whisky?"

He grimaces. "The last few days . . . shitty."

"You're going to have to pull it together, Max. Like, soon."

"Yeah. Probably hard to believe right now, but I'm working on it."

"Well, work harder. Because I can't keep reliving this same experience. You mess up and somehow I get involved, and we both end up suffering."

"I get it," he says. "It's hard on me, too."

"Then *fix* it."

He gazes at me for a long, pensive moment. Finally, quietly, he says, "Thanks for coming to get me."

He climbs out of the car and makes a slow, stutter-step trek to his front door. When he's safely inside, I back down the Holdens' driveway and into my own, blinking back tears.

20

WHEN I WALK IN THE FRONT DOOR, Meredith's in the living room, and for a half second, I assume she's been exercising—she's perspiring and she's flushed, grimacing under the strain of whatever she's put her body through. Then I notice that she's holding her phone and, *oh my God*, her trusty contraction timer is open on its screen.

With a rush of terror, I comprehend what's *actually* going on, and my bag slips off my shoulder. It lands with a thump as I stand, gaping.

Meredith's head snaps up. She grits her teeth—she's biting back a curse or a groan or a scream—and pinches her eyes closed so tight she's nearly unrecognizable. For a long minute, she breathes shallowly, in and out, in and out. Then she opens her eyes.

I haven't moved a step.

She grunts, "Baby."

Meredith is a woman of beauty and poise and control. This sweating, snarling beast before me . . . she's petrifying.

"Jill," she says, jerking me back to reality. *"Baby."*

My stomach flip-flops with a bizarre combination of bewilderment and trepidation and . . . excitement? I hurl into action, dashing across the living room. "Why are you just sitting here?!" And then I realize: I've had her car all afternoon. "Meredith! Why didn't you call me?"

"I was planning to, but I was trying to reach your dad first."

"We have to go to the hospital," I say, trying frantically to catalog what we need to take with us.

"I can't"—she pauses to take in a great gulp of air, one that seems to bring her back to herself—"go anywhere without your dad."

"Where *is* he?"

She dabs her forehead with a dampened washcloth. "I've been trying to call him for the last hour. No one's at the office, and he's not picking up his cell."

"But he knows the baby's coming?"

She shakes her head, nearly hysterical. "I haven't spoken to him since this morning."

"We have to get you to the hospital, Meredith. You can't give birth on the couch just because Dad's disappeared!"

Tiny fissures run like rivers through my heart when she says, "But I *need* him."

"What about Marcy?" And then I remember—

"Seattle," Meredith moans.

"I'll call Mrs. Tate." A hospice nurse is better than no nurse.

Meredith nods, but her face is contorting again, and she's found my hand. She squeezes. My fingers are turning blue, and I'm paralyzed with fear—of Meredith and her new herculean strength, and of the leech baby, who might be trying to claw its way out of her.

I find Mrs. Tate's cell number in Meredith's list of contacts, but get her voice mail. The Tates' landline, too, goes unanswered. Panic fills my throat, fizzing up like champagne in a flute.

Meredith struggles through another fit while I try Dad's cell, then his office. He doesn't pick up the phone and neither does Natalie, who's paid to sit at a freaking desk and do just that.

I toss my own cell onto the coffee table and try not to cry out as Meredith grips my hand again. I find myself breathing along with her, quick, shallow puffs that make my head feel like it's floating away. When it's over and she lets me go and my fingers regain feeling, I say, "Meredith, we have to go to the hospital. I'll come in with you—I'll stay with you the whole time, if you want."

Because fear, apparently, breeds impulsivity.

She's shaking her head. "I can't ask that of you."

"You're not asking—I'm offering. The least I can do is get you there, and then I'll help however I can until Dad shows up."

Her expression is insultingly cynical. "Jillian, you don't know anything about childbirth."

"Doesn't matter. You can't have the baby here."

I watch it happen: my words permeating her pain-addled mind, her slow acceptance, her swelling hope. "You'll coach me until your dad arrives?"

I falter at the word *coach*, picturing myself in a baseball cap, holding a clipboard and pumping my fist as Meredith *ooh-ooh-aahs* her way through labor.

What have I gotten myself into?

"Of course, Mer." Dad's left me with no other choice.

I grasp her elbow and attempt to pull her up off the couch. My effort combined with her lack of assistance reminds me of a tugboat hauling a barge through a choppy harbor.

Once she's standing, leaning up against the wall of the foyer while

I collect my wallet and keys, she says, "Oh! The bags! Run to my bedroom and get them, will you, Jill?"

I dash to the back of the house, into Dad and Meredith's bedroom. The bags sit on the checkered chaise next to the window. The large duffel's been packed for weeks, full of brand-new nightgowns and slippers, mini shampoos and a travel hair dryer. The second bag's much smaller, stuffed with diapers, flannel blankets, and what Meredith calls a "coming home outfit," a frothy white ensemble with layers of lace and tulle—in other words, totally practical. I grab them both and hightail it down the hallway. I help Meredith out the front door and into the passenger seat of the Saturn before buckling into my own seat.

We *fly* out of the neighborhood.

My skin feels tight and itchy; the unknown freaks me out, and childbirth is about as far out of my realm as Arabic literature and quantum physics. Sure, a few months ago I happened into the basement while Meredith was watching *From Conception to Birth* on Dad's gigantic high-definition TV, but I can't say I learned much. There was so much screaming and . . . *anatomy* . . . I was at once frozen in horror. That only lasted a moment, though, before I spun on my toes and zoomed right back up the stairs. It'd been a challenge to keep my lunch down.

I weave through traffic. In the lulls that break up Meredith's apparently intensifying contractions, she alternates between calls to my dad's cell and his office. There's still no answer, and my concern peaks. Not only do I have no idea how to help Meredith, but now I've got Dad to worry about. I grip the steering wheel, swerving right to exit the freeway.

After pulling into the hospital parking lot, I dump Meredith at the emergency room entrance. I park the car crookedly in the first empty space I see, then hurry into the hospital to find her hobbling up to the triage desk. Chaos ensues. A particularly nasty contraction overtakes her, and she folds over the desk, gasping and moaning and scaring the hell out of me. The admitting nurse also appears alarmed. She makes a quick, quiet phone call, eyeing Meredith like tentacles might erupt from her stomach at any moment.

When another nurse comes hustling around the corner with a wheelchair, Meredith crumples into it. I follow with the bags as she's shuttled down the corridor toward an ominous set of doors marked LABOR AND DELIVERY; it surprises me to learn that an entire section of the hospital is reserved just for women having babies. And with that little *aha* moment comes a wave of sheer terror. . . .

I'm about to become the world's least helpful person to a woman in the throes of one of life's greatest miracles.

21

IT'S OFFICIAL—I'M NEVER HAVING BABIES.

Though Meredith's labor was (relatively) quick and (supposedly) not all that painful, I've seen enough to make me want to stay on birth control indefinitely. Through an hour of testing and monitoring, I endured the pain of her hand, vise-gripped around mine. Through thirty-five minutes of pushing, I stood as close to her head as possible, squashing my eyelids closed anytime things even hinted at a turn toward the graphic. I tried my best to be encouraging but, well, I was quietly panic-stricken. Meredith was just *out there* for the world to see, whimpering and howling and carrying on in this gruesome, feral way.

It was awkward. It was disgusting. It was appalling.

And then it wasn't, because when the doctor held a squirming Allyson Claire in the air, cherry red and crinkly, she let out this woeful little cry and my heart just . . . *melted*.

Now Ally's clean and calm, wrapped in a butter-yellow flannel blanket. Meredith passes her to me, and I hold her in the rigid cradle of my arms. I probably look exactly like the newbie I am, but her weight and her warmth are grounding.

Gazing into her gray eyes, I wonder if she might not be such a leech after all.

A nurse comes to whisk her away for a checkup, leaving Meredith and me alone. She's resting in the sloped bed, sucking down gallons of icy water. Her hair appears stylishly tousled and her cheeks are rosy—glowing, a nurse observed earlier. She looks tired, but serene.

I can't imagine surviving what she just went through, not in a million years.

I collapse into the vinyl recliner provided by the hospital for bunking dads—mine is still absent, incidentally. The dusty lavender glow of twilight peeks through the window blinds, and I can barely keep my eyes open.

"Jill," Meredith says, waving me over. The pastel hospital bracelets on her wrist whisper with the movement. I cringe at the repulsive gaseous noise the chair makes as my weight leaves it, and cross the room in three steps. Meredith pats her bed and I perch on it, careful not to jostle her. She reaches out to smooth a lock of my hair. "Thank you," she says, "for everything."

I shrug, her attention making me bashful. "You're welcome."

"I'm serious," she says. "There's no way I could have done it without you."

"I'm glad I was here." *Now* this is true. If you'd asked me an hour ago, my answer would've been the exact opposite.

"She's beautiful, isn't she?"

"I've never seen a pinker, wrinklier, noisier newborn."

She laughs. "She's exactly what I've imagined since I married your dad. I just—I wish he could've been here."

"Do you think . . . ?" I pause because I need to get my emotions under control. I swallow and start again. "Do you think he's okay?"

She's slow to answer, and that scares me. *Say yes*, I think. *Tell me he's fine.*

"We're at the hospital," she says. "We've been here a few hours. They would have notified us if he'd been in an accident. . . . So, yes, I think he's fine." She gives a measured lift of her shoulders. "He knew I could go into labor at any time, and he made himself unavailable."

"It must have been something he couldn't get out of." I'm skeptical even as I say this, but instinct says I should try to defend him. "Whatever he's doing, wherever he is, must be so, so important."

"Wouldn't it have to be? To close the office? To turn off his cell? I can only imagine . . ."

"Are you mad?" I ask, wondering if I'm overstepping. But then, Meredith seems willing to talk. I *need* to talk; I need to understand what might've caused my dad to flake so tremendously.

She reclines, resting her head on the mountain of pillows behind her. "I don't have enough energy to be mad. More than anything, I'm sad. The last few hours are locked in my memory and yours, but he'll never know them."

I lean back until we're side by side. The nearness is strange, but not in a bad way. Over the course of the afternoon, my connection with Meredith morphed into something new, something different, something real.

"I really am glad I'm here," I tell her.

"Me too," she whispers.

The door flies open, slamming against the wall with superfluous force, ushering in a waft of medicinal air from the hallway. My dad tumbles in after it.

Part of me is relieved to see him, alive and well. A bigger part of me is furious to see him, alive and well. His hair is messy in the front, where he's likely been tugging at it, and his tie is loose around his neck. He hauls a flour sack of anxiety in on his back. His expression, worn and contrite, makes me thankful Ally's in the nursery. I don't want this man to be my baby sister's first impression of her daddy.

He walks toward us. Meredith stiffens. He must notice, because he stops short of the bed. He looks from me to her, then back to me again. "Jillian, can Mer and I have a minute?"

"Where were you?"

He sighs, as if he has a right to exasperation.

"Dad, where *were* you?"

"We'll talk later. Go find the cafeteria, would you?"

"I'm not hungry." And, jeez, I think I've earned an explanation.

"I'd love a decaf coffee, sweetie," Meredith says. She looks at my dad, then gives me a smile. "You've been an enormous help already, but would you mind one more task?"

Traitor.

I leave, but I'm no idiot. Instead of closing the door behind me, I let it fall to barely cracked and step to the side—cafeteria, my ass. I lean against the wall and cross my arms like I have permission to loiter in the hallway. Break the rules blatantly and people rarely question you—a lesson I learned from Max.

I hear the vinyl chair creak and imagine my dad sinking into it. "I'm so sorry," he says.

"Where were you?"

"Tacoma. Meetings. I had meetings all day."

I hear Meredith sigh. "I don't believe you."

"Why would I lie?"

"You tell me. In this age of constant communication, how in God's name could you have been inaccessible on a day like today?"

"I left my phone in my car. You know I don't take it into meetings."

"And you knew I could go into labor anytime. Jill and I called your office dozens of times. Where was Natalie?"

"She had the day off."

"How convenient."

The chair protests as my dad shifts his weight. "What the hell is that supposed to mean?"

"You know *exactly* what it means."

Dad, apparently, is speechless—a rare occurrence. But what is there to say? *Sorry I missed the birth of our child, the baby we've been trying to conceive for years*, seems glib. He's so far up shit creek, I almost feel sorry for him. But then I recall Meredith, small and helpless in her hospital bed, without him.

The silence swells.

Finally, quietly, Meredith says, "You should have been here."

"I know."

"You have no idea what you put me through. What you put Jill through."

"I'm sorry."

"Are you?"

"Christ, Meredith. Do you think I didn't want to be here?"

"I don't know what to think."

"I said I'm sorry. Isn't that enough?"

Is he apologizing because he regrets missing his baby's birth?

Because he failed his wife and scared the crap out of me? Or is he sorry because Meredith's angry?

This was supposed to be the happiest day of her life, but instead of celebrating Allyson's arrival, she's stuck sorting out the mess Dad's carelessness caused.

It's so unfair.

22

I TAKE MEREDITH'S CAR HOME, SINCE MY parents will be spending the night at the hospital with their new baby.

The house is gloomy and too quiet. I consider calling Kyle or Leah, but I have no idea how to describe Ally's birthday to my friends. *My father missed the entire ordeal. In brighter news, I got to snip the umbilical cord!*

It's nearing midnight and I'm exhausted, but I'm also too keyed up to sleep. I take to the kitchen, dirtying all the measuring cups and spatulas in my arsenal. As I bake to the gentle whir of my new mixer, my posture loosens and my worries recede. I find my groove, that wonderful, intangible place where I'm scooping and sifting and stirring with an empty head and a satisfied heart, and I never, ever want to stop.

When the sky begins to lighten, I line my confections on the counter, wrapped and ready for transport. I've made Meredith's favorites: a spongy almond-flavored butter cake with a crisp sugar glaze, chocolate babka, and lemon blueberry tarts, which I baked in the fluted tart pans she gave me for Christmas. As I admire my work, my stomach rumbles. I snag a tart—it's to die for, just the right combination of sweet and sour—before retreating to my room and falling into bed.

．．．．

When I wake, the day's in full swing.

I send my dad a text, asking him to call my school so my absence will be excused. Then I scrub the kitchen, fold laundry, and set up the Pack 'n Play that's been sitting, boxed, in the nursery. I pause only briefly to wonder if Max made it to school, if he's hungover, if he's aware of how completely my life has changed since yesterday's roadside rescue.

Seems like ages ago.

Dad calls at lunchtime and suggests, since I'm playing hooky from school, that I come to the hospital for a visit. "Don't forget to grab the camera," he says. He hangs up before I have a chance to dissect the nuances in his tone, but if I had to guess, I'd say his marital problems haven't disappeared overnight.

I indulge in a leisurely shower, then blow my hair out. I'd like to take Meredith her baked goods and I'd like to see Ally, maybe hold her again, but the anger and accusations of last night have made me gunshy. It's midafternoon when I finally leave for the hospital.

Meredith tears up when I present her with the pastries. "How will I ever eat all of this?" she asks, half laughing, half crying.

Apparently she has no plans to share with my dad.

He remains in the corner, holding a pink-swathed Allyson, looking on while Meredith and I chat about the baby's first night. She tells me about the challenges of diaper changing and how gross spit-up is and how helpful the nurses have been. She devours two tarts, a slice of babka, and a good chunk of the butter cake as she talks. I try not to laugh, watching her pig out so enthusiastically. When she's done, Dad passes her Ally and gets comfortable in the recliner, picking at one of the pieces of chocolate babka that escaped Meredith's binge.

Since the three of them seem peaceful enough, I wander to the cafeteria. When I return with a large, heavily sugared coffee, everyone's napping. Meredith's in bed, and Dad's crammed into the vinyl recliner beside her, one elbow crooked under his unnaturally bent neck. Ally's snuggled into her hospital-provided crib, its clear plastic sides a window into her world. I use the camera to snap a few quick pictures, then plop down in another chair—a hard, plastic thing brought in by an attentive nurse—to drink my coffee and watch my sister snooze.

Her round face is placid, and her peach-fuzz hair is covered by the rose-colored hat Marcy knitted for her. She's wrapped tight in a flannel blanket, but her eyelids twitch, like she's having a vivid dream. I want to pick her up and hold her, but her fragility intimidates me. Babies are all too easily droppable.

Dad lets out a jagged snore. I hold my breath as Ally stirs. Turning her head slightly, she peers at me with graphite eyes.

"Newborns can't see very well," Meredith told me a few weeks ago, during one of her many baby lectures. I was only half listening, but that nugget of information resurfaces, spoken in the slightly haughty voice she often used while educating Dad and me on the ways of the enigmatic newborn. "It's hard for them to focus on anything more than a foot or two in front of them, and they can't fix their gaze until they're nearly two months old."

This I find hard to believe. My sister is staring at me as if she wants to sit up and have a chat, maybe hear the latest McAlder gossip.

Feeling like an idiot, I smile and give her a little wave.

She makes a soft gurgling sound and flails her tiny fists. I bend over the crib for a better look. She makes it again, the coo that sounds sweet and pure.

Worried she'll wake my parents (*our* parents, I guess), I slide one hand under her head and the other beneath her rear, careful not to unravel the burrito-like swaddling Meredith wrapped her in. She weighs almost nothing, though she's living and breathing and squirming a little. Gingerly, I bring her against my body and sit back down. She's warm and she smells good: clean, the softest lilac. There's a certain comfort that comes with holding her, like she might be capable of making life okay again.

My tranquil moment is interrupted by muffled voices in the hallway. I look to the door and see Marcy peering through the glass. She pushes into the room, tears streaming down her face. She's carrying gorgeous fuchsia tulips and a WELCOME BABY GIRL balloon. School's apparently out for the day, because Max is with her. He hangs back, hands buried in the kangaroo pocket of his sweatshirt, while his mom places the flowers on the counter.

She comes closer, squeezing my shoulder as she gazes down at Ally. "Oh, my . . . She's so beautiful."

I'm about to offer to let her hold the baby when Meredith shifts. She opens her eyes, smiling at the sight of our neighbors. I drop my eyes to Ally, listening to softly spoken words of *lucky* and *perfect*, wondering at Max's surprise appearance. When Dad wakes to the quiet commotion, the room erupts in congratulatory hugs. It seems the misery of last night is forgotten when he retrieves Ally from my arms and sits down next to Meredith on the bed. I'm not sure if they're putting on another show or if they've decided to let last night go, but the sight of them beside each other is reassuring. I find myself relaxing into my seat.

Then Max crosses the threshold, moving toward me. After yesterday's display by the river, I should harbor nothing more than ill will, but to be honest, I want to fall into his arms. He squats next to me, and his proximity sends my heart spinning.

Why can't I ever stay angry with him?

"Congratulations," he says.

"Pretty crazy, huh?"

"I don't think I've ever seen you hold a baby."

Breathe, I remind my failing lungs. "I don't think I ever have, until yesterday."

"I heard you coached Meredith through it."

I shrug, peeking at my dad; he's consumed by his role of doting husband, paying no attention to Max and me. "That wasn't what was supposed to happen, but I guess it worked out."

He goes quiet, and I wonder if he's thinking about how contemptuous he acted at the river yesterday, like I am.

Fix it, I told him while we sat in his driveway. I want to believe him when he says he's trying, but how many times am I supposed to accept his regressions? He can be adorably charming, but there's a bold line dividing *supportive friend* from *dangerous enabler*. Becky crossed it and never looked back, and I'm toeing it. I know I am.

He glances at our parents, fawning over Ally, who's drifted back to sleep. "Hey, do you want to get out of here for a while? Go for a walk or something?"

"I don't think so."

"Come on, Jill. I wanna talk to you about yesterday."

I look at him, hard, my frustration poking its head around the corner. Why does he presume I'm a sure bet?

I shift my attention to the pale, pencil-point scar on his forehead. I'm not sure why, but I've always liked it. Maybe because it gives his otherwise perfect face a flawed sense of character. Or maybe it's the story behind the scar: the two of us exploring the woods behind his house years ago, me stumbling into a wasps' nest, the buzzing, militant insects and the pain of their stings immediately disorienting. Max rushed into the mayhem to pull me to safety, another near-death experience thwarted by his bravery. He ended up getting stung almost as many times as I did, mostly on his bare arms, but once above his eyebrow, too.

"I don't feel like talking," I tell him.

He frowns. His gaze skims my hair, loose around my shoulders, and I suffer the memory of his fingers running through it, pushing it back to reveal my neck. I shiver.

He notices, then looks meaningfully in Dad's direction. "Let's go out in the hall, then."

"I said I don't feel like it."

"Jesus, Jillian. Are you never gonna to talk to me again?" Even whispering, he sounds wounded. It surprises me, this knowledge that I'm capable of inflicting hurt on him. I could start torturing him, just as he tortures me, though I would never. Power over his happiness is a taxing thing—so much so, it's tempting to agree to that walk after all. But I have some pride.

"No, Max. Not today."

I stand and grab the camera from the counter, then approach the baby lovefest. Marcy's cradling Ally, staring down at her while Dad and Meredith look on. They're speaking in hushed tones, which is probably what you're supposed to do when a baby's napping. I make a mental note for the future before bringing the camera's viewfinder to my eye. I take a few candid shots before Dad says, "Jill, will you get one of Mer and me?"

Marcy lays the baby in Meredith's arms. Dad sits on the edge of her bed. He wraps an arm around her shoulders, dropping his free hand to Ally. They stay like that for a long moment, unmoving, until Meredith looks up at him and, unbelievably, smiles. I capture a picture of the three of them; they appear a lovely little family.

Sucks that I can't stop circling back to reality.

"Max, do you want to hold her?" Meredith asks.

He nods. Carefully, he takes Ally, tucking her in the crook of his arm like a football. He walks her to the chair I occupied earlier and sits down, totally at ease—the exact opposite of how I felt on the two occasions I held my sister.

"Get a picture, Jill," Meredith whispers, nodding toward Max.

Something about viewing him through the camera's lens brings sharp focus to my feelings, feelings that've been mixed up for months, feelings that were jumbled only seconds ago. I see him differently, in a startling new light. He's not my neighbor or my childhood playmate, he's not a screwup who's forever making dumb decisions, and he's not a boy I had a meaningless fling with, either. Thanks to the stark clarity of the lens, he's Max, the only boy who's ever made me feel like *me*.

My skin goes hot so quickly, I'm dizzy.

"Jill?" Meredith says, sounding far away. "Are you going to take the picture?"

I swallow the emotion scaling my throat, then click the shutter, capturing Max and Ally together. Short of breath, I trip over my feet trying to make my way across the room, lurching forward before recovering inelegantly. I dump the camera, which suddenly weighs a hundred pounds, on the counter. I feel Meredith, Dad, Marcy, and Max watching as I scramble to gather my jacket and my bag and my coffee. I don't say anything, though their matching expressions of bewilderment beg for explanation.

I need to get out of the room before I cry, or pass out, or say something I'll later regret. I need to collect my bearings, away from them.

Away from *him*.

I step into the cool, quiet corridor and press my back against the wall's solid surface, reeling, thanks to one astonishing realization. . . .

I'm in love with Max Holden.

23

EREDITH AND ALLY ARE SET TO BE discharged from the hospital the next afternoon. As soon as I get home from school, I sit by the living room window, a one-girl welcoming committee, keeping an eye out for the Durango. I smile when I see Marcy, pulling Mrs. Tate along by the hand. They scamper through the rain and into our yard, speedily tying pink-and-yellow balloon bouquets to our mailbox and a few of the leafless shrubs in the soggy flower beds. Marcy stakes a garish wooden stork holding a swaddled baby in its beak. Though I'd die before admitting as much out loud, the decorations are sort of cute.

When the Durango finally pulls into the driveway, Dad climbs out, takes Ally's carrier from the backseat, and hurries toward the house. When he opens the front door, his hair shimmers with raindrops and the shoulders of his jacket are polka-dotted by the drizzle. He leaves Ally in the living room with me, then jogs back outside to help Meredith out of the car. He walks beside her, his hand clasped around hers, until they're through the front door.

It's official: We're a family of four.

For the next couple of hours, neighbors cycle through—Marcy, the Tates, the Rolons, others—all bearing slightly varied versions of the same casserole, all eager to lavish Ally with attention and compliment my parents on their baby-creating skills.

I'm not sure if Dad and Meredith have settled their argument, but they're civil. They cooperate through what sounds (and smells) like a particularly messy diaper change, and Dad brings Meredith a mug of tea while she feeds the baby on the living room couch. They both catch a quick nap during Ally's snooze in the baby swing. I ride out what's left of the afternoon by whipping up a dulce de leche cheesecake, hesitantly optimistic. Maybe the crazy's ceased.

Before dinner, Kyle and Leah stop by to meet Ally, who's asleep in Meredith's arms. Kyle takes a quick peek, mutters his congratulations, and backs away, but Leah's smitten, full of starry-eyed murmurs like, "Aww, she's *so* adorable."

"Thank you," Meredith keeps saying, radiating pride.

Dad, on the other hand, has barely looked up from his laptop.

My friends and I head for the kitchen, where I dole out slices of cheesecake and pour Cokes over ice. We sit at the table, and Leah holds her glass in the air. "To Jillian," she says formally, "the world's latest and greatest big sister."

"Thanks," I say with a smile. The three of us clink our glasses in a toast and for a second, everything's perfect. Then Kyle opens his mouth.

"I hear you weren't very nice to Max yesterday."

I nearly choke on a sip of soda. "What?"

"We hung out last night."

"And?"

"And he said you wouldn't to talk to him at the hospital. He said you grabbed your jacket and bounced."

"Jill." Leah's voice is gently admonishing. "I thought we agreed to be there for Max."

"I am there for Max." *On Monday, I picked him up, drunk, off the side of the road*, I want to tell them. *What are friends for?* Instead, I exhale a weary breath. "I was tired. I'd been up the entire night before, and then there was the birth, and my dad, and everything was just . . ." I'm making zero sense, I realize, and my friends are staring at me like I've got chocolate chips for brains.

Leah glances at Kyle. He gives her a subtle nod, and she says, "We get that things have been chaotic, but you heard about him and Becky, right?"

"Uh . . . no."

"They're through."

"What?"

"Broken up," Kyle says, grinning like the demise of his buddy's relationship is the world's best news.

It's a struggle to maintain a politely bland expression. "When?"

"Last week," Leah says. "That's why she was such a mess when she crashed Movie Night—she was in denial about the whole thing. Then, Monday at school, Max marched up to her and told her he really was done, and that he didn't want anything to do with her anymore. It was a spectacle. I can't believe you missed it."

I can't, either. God—Monday. That was the day Becky rammed into me on the quad. The day Max guzzled whisky at the river. No wonder he couldn't call her for a ride—they broke up.

"Max didn't bend," Kyle tells me, swirling the tines of his fork through the caramel left on his plate. "He kept saying, 'We're over,' and 'There's nothing between us.' He wasn't a jerk about it, but you could tell he'd had enough, you know? For the first time in a long time, I was really proud of him."

"I'm so glad he finally cut it off," Leah says. "Jesse is, too. Max is better off."

"Agreed," Kyle says.

I mumble my assent because in theory they're right. But if Max is so much better off, why didn't he tell me about Becky during Movie Night, or our forlorn walk through the neighborhood? Why'd he leave school to get wasted at the river?

You don't know anything, he said when he called to ask for a ride. I countered with a diatribe about what an asshole he was. At the hospital he tried again, and I shut him down.

I blink, trying to make sense of it all.

"Max has a good heart," Leah's saying.

"He deserves to be happy," Kyle agrees.

I nod, because *yes* and *yes*.

. . . .

After my friends leave, Dad and I head out to pick up a late dinner. He suggests I drive, and I'm glad. When my hands and head are busy, it's easier to keep from fixating on what he pulled the other night. We never did get to "talk later" like he promised, and while I'm hopeful he and Meredith are on their way to working things out, my worries haven't gone anywhere.

"Chinese?" I ask, braking at a stoplight.

"Whatever you want."

The quiet pulls thin. Dad fiddles with the heat and the defrost, then checks the glove box to make sure all the proper documents are there. A wall of discomfort stands between us.

It's clear he senses it, too, when he says, "Thanks for being there for Mer at the hospital."

"Where else would I have been?" I don't mean it as a dig, but it comes off as one, and I don't feel sorry. I stare straight ahead, unblinking, until the stoplight looks like red smears in an impressionistic painting. The wipers swish across the windshield, back and forth, back and forth.

"She's still upset," Dad says.

The light flashes green and I stomp down on the gas pedal. "Can you blame her?"

"I was working."

I recall a drizzly afternoon several years ago, when Max and I discovered Bill's old record player in the Holdens' garage. Having never seen a record, we had no idea how to set the needle, but we got a laugh trying. The songs skipped and popped and jumped, and the two of us cracked up listening to phrases repeating. *I was working—I was working—I was working.* If I had a dollar for every time I've heard Dad use that phrase over the last few months, well, I wouldn't have to worry about how to fund my culinary education.

"What are you thinking, Jillian?"

That you've been really self-centered.

That there's more to your "I'm working" story than you're letting on.

That I'm too scared to ask the important questions.

"Nothing."

"I love Meredith."

I nod, because I have no concrete proof against his claim. I've seen their affectionate moments: Dad's hand on Meredith's previously pregnant belly, her brush of a kiss across his cheek as he rifles through case files. And I've witnessed their more significant gestures of love: Dad driving Meredith to countless fertility appointments, writing checks to chip away at mounting debt. And Meredith, managing the Eldridge household with zeal. Still, I've seen enough reality TV to know that love doesn't stop some people from exploring other avenues.

"I imagine this is hard for you to understand," Dad says, reaching over to pat my knee.

I cannot believe he has the audacity to be so condescending.

"I understand more than you think," I shoot back, making a hairpin turn into the parking lot of the local Chinese restaurant. An enormous neon panda rotates lazily on a signpost; its cartoonish apathy amplifies my irritation. I throw the car into park and yank the keys from the ignition.

Dad backpedals. "I didn't mean it that way. It's just that marriage takes effort. Sometimes it's wonderful. Sometimes it feels like a job—like the most tedious job in the world."

His honesty dampens my frustration. "I know about effort, Dad."

"You do—more than I did at your age, that's for sure. You're growing up, and that's hard for me to come to terms with. You did good, though, stepping in to help Meredith."

I shrug. "I guess."

"You did. She's told me time and again that she couldn't have done it without you. Plus, you're staying focused on school, and staying away from Max."

On one hand, I wish I could tell my dad what I *really* think: There's not an excuse in the world good enough to pardon what he pulled on Ally's birthday. And I'm focused on school because I suddenly need scholarship money, in large part because of him. And his assumptions regarding Max are unfounded and stupid. On the other hand, this exchange, his honesty and warmth, the bountiful compliments he's sending my way . . . I'm clinging to all of it, tucking it away for safe-keeping.

"Anyway," he says. "You're a good kid, Jill."

He gives my hair a ruffle before climbing out of the car and heading into the restaurant.

24

ALLY IS NOT A SOUND SLEEPER.

I mean, I assumed she'd wake up during the night, but I figured Meredith would get her, change her, feed her, and put her back to bed.

That's not how it works.

Ally's up at all hours, crying and carrying on. I'm shocked out of sleep by her wails, then forced to lie awake listening to Meredith's singing—"Twinkle, Twinkle, Little Star" or "Rock-a-Bye Baby"—her footsteps echoing up and down the hallway as she paces with the baby. Occasionally it's Dad who gets up, and then it's the theme song from *Star Wars* I hear, hummed low and lethargically. Over and over and over.

She really is a leech baby; she purloins sleep.

According to Meredith, Ally naps all day. I wouldn't know because I've spent the last couple of days suffering through school and work with a wicked case of exhaustion. Call me crazy, but common sense seems to dictate that *someone* should be keeping the baby busy during daylight hours so she—and the rest of us—can sleep at night.

I plan on spending my Saturday in sweats, experimenting with a classic chocolate soufflé recipe and napping sporadically. That's until Meredith calls me into the nursery, where she's dressing Ally in a cheerful pink onesie. "Marcy and Max are coming for a visit."

"Max? *Why?*"

She glances at me, one hand resting on the baby, surprise widening her eyes. How's she to know I'm head over heels for our neighbor, the very boy who's made the last few months of my life agonizing? How's she to know I have no idea what to say to him about his suddenly single status? How's she to know that when I'm in his presence I feel like a hot-air balloon—swollen with heat, in danger of floating away?

"I mean, I just don't get why he'd spend his Saturday sitting around with you and Marcy and a baby."

"Because he wants to? And you make a good point. It'd be nice if you sat with us, especially since your dad's working. I don't want him to get bored."

"If boredom's an issue, maybe he shouldn't come."

"Jillian! I thought Max was your friend?"

"He was—*is*—but I planned to spend the day baking."

Meredith bends to kiss Ally on the forehead; the baby squirms, kicking the air. "Can't you bake later?" she coos. "This sweet girl and I want your company."

I frown. "Using the baby against me? Manipulation much?"

Meredith grins, triumphant. "Thanks, Jill. I owe you one. They'll be here in an hour."

I sigh and head for the shower. So much for sweats.

It's almost lunchtime when the doorbell rings. My stomach drifts to the ground, fluttering like a leaf in a downdraft, though I pretend I don't hear the chime. I steal a cracker from the platter Meredith's set out, loaded with Brie, grapes, and apple slices. There's a big pitcher of lemonade, too. I don't mention that lemonade seems unfitting for a day cool and cast in impenetrable cloud cover, though, because it's nice to see her bustling around the kitchen the way she did before her pregnancy.

The bell sounds again. Meredith must give up on me being any help, because she hurries out of the kitchen to open the front door.

Marcy makes a beeline for Ally. She lifts her from her bouncy chair, snuggling her close. Meredith looks on, beaming. And then Max saunters into the room, pilfering my attention. He's in jeans and a long-sleeved gray T-shirt, his hair covered by a Seahawks hat. He hugs Meredith and tells her how great she looks, then glances over his mom's shoulder at my sister. Resting his big hand on top of Ally's little head, he says, "She's growing fast."

I'm pretty sure that's a good thing, because Meredith grins and says, "I think so, too!"

He turns to me and, with a decorous nod of his head, says, "Jillian."

I counter with my own stiff greeting. "Hello, Max."

He and Meredith gather the snack platter and lemonade, and we head for the living room. Marcy sits down with Ally in one of two chairs while Meredith snags the other, leaving Max and me with the couch. Fantastic.

I claim an end for myself. It's big enough to seat three, but Max sinks down right beside me, so close I have to tuck my feet under so they're not resting against his leg. I can't decide if he's oblivious to the fact that I value personal space or if he's trying to tempt me, but either way, his nearness is taxing. I don't trust myself to touch him in the most platonic of ways, yet we're inches away from cuddling in front of his mother and Meredith.

He and I sit in silence while the two of them chat. He swallows truckloads of food. I try not to think about him.

Time trickles by, until I jump to attention at the sound of my name; Marcy's looking at me expectantly. "Um . . . What?"

"Your middle name? What is it?"

"Oh, it's Grace."

Max peers at me. "Jillian Grace . . . Why didn't I know that?"

Because you're an ass, I want to say. I've known his middle name—William, after his dad—since I was eight.

"And Allyson Claire," Marcy says, gazing down at the baby.

"Ally sounds good with Jilly," Max remarks. Odd, considering he's the only person who calls me Jilly. I bite my lip to conceal a spontaneous smile.

"Mer," Marcy whispers. "She's dozed off. How long will she sleep?"

Meredith checks her watch. "Probably an hour. She's not due to eat until two."

"Can I treat you to a cup of coffee in town?"

I'm pretty sure the panicked expression Meredith's wearing mirrors my own. There's no way I'm comfortable babysitting a newborn, and I doubt she's cool with letting me try. "I don't know," she says. "I haven't left Ally for a minute since she was born."

"That's why you need to get out," Marcy says. "You have to take care of yourself, too."

"But she's so little, and Jill doesn't have any experience with babies."

"Max does. He's been watching Oli since he was a few weeks old. We'll be gone thirty minutes, tops."

"I don't mind sticking around," Max says. Of course he doesn't—tormenting me is his favorite pastime.

Meredith looks to me. She knows how unprepared I am for baby duty, and she knows I'm not supposed to be with Max unsupervised. Surely she won't leave.

"Well," she says. "What do you think, Jill?"

I blink, dumbfounded—I thought we'd made headway in our relationship!

"I can handle it," I lie, because how can I refuse without sounding entirely self-centered?

Max wraps an arm around my shoulders. "We'll be fine. Ally'll probably still be sleeping when you get back."

Meredith nods, but her shifty gaze says she's unconvinced. She gets up and lifts Ally from Marcy's arms. She kisses her cheeks, then snuggles her into the swing. "I'll get my purse," she says, glancing back at the baby like she might never see her again.

A few minutes later, Marcy pulls her out the door, leaving Max and me alone.

I shrug away from the warmth of his arm and move to the chair Meredith vacated. "You don't have to stay," I tell him. "I'll be fine for a half hour."

"I don't mind hanging out, but if you don't want me here, I'll go."

I keep my mouth shut. Even greater than my fear of babysitting alone is my often ill-fated desire to spend time with Max Holden.

He snags a bunch of grapes from the platter and pops one into his mouth. "So, what do you want to do?"

"Read, I think. You can watch TV."

If he's offended, he doesn't let on. It's not like I'm trying to insult him; I just need time to collect myself, to figure out how far I'm willing to let this impromptu bonding session go. It seems like every time Max and I start to make forward progress, we're blown backward by an outside force or, sometimes, a mess of our own making. My heart winds up bruised, and he does something undoubtedly stupid, and I hesitate to put myself out there, again, when I'm not one hundred percent sure where his head's at. I want things to be good, for me and for him and for *us*, and I think they could be, but the very real possibility that they could just as well fall apart terrifies me.

I pluck a Williams-Sonoma catalog from the coffee table and curl up in my chair. I open it, but instead of perusing its pages, I spy on Max. He looks so cozy, stretched out on our couch in that shirt that appears superbly soft.

I miss him. That's the simple truth of it.

When he clicks on the TV, finds *SportsCenter*, and gets involved watching a panel of experts discuss Super Bowl odds, it hits me how ridiculously marital this scene is: Max and the remote, me and my cookware catalog, the snoozing baby. But I can't stop watching him, and I can't stop thinking about his hug outside True Brew, and the fun we've had hanging out over the last few weeks, and the way his mouth feels on mine.

He glances up and catches me looking. He smirks. "How's the magazine?"

"Fine."

"Which one is it?"

Why do I suddenly feel out of place in my own house? "Um, what?"

"Never mind," he says, chuckling.

I'm fumbling for a comeback when Ally startles in her swing. She whimpers, and I look wide-eyed at Max.

He holds his hands up. "I didn't do anything."

"They've only been gone ten minutes!"

He turns the TV down. "Read your magazine, Jillian Grace. She'll go back to sleep."

But the baby's fusses quickly progress to full-on cries, and I'm becoming increasingly alarmed. "Should I call Meredith?"

"Nah. She probably just wants to be held." He goes to the swing, turns it off, and lifts Ally into his arms. He hushes her and bounces on his knees a little. It's endearing, the way this jock of a guy holds a helpless little person with such care. Miraculously, Ally's cries fizzle, and I find myself envious of Max's magic touch.

"Maybe she woke up because she wants to eat," he says.

"It's nowhere near two o'clock."

"So she's not hungry. I don't think she's cold. Maybe she needs her diaper changed?"

"Ew."

"What do you mean, 'ew'? Don't tell me you haven't changed her diaper yet."

I stare at him.

"Okay, wow. You haven't changed her diaper yet."

"Meredith does that stuff."

"Still, you should know how."

"Why?"

"Are you kidding? So you can be a kick-ass big sister. Come on," he says, nodding toward the hallway. "I'll talk you through it."

With a sigh, I follow him to Ally's nursery. He situates her on the changing table. "Okay, step up there," he says, rubbing his hands together like he's a sideline coach or something.

I do, and draw a complete blank.

He rolls his eyes. "Unwrap the blanket and unsnap her onesie."

I'm tempted to make a joke about Mr. Football knowing what a onesie is, but the truth is, I'd be lost without his help. I bite my lip and follow his directions. "What now?"

"Get the wipes and the new diaper ready before you take the old one off. You don't want her diaperless for longer than a second."

"Sounds like you're speaking from experience," I say, unfolding a clean diaper.

"Oh, yeah. Oli peed on me more than once. Not cool."

I giggle at the mental image. "Ready with the new diaper."

"Okay, hold her feet like this." He shows me how to corrall Ally's wriggling ankles, then says, "You'll unfasten the old diaper, use the wipe, and slip the fresh diaper underneath."

I follow his directions, fastening the tabs of the clean diaper, feeling accomplished. "Now I snap the onesie back up?"

He nods. "Simple as that."

I finish dressing my sister, my heart filling with hope. This amiable rapport Max and I've got going feels good—like it could be *more* than good.

I carry Ally back to the living room and sit down on the couch. She rests contentedly across my lap, focusing on the slowly rotating ceiling fan above.

Max joins me, this time leaving a good foot of space between us. "You did good," he says. "*Now* you're a kick-ass big sister."

"Thanks for teaching me."

He shrugs. "It was nice to have you talking to me again." He tilts his head, looking over at me. "Kyle told you, didn't he? About Becky and me?"

"He might've mentioned it."

"Yeah?"

"Yeah. I'm not sure if I should say I'm sorry, or congratulate you."

His smile's like a pinch of salt—minuscule, but enough to affect me. "You don't have to say anything. I just want you to know that she's not a factor anymore. Not at all, okay?"

I nod, and as an offering of peace, I pick up the remote and turn *SportsCenter* up.

He grins his Max grin, wide and open, eyes crinkling at the corners, and I feel a rush of emotion so intense I can't dismiss it—I don't *want* to dismiss it. He stretches his hand in my direction, letting it rest on the couch cushion, palm up, and my hesitancy melts away.

Holding his gaze, I slide my hand into the warmth of his, and his fingers find their way into the space between each of mine in this deliberate, intimate way that erases the last of my doubt. Without the darkness of Becky's shadow, without the difficulty of the last several months clouding my vision, Max is what I see.

Max is *all* I see.

25

AFTER DINNER AT HOME WITH MEREDITH AND Ally, I sit at my desk with my computer, a notepad, and a pen. The more I think about the International Culinary Institute and its meager smattering of scholarship options, the less likely my Grand Diplôme of Professional Pastry Arts seems. Even if I'm awarded all the money I apply for, and even if I save every penny I make at True Brew, I'll just barely have enough to cover tuition. Short of taking out a gigantic loan (what's that my dad said about debt being no way to live?), I'll have nothing left to pay for housing and food and transportation—essentials. That means . . .

New York isn't going to happen for me.

The realization is like lemon juice in a fresh wound, and I'm doing my very best not to wallow in self-pity. Diversion number one: research Seattle culinary schools.

There are some good ones, but the International Culinary Institute's been my dream for so long, anything else feels like settling. Still, I take halfhearted notes on a few possibilities—programs at the Art Institute of Seattle, the Seattle Culinary Academy, and Le Cordon Bleu—but the more I scribble stats and figures, the less stock I put in my future pâtisserie. Without the International Culinary Institute, I'll probably end up baking at the local doughnut shop.

I'm distracted by a slam of the front door. Dad's home, and he and Meredith get right into it. I toss my pen down; if they knew how much I can hear, they'd shut up.

"It's Saturday," Meredith says. "It's bad enough you were gone all day. You could've come home for dinner."

"I was *working*," Dad says.

I close my laptop with a sigh.

"You're always working. Prepping for a case. Mid-case. Wrapping up a case. I wish you were as interested in spending time with your daughters as you are in your job."

"I'm interested in paying the mortgage, Meredith."

"Ally's not going to be a baby forever. Look how quickly Jillian's grown up. Someday you'll regret not being around more."

"And someday you'll regret being such a nag."

The living room falls quiet. I imagine Meredith's face twisted with hurt. Dad's being so unappreciative, so nasty. Lately, I've found Mer's nagging to be pretty damn warranted.

Footsteps pad down the hall. Her shadow passes by my door, and I consider checking on her, but I don't know what to say or how to help. Besides, she'd probably put on her happy face and pretend everything's fine, like usual.

My phone dings with a text. I grab it and fall onto my bed.

Max: *What are you doing?*

I type: *Homework*, because the truth, *listening to Dad and Mer fight*, is too much information.

On Saturday night? You know better.

I smile and respond: *OK, Life of the Party. What are you doing?*

Thinking.

About?

I await his response, buzzing with anticipation. There's something about our conversation—texted or not—that feels monumental.

My phone chimes. He's sent one word: *You.*

Thank God I'm alone, because I can't help my little gasp of surprise. I reply: *Don't play games with me, Holden.*

No games. And then: *I had fun today. You?*

Yes. I send the message and let the admission sink in. I *did* have fun. When there's no drinking or drama or dysfunction, Max and I are great together.

He sends another text: *Guess what I want . . .*

I can only imagine. *Ooh, tell me.*

Ice cream. Out front in 5?

I confirm, grinning, then swap my leggings for jeans. I leave my sweatshirt on; *this isn't a date*, I remind myself. Still, I run my fingers through my hair and swipe lip gloss across my mouth. Then I head down the hallway to Dad and Meredith's room.

She's in the master bath, on her knees, scouring the tub with a scrub brush. The harsh smell of cleanser burns my nose. I lean against the doorjamb. "Meredith?"

The brush falls, landing in the tub with a clatter. "Oh! Jill, you startled me." With the back of her hand, she wipes perspiration from her forehead. Then she notices my shoes. "Where are you off to?"

"Just out for a bit."

"With who?"

"Well, remember this morning, before Marcy and Max came over? When you said you'd owe me one?"

"Sure," she says. "Cashing in already?"

"I was going to go out with Max for a little while, and Dad . . ."

Meredith straightens, her gaze narrowing. "You don't want your father to know."

"He doesn't get Max," I say, hoping she does. The implausibility of this moment, confiding in Meredith, is not lost on me. But I want to trust her—I *need* to trust her. "He thinks Max is trouble, but he's not. He thinks Max will change me, but he won't."

"Please. You're better than letting a boy rub off on you. But wait . . . Is this a date? Because this morning you seemed pretty *eh* about Max."

"We're just going to get some ice cream. I'll be home before Dad notices I'm gone."

She smiles conspiratorially. "Your secret's safe with me."

I leave through the back so as not to attract attention. Max is waiting in his truck, parked on the street between our houses with the passenger door wide open. He's listening to early Tim McGraw, classic enough to satisfy his tastes, I suppose, but contemporary enough to keep me from going batty.

When he sees me, his face, illuminated by the cab's dome light, comes alive with a smile. There's a new energy between us, a palpable, the-possibilities-are-wide-open kind of energy.

I like it.

. . . .

We pick up ice cream from Rainier Creamery. Then Max drives down to the river, where he parks on a deserted overlook. The sky is pitch black and wind whistles through the truck's tiny entry points, but inside the cab we're warm and comfortable. We dig into our ice cream, country music's all-stars crooning ballads over the radio's waves. As far as non-dates go, the whole scene is pretty dreamy.

Max quickly interrupts it. "Level with me. How thoroughly have I pissed you off over the last few months?"

Leave it to him to get right to business.

"Pretty thoroughly," I admit, studying a spoonful of coconut ice cream. "When you called me from the river, finding out later it was about Becky. That was . . . unpleasant."

"It wasn't about Becky. Shit, Jill. Is that what you think?"

"You drink yourself into oblivion right after you break up with your girlfriend. What am I supposed to think?"

"Not that it had anything to do with *her*. That day . . . Seeing you in the parking lot after school, knowing I'd probably fucked things up beyond repair, I felt like nothing was ever gonna be right again." He looks at me, his expression quizzical. "Haven't you ever felt that way?"

"Honestly? I've been feeling that way a lot lately."

He drops his ice cream dish into a cup holder. "I've been taking my shit out on you, and I know that's unfair, but after Halloween, after Bunco, I knew you had regrets—"

"Wait. You *didn't* have regrets?"

"I was freaked out, yeah. You're *you*. If I hurt you, my parents will disown me. Kyle will beat my ass. Shit, your dad'll bury me in his backyard. But I was never sorry."

Bits of reality replace the conjecture that's been clouding my head for weeks. I take another bite of ice cream and let it melt on my tongue. It's sweet and tropical, and makes me think of sun-drenched beaches and palm trees and warm ocean air. I glance out the window at the black, black sky, feeling conflicted. "What about Becky?" I ask, because if I'm going to do this, give Max and me a real shot, I need to know everything.

"What about her? We were a cluster-fuck."

"Then why did you stay with her so long?"

He expels a hefty *I was hoping you'd never ask me that* sigh. "She's not a terrible person, Jill—not like you think."

"Yes, she is. She's manipulative, and she's mean to you."

"Yeah, well, I haven't been all that great to her."

"She makes you drink."

He laughs, a dry, drained sound. "I do stupid things all on my own, in case you haven't noticed. Becky's never made me do anything. And for what it's worth, I'm done getting sloshed every time the world gives me the finger."

"Really?" My tone is part dubious, part dazzled. I want to believe him; I want him to prove he means it.

"Yeah, really. And you're right—Becky can be a royal pain in the ass, but to be fair, a lot of the time, she was reacting to shit I pulled."

"Then . . . *why?*"

He's staring out the windshield, into the night, when he says, "She was supposed to go to Italy in the fall, for this semester-abroad program she was accepted into. She deferred a year because she wanted to be around for Ivy and me. I didn't care whether she stayed or went, which should've been a red flag, but she stuck around, and I felt like I owed her. Plus, she's Ivy's best friend, and she's at the house all the time, and tolerating her seemed easier than making waves. Jesus, Jilly, I don't know. My dad's stroke . . . It screwed me up."

My heart squeezes at the way his voice breaks over those final words. "What happened to your dad had nothing to do with you. You know that, right?"

"It had *every*thing to do with me. I was home. I could've—*should've*—mowed the lawn. He asked me to, but I was getting ready to go out with Becky—some midday party at a lake an hour outside town. I should've told Becky I was bailing on the party. I should've helped my dad. At the very least, I should've found him sooner. A minute or two might've made a difference."

"God, Max. It wasn't your fault." I reach over to touch his arm, wondering if anyone's ever told him as much.

"He's just . . . He's *so* different now."

"But he's still your dad. He still loves you and your mom and your sisters, and he's still wild about football. Wheelchair or not, he'd find a way to move mountains if it meant you'd be happy."

"I know." He runs a hand over his face. "God, I *know*. I'm trying—I swear I am—but for a long time, I just wanted to be away—anywhere but home. Becky . . . When I needed an escape, she was there."

I slip my hand from his arm and say, quietly, "Is that what I am? An escape?"

He huffs out a laugh. "Hardly. Everything's different with you. Right now, the way you're asking me to explain myself? Nobody else does that. My mom and my sisters take my crap in stride, like they've written me off, but you don't. After the river and the whisky, I felt guilty as hell about the way I treated you. You . . . You make me want to get my shit together."

I ditch my ice cream bowl in the cup holder next to his. Since he's laying his playbook on the table, for once completely forthcoming, I swallow my hesitation and broach a new topic, one far less appealing than the idea of Max getting his shit together. "I recently heard a rumor about you, Becky, and a biology classroom. True or false?"

He makes a grim sound. "Jill. False. Becky and I haven't . . . Well, it's been awhile. Since before Thanksgiving." He adjusts his hat, looking tremendously uncomfortable, and I get it. Ice cream followed by talk of Max's sex life—totally awkward. He says, "There hasn't been much interest in risky biology hookups, at least not on my part."

"Huh. I suppose that's good to hear."

He smiles, then lifts the center console and takes my hand in his, warm and a little rough, like worn leather. "My parents have never liked me with Becky. Not because of anything she's done, really, but because she's not the girl who lives across the street. You know, the moody baker girl who sometimes pretends I don't exist even though she has this massive crush on me?"

"Oh, yeah? Well, *I* live across the street from a cocky jock who once coerced me into the world's cheesiest mistletoe kiss."

He laughs and I move to poke him in the ribs, but he catches my wrist and pulls me into a hug. I breathe him in; his evergreen scent cocoons me, making me feel safe and wanted and really, really happy.

Our linked hands rest on the seat between us the whole way back to our neighborhood, where Max parks in his driveway. "Stay there," he says, opening his door and hopping out. He circles around to open my door for me.

"Just like a real date," I joke, standing beside the truck, where it'll hopefully shield us from the wide-open view of my house and his.

"I owe you dinner, remember?"

"Have you been holding on to your Bunco winnings all this time?"

"I have, actually." He steps closer, circling his arms around my waist. He's looking at me like I'm a galaxy of twinkling stars. "So, how 'bout it?"

I can't believe he thinks I need time to consider. Of course I'm going to let him take me out, but that doesn't mean I'm not going to keep our outing on the down low, at least until my parents quit it with their nightly blowups. In good conscience, I can't add another layer of strife to their dynamic. I'll tell my dad about Max and me when the time's right—like, when I move out, because I'm not sure he's ever going to understand these feelings of mine.

"If we go to dinner," I ask, "will you kiss me good night after?"

Max smiles. "I can probably manage that, although I kind of want to kiss you right now."

"But there's no mistletoe," I say with mock solemnity.

He leans in, letting his nose brush mine, and whispers, "Like I give a shit." His kiss is sweet and lingering, a pulled-taffy kiss, and when he moves away, he's grinning, arrogance personified. "You working tomorrow?"

"After lunch."

"Come over for breakfast?"

I think of Ivy, who can set ice water to boil with a single scathing look. My connection to Becky's heartbreak has planted me firmly on her shit list, and there's no way she's going to welcome me to the Holden family breakfast table. I'm about to raise my concerns with Max, but then I look into his ocean eyes and warmth spreads through me. I'm sinking . . . smiling . . . reaching for his hand.

"Okay," I say as he tugs me into him.

He dips his head and presses his mouth to mine, and a solitary thought makes a cinnamon swirl through my head: *I will never, ever get enough of this.*

26

THE NEXT MORNING, I PEER NERVOUSLY AT the Holdens' house from our front window. Their driveway looks like a parking lot. Marcy's and Ivy's cars are there, alongside Max's truck, and Brett and Zoe's minivan. I groan; it's going to be a full house.

Dad's out—*shocking*—so I let Meredith know where I'm headed. She smiles sort of knowingly and waves me off. Pulling my hood up over my head, I dash across the street, dodging raindrops. Max meets me at the front door in a chartreuse T-shirt and faded jeans. He's hatless, which doesn't happen enough, in my opinion. Before I have a chance to comment, he tugs my hood back and pulls me into a hug.

"Morning," he whispers.

I duck away, worried Ivy will walk into the foyer. It's bad enough that she'll most certainly report my presence at breakfast to Becky. I'm not about to give her the added ammunition of witnessed physical contact.

Max gives my shoulder a squeeze. "Don't stress, okay?"

"Easy for you to say."

"Seriously. We'll keep it low-key." He grins, a sun-cresting-the-horizon sort of grin, and I want to lock it up and keep it forever.

His family is gathered in the kitchen. Marcy's at the stove while Brett and Zoe sit at the table with Bill. His mouth is turned up in a slight smile as he listens to the conversations floating around him. He's a fan of the big weekend breakfast. He used to swear he needed a full gut for game day, but we all know the truth: Bill's happiest when he's with his brood, and nothing brings them together like a home-cooked meal. I give him a wave, inhaling the scents of bacon and maple syrup. My stomach rumbles, but my appetite diminishes when I make eye contact with Ivy, who's leaning against the counter.

"Look who's here," she says, snarky.

Max flips her the bird, steering me to the kitchen table. He sits beside me and Ivy claims the spot directly across from us, like she's our chaperone or something. She takes her phone from her pocket and, eyeing me over its top, taps out what appears to be a lengthy message. To Becky, I'm sure.

When she finishes, she says, "Nobody mentioned you were coming over, Jillian."

"Uh, I did," Max says.

"Not to me."

"Didn't know I needed your approval."

"Would've been nice," she says, tossing her hair.

He lowers his voice. "You know, you're not Becky's informant. It's not her business what I do, so how 'bout a little loyalty?"

Ivy's opening her mouth to respond when from the stove, Marcy calls, "We're always happy to have you, Jill."

"In fact, you should come more often," Brett says, defusing the tension. "It's nice to have another outsider at the table."

Zoe prods his shoulder. "You're not an outsider."

"But I'm not a Holden, and Jill's not, either." He winks at me. "Solidarity."

"You're all welcome for breakfast anytime," Marcy says, dusting her hands off on her apron. "I think we're ready."

Oliver bounds into the room, a sippy cup of what I hope is diluted juice grasped tight in his hand, and sandwiches himself between his parents. Zoe cuts a pancake and a banana into tiny bites for him. Marcy tops off mugs with coffee from a carafe, and Brett uses a remote to turn the small kitchen TV to ESPN. He and Max debate defensive strategies while Bill follows along, contributing a bouncy nod here and there. Ivy picks up her phone to respond to a newly received text, simultaneously rolling her eyes at the way Zoe hovers over Oliver like a helicopter. We devour plates of buttermilk pancakes and crispy bacon, and all in all, things couldn't be more normal.

My attention remains divided between my breakfast, which is delectable, and the attentive way Ivy feeds her father. Bill's kind of a mess when it comes to eating now, but his fancy-pants daughter seems unfazed. She uses a napkin to dab gently at his chin; selfless acts on her part are so few and far between, I'm mesmerized.

That is, until Oliver tosses a piece of banana onto the floor, grinning expectantly at his audience. Max laughs, breaking the food-induced hush. Zoe frowns at her child, then shoots her brother a reprimanding look.

Max, still laughing, shrugs and says, "What?"

"Grow up," she scolds, though she looks more amused than upset.

"Never." He tosses a piece of bacon and nails her right in the nose.

The meal continues, and aside from Max sliding his hand along my leg—low-key, my ass—this morning's breakfast turns out not so different from the hundreds of other meals I've shared with the Holdens.

By the time I get up to help Marcy clear the table, I can't remember what I was so worried about.

We can do this, Max and me.

When the food's gone and the kitchen's clean, he and I sneak up to his room. Clothes and sports equipment are strewn about, his bed is unmade, and there are school papers littering his desk. The space smells clean, though, like him. He closes the door, locking it, I notice, then peers at me like a lion stalking a tasty zebra. "Come here," he says, holding out a hand.

I step forward, slipping my hand into his. I laugh when a mental picture flashes in my mind: a zebra, eager and naive, trotting into the trap of a hungry lion.

"What's funny?" he asks.

"Nothing. This is just . . . weird."

He loops my arms around his neck, then clasps his hands at the small of my back. "It's good, though, right?"

I lift up on my toes to kiss him. "Very good."

He walks me backward until we reach the futon under his window. We sit, intertwined.

"How long can you stay?" he asks.

"Not long. I have to work, remember?"

"I don't want you to go. How's that for weird?"

What's really weird is that I get what he's saying. I've lived within fifty yards of him for more than half my life, yet suddenly it seems like we never have enough time together. "Trust me. I'd rather stay here."

"Ask Kyle to cover your shift."

"The two of us are supposed to close together."

"So I won't see you till tomorrow?"

I tense. I haven't given much thought to tomorrow. To school.

It's clear he knows me well when he says, "Jill, who gives a shit? People are gonna find out."

"An hour ago you were fine with keeping things low-key."

"Yeah, then I sat through breakfast feeling like I couldn't touch you. It sucked."

"That's just it. Your sister saw us consume a meal together, and she couldn't have been snottier about it."

"She'll get over it."

"What about Becky?" Becky, who belittles me as often as possible. Becky, who didn't give a second thought to smacking into me on the quad. Becky, who hates me because she believes I stole her boyfriend. "If you think she's not going to assume it's my fault you guys broke up, you're deluded."

"Like I'll stand by and let her give you shit."

But what if you're not standing by? I want to ask, suffering the phantom ache of her shoulder check. "You have no idea how terrible girls can be when they feel like they've been wronged," I say. "Let's just play it cool, okay? I can't have another thing to worry about. Not right now."

He rests his cheek on top of my head. "What else are you worried about?"

I stall, then stammer, "Things at home are . . . not great." I'm uncomfortable talking about this, even with Max, and besides, the friction that is life under the Eldridge roof isn't exactly new-relationship fodder. "I'm trying to get back to a good place with my dad, but he doesn't understand you. He can't let go of Halloween, or Bunco, or the night Officer Tate found beer in your truck."

Max pulls away, sitting upright. "Oh, hell. That's all in the past."

"I know, but it'll be a while before he comes around. If he finds out about us now, he'll be pissed and I just . . . can't. For now, can you and me just be *you and me*?"

His expression softens. He slides his hand under my hair, along the back of my neck, pulling me toward him until my forehead rests against his. "Jilly," he breathes, "I don't like secrets, but more than anything . . . I just wanna be with you."

"Ditto," I whisper.

• • • •

When I swing the door to True Brew open, the shop is empty but for an elderly couple sipping coffee at a corner table. When I make my way behind the counter, Kyle looks up from the espresso machine, where he's vigilantly wiping down the grates. He stops whistling— "Whistle While You Work," naturally—and his expression morphs from friendly to suspicious. "Jelly Bean, what are you looking so cute for?"

I glance down at my clothing: my True Brew T-shirt and my work-only, coffee-stained jeans. "Are you kidding?"

He rolls his eyes. "Not your clothes." He studies me as I tie on my apron. "Is that *eyeliner* you're wearing?"

I stick my tongue out. "So what if it is?"

"I'd just like to know why, is all."

"Maybe because I had breakfast at the Holdens'."

His eyes light up. "And?"

"*And* . . . Max and I are good."

"I sense you're watering things down."

I can't help a little smile. "We talked yesterday. A lot. And this morning."

"I *bet* you talked." He tugs on my ponytail, messing it up.

"Kyle, stop!" I dart away, catching a glimpse of the ancient couple at their corner table. They're craning their necks to see over the counter—oh, the mischief their baristas are making!

I pull the elastic from my hair, comb my fingers through, and gather it back up. "You better chill, buddy. You're going to get us fired."

"Nah. I know the owners. And don't try to distract me. Max and you . . . ?"

I busy myself topping off milk pitchers. "Are friends again."

Kyle cocks his head, his skepticism flagrant. "You're not telling me everything."

Max and me . . . We're so new, so fragile. I'm hesitant to share with anyone—even Kyle—for fear of popping our iridescent bubble. "I'm telling you what you need to know."

He stares at me for a long moment, then turns away to fill a cup with drip coffee. Handing it to me, he says, "You like him. It's written all over your face—thirsty eyes and kissy lips, puppy love in all its glory. I mean, keep your secrets if you must, but know that *I* know exactly what you're feeling."

I roll my eyes. "Fine. We spent the better part of the morning making out. Is that what you want to hear?"

He laughs, gleeful. "That's *exactly* what I want to hear!"

"But listen—not everyone will be as delighted as you, so keep quiet, okay?"

"Please. You and Max? It'll be old news before you know it."

"Not as far as my dad's concerned. He'll see red if he finds out. Becky will, too."

"So, what . . . ? You guys are gonna be all covert? Max is cool with that?"

I shrug, refilling the grinder with espresso beans. "I'm not sure I'd use the word 'cool.'"

"Jill," Kyle says, sidling up to me. "Please tell me you're not complicating things. If you think your dad'll be pissed now, just imagine how furious he'll be if he finds out you've been hiding this guy he didn't want you to go out with in the first place."

"I'll tell him. I just need time, is all."

He shakes his head. "Jelly Bean knows best, I guess."

27

COME MONDAY MORNING, I'M SEVERELY LACKING IN the sleep department. I spent most of last night whispering on the phone with Max, and the remaining hours of darkness listening to Ally's wails and Meredith's out-of-tune lullabies.

I drive her car to school again—she doesn't have much need for it, since Ally's not old enough to venture out into the world much—and arrive a few minutes early. Kyle meets me on the quad, tossing a football into the foggy air, catching it as it spirals back to earth. "Leah ran off with Jesse," he says as we navigate bunches of people. He tucks the football under his arm, his eyes flickering with sudden curiosity. "Tell me—what if you were to see Max right now? What would you do?"

"I don't know. I guess I'd say hello and go about my business. What do you care?"

He blinks his big blue eyes at me. "I'm just trying to work out the details so I'll understand why you wouldn't drape yourself all over this guy you're obviously nuts for."

Maybe so I don't get walloped on campus, I think, scanning the crowd for Becky's burnt-orange hair. I make an irritated noise in Kyle's direction. "We've been over this."

"Yeah. And I'll try not to say 'I told you so' when your secret becomes everyone's business and all hell breaks loose."

"Thank you, Nostradamus. Consider your prediction noted and ignored."

The bell blares, and we file into the locker bay with the herd. I spot Max hanging out with Leo and Jesse near my locker. He thumps Kyle on the back as we pass—"Asshole," Kyle mutters good-naturedly—then catches my eye and tosses me a smile.

I smile back and continue down the hall, struggling to ignore the invisible threads tugging me back toward him. I spin the dial on my locker clumsily. Kyle offers a haughty know-it-all snicker.

I sense Max moving closer even before he taps my shoulder. I turn to find him wearing a look that promises fun whirled with a dash of trouble. "Morning, Jillian," he says.

Over his shoulder, I see Leo and Jesse watching us. They're in listening range, Kyle might as well be on top of us, and the hallway is swarming with people. Becky's still nowhere to be seen, though, and that's a relief. "Hello, Max," I say, matching his formal approach.

He grins as he realizes I'm going to play along. "I wanted to see if you'd like to ride to school with me tomorrow."

So your ex can catch us walking onto campus together? "Oh, um, wow," I splutter, foraging for an excuse that makes sense. "Thanks, but I'm pretty sure Meredith will let me borrow her car."

"Seems kind of stupid for us to drive separately when we could easily ride together."

"But your taste in music sucks," I say, saccharine sweet.

Kyle snorts.

Max doesn't miss a beat. "I might be willing to let you choose the music."

"Really?" He'd give up his beloved classic country just for me?

His voice is a hum suspended in the space between us. "Anything for you, Jilly."

God. He's so good at this. The tips of my ears are hot, but I affect an unflappable air because this is a game, that's all. "What if we hang out after school?" I propose. "We can study. Or . . . something."

"Yeah, okay," he says, his smile turning suggestive. "I'll see you later, then." He brushes a lock of hair from my face, out of bounds, but it's hard to make myself care because his touch sends pitter-patter pops of electricity across my skin. "You won't regret it," he says in that same quiet voice, the one that's meant just for me (and Kyle, I guess, though I've mostly forgotten about him).

The exchange has run its course, but Max remains in front of me like his shoes are rooted to the scuffed linoleum. I gaze at him with what I suspect are googly eyes.

The warning bell pierces the din of the hallway, and Kyle grabs my elbow. "See you later, dude," he tells Max, dragging me down the hall.

"See?" I say once we've rounded the corner. "We're totally capable of keeping things chill."

"Okay, Miss Delusional. That was the most charged exchange I've witnessed . . . ever. I'm not sure which of you's going to screw this up first, but it's bound to happen."

I shake my head, wondering if there's something to his conjecture, and hoping there's not. I recall Max's whispered words—*I just wanna be with you*. Like a spring breeze, they drop seeds of uncertainty into the soft soil of my mind.

Should I be open with Max, and take Becky's wrath as it comes? Should I tell my dad about us, and go back to being the letdown he thought I was after Halloween? After Bunco?

As I walk into French, those seeds of uncertainty shoot into sky-high evergreens of doubt.

28

IDWEEK, SHOUTING ROUSES ME FROM SLEEP, HOT words blistering my subconscious before I'm alert enough to comprehend them. Bleary-eyed, I glance at my clock; it's just after midnight.

A thud from the living room makes me jump—a book hitting the coffee table?

The arguments are getting worse. No longer does Meredith attempt to keep her voice down, and Dad has abandoned his evasive *I was working* mantra. Hurling thinly veiled insults with no concern for hurt feelings has become okay—*normal*. I hate that it's all Ally knows.

I sit up in bed as Meredith shouts, "You could tell me where you're disappearing to!"

"The last thing I need is a babysitter. Get off my back!"

"You're hiding something. I know you are." Her razor-sharp accusation cuts the sleepiness from my brain.

"Bullshit!" Dad says. "The only thing I've hidden is how much work it takes to keep this family afloat. Your lifestyle isn't free."

"Don't you dare patronize me. I'm your wife, not a financial burden, and you're smack in the middle of a midlife crisis."

"Can you blame me? You have no idea what kind of pressure I'm under at work, and you have no idea what kind of debt you racked up with those specialists—even after we pissed away Jillian's money. All you cared about was having a goddamn baby, and look where that's gotten us!"

Ally starts to cry. Dad's pitching low blows, and the hostility in his voice digs into my skin like a thorn—I can only imagine how Meredith must feel. My frustration with him, once a snowball tumbling innocuously downhill, has become an avalanche.

Instinct says I should take his side, but he's being *such* a jerk. Meredith could leave him—I'm not sure I'd blame her—and she'd take my sister, who I'm only just getting to know. All I'd be left with is my father, who's become so dispassionate he's hardly recognizable, and a future full of uncertainties.

The house falls quiet. I imagine Meredith settling down to feed Ally. Dad probably has buried his nose in his laptop, as if he hasn't just spewed a deluge of hurtful words. I close my eyes and think of Max, our after-school visits, cruising around in his truck, our final destination the secluded road by the river, where we talk and laugh and kiss like we're the only people in existence. . . . The best hours of my day.

I'm sinking back into sleep when Meredith's voice floats down the hall. "Jake?"

"What?" Cold, brittle.

"Are you having an affair?"

I sit up, straining to catch his answer.

"I'd rather know now," Meredith says. "Considering your past, you can understand why I'd be suspicious."

"What the hell is that supposed to mean?"

"You've got a new baby. Your closest friend's had a health scare. You're stressed. You're unhappy." She pauses, letting her words sink in. "Beth left you because after Jillian was born, you strayed. Now you're in a similar situation. Who's to say you won't cheat again?"

Beth . . . *my mother* . . . moved halfway around the world because Dad couldn't keep his pants on?

A wave of vertigo rolls through me.

I reach for my nightstand and grab my phone. Briefly, I consider calling Beth. She's the only person who can confirm Meredith's accusation. But what's the point? Dad's lack of contradiction is proof enough.

My fingers dial a different number.

He answers after four rings, his voice textured like sandpaper.

"Max?" His name slips out, wobbly and small.

I hear a rustling. "Jill? You okay?"

I swallow the sob that arrives with his concern. "Can I come over?"

"Yeah, of course. I'll meet you at the door."

I don't change out of the flannel pajama pants I'm wearing, but I pull a sweatshirt over my tank top and slip on a pair of flip-flops. I climb out my window with far less finesse than Max manages, and my shoes slap pavement as I run across the street.

True to his word, he's on the front porch, in gym shorts and a white T-shirt, his hair haphazard, dark spikes jutting every which way. Somewhere between my window and his front door, I've started to cry in earnest. He scoops me up and holds me as I shudder against him, trying to muffle my sobs.

After a few minutes, he leans back, hands on my cheeks, angling my face up. I'm sure I'm a mess—I get very splotchy when I cry—but he's gazing down at me with such concern, I doubt he's noticed. He whispers, "If you can be silent for ten seconds, we can go upstairs."

I nod and follow him inside. He closes the door without a sound. We tiptoe through the living room and kitchen, beyond the closed door of his parents' bedroom, to the staircase that leads to the second floor. We creep past Ivy's room and the bonus room before making our way into his bedroom. He locks the door before guiding me to his bed and nudging me onto his rumpled sheets. Sinking down beside me, he moves his hand over my back in slow circles as fresh tears trail down my cheeks.

"I'm not gonna lie," he says. "You're freaking me out."

"I'm sorry." I wipe my eyes with the sleeve of my sweatshirt. "My parents . . ."

He shakes his head, brows lifted enough to tell me he has no idea what I'm talking about.

"They're fighting," I explain. "A lot. Horrible arguments."

"Jesus, Jill. Since when?"

"Last summer. But lately, since Ally was born, it's gotten really bad. And my dad . . . He's cheating on Meredith."

Max's mouth falls open. "Like, an *affair*?"

I nod. "He's never home. He's evasive. He's being *so* mean. And he was MIA the day Ally was born!" I remember with alarm where I am and pause to find my composure. When I speak again, my voice is quieter, safer. "What kind of man would miss his daughter's birth?"

"I don't know . . . a stupid man? But not one of those things makes your dad a cheater."

"All piled up they do."

He reaches for my hand. "I'm not gonna argue that he's being a dick, but don't you think you should give him the benefit of the doubt? Maybe he's busy at work. Maybe he doesn't know how to deal with the baby and he's making a mess of things."

"You're wrong."

Max regards me, his mouth set in a deep frown, making me uncomfortable, squirmy. I busy myself trying to remember the last time he saw me cry. . . . Seventh grade, I decide, riding bikes. I fell (trying to keep up with him) and scraped the hell out of my leg. He helped me, bloodied and bawling, as I hobbled home, then stayed by my side while Meredith (Dad's fiancée at the time) rummaged through medicine cabinets for gauze and Bactine.

Having read enough from my expression, he says, "What aren't you telling me?"

"He's done it before," I say, and the admission makes me heartsick. "He cheated before, on my mother. He's the reason she left."

Max sighs, a sorrowful sound, and draws me into his arms. I cry, hating my helplessness, my vulnerability, despising the tears that scatter like rain across his shirt.

When I'm reduced to rosy cheeks and sniffles, he helps me out of my sweatshirt and shoes, and even though I feel a little like a child, it's nice to be taken care of. He fluffs a pillow for me, then tucks layers of blankets up to my chin. I've never been in his bed before—it's been years since I've even sat on it. It's so intimate, being wrapped in the sheets he sleeps in, cloaked in his scent and his personal space. I want to hibernate here until winter's over.

As I watch him stride across the room to flip off the light, I realize he's replaced Kyle as my go-to friend, the person I reach out to intuitively. When he climbs into bed, I scoot into the cocoon of his embrace and whisper, "Thank you."

"I'm glad you called."

"I hate that I woke you."

"Please, Jill. How many times have I bothered you with my shit? Call whenever you need me, no matter where I am or how late it is."

"I will," I say, and then, "Same goes for you."

He nods, running his hand over my hair. "How come you didn't tell me about your dad and Meredith?"

"I haven't told anyone."

"Not even Kyle?"

"Not even Kyle. It's not exactly fun to talk about."

"But you shouldn't have to deal on your own." He's speaking from experience, his voice deep, startling in its seriousness. "Talk to me, okay? Whenever you feel like it. Even if you don't want me to talk back . . . I'll hear you."

I could cry all over again. I burrow into his sleepy scent, pressing my lips to the warm skin of his neck. God, I love him. I sensed it before, but now I *feel* it, prickling my skin, seeping into my bones, consuming me from the inside out.

"Saturday's Valentine's Day," I say. "Can we hang out?"

"Of course. What should we do?"

I ponder while he toys with the ends of my hair, and then inspiration strikes. "Seattle. I want to take you to my favorite restaurant."

"Cool. Can I plan the rest of the day?"

"Depends on what you've got in mind."

"Fun stuff. Stuff that'll cheer you up."

"But it's not your job to cheer me up."

"Uh, yeah it is. Maybe you haven't noticed, but my happiness relates directly to yours. I never want to see you cry again."

"That might be the sweetest thing you've ever said, Holden."

"I have my moments." I hear humor in his voice as he goes on,

"Remember when you had that horrible summer job walking the Rolons' dog?"

They hired me a few years back to take their grouchy terrier around the block once every weekday while school was out. It was a thankless job full of ankle nips and poop scooping, worsened by the fact that it was one of the hottest summers on record. "Ugh. Yes, why?"

"Remember how I used to walk with you?"

"I do." Max's company was the only thing that kept me from strangling that dog.

"Do you know why I walked with you?"

Curious, I fold my hands across his chest, drop my chin, and work to make out his features through the darkness. "Why?"

"Because I thought I was in love with you."

I laugh out loud, only quieting when I remember I'm in Max Holden's bed in the middle of the night, down the hall from his sister and a floor away from his parents.

"Seriously. I was convinced you were, like, my soul mate." He pauses, smiling at the memory. "Even back then, watching you drag that shitty little dog down the block, I thought you were the most beautiful girl in the neighborhood."

"I can't imagine why," I say, only able to recall braces, knobby knees, and a flat chest.

He brings my hand to his mouth and kisses my palm. "I still think you're the most beautiful girl in the neighborhood."

I wriggle up so we're face-to-face and run my fingers through his hair; it's deceptively soft. "Do you think it's weird that we know each other so well, even though this"—I gesture between the two of us—"is new?"

"No way. I like that I know everything about you." He gives me a lazy grin. "Makes you easier to put up with."

"You don't know *every*thing," I say, indignant.

"Wanna bet?" He plows ahead without waiting for an answer. "I know you like soda best from a fountain, and I know your cookbook collection's the first thing you'd save in a house fire. I know you drink your coffee with cream and a shit-ton of sugar, and I know your favorite book is *The Giver*. I know you like dark chocolate more than milk. I know you have a tiny freckle on the inside of your left wrist." With the pad of his thumb, he grazes the spot he's referring to. He sits up and trails his fingers down my spine, over my hip, and along my thigh. With his eyes locked on mine, he wraps his hand around the back of my knee and says, "I know this is the only place on your body where you're really, truly ticklish."

I giggle and squirm until he stops, then work my way back into the crook of his arm. He tilts his head and waits for me to brush my lips against his. "Saturday," he says. "You figure out dinner, but I've got the rest." The hopeful timbre of his voice, the impish gleam in his eye—they're very cute.

"Deal."

He kisses me again, softly, then sprinkles kisses all over my face—across my cheeks, along the line of my jaw, and once on the tip of my nose. He finds my mouth again, and his lips taste of seawater, the last evidence of my tears.

29

I'M ROCKING ALLYSON CLAIRE IN HER ROOM Saturday morning, trying to give Meredith a few minutes to herself because, of course, Dad's nowhere to be found. Ally's dozed off and I'm feeling very proud of myself, having lulled her to sleep for the very first time, so when the doorbell rings, I wait for Mer to get it. I listen as she and Max greet each other, then smile when he peeks around the corner. "Almost ready?"

I nod. "You can come in."

He does, leaning up against my sister's crib, sorely out of place among the chic white furniture and frilly pink linens. He's wearing jeans and a plaid button-down in shades of blue, and he's hatless again, which I love.

I lay Ally in her crib. She does that funny twitchy thing Meredith calls startling, and Max does a poor job of stifling his laughter. I drag him out of the nursery before he wakes her.

He stops me in the hallway. "You're the greatest big sister ever."

"Oh, really? What would your big sisters have to say about that?"

"Who cares? They were borderline abusive when I was a kid. Ivy still is, sometimes. You're, like, gentle and caring and sweet."

"I can be gentle and caring and sweet with you, too."

"Yeah? Prove it."

I lift up on my toes to kiss him. Pressing his hands against my back, he eases me closer. He lets go of a sigh when I tease his mouth open, and then we're full-on making out in the hallway—until the dainty sound of Meredith clearing her throat interrupts us. Max shoves me away like I've burned him.

"Just checking on the baby," she says, breezing past. She avoids my eyes, but she's biting her lip, hiding a smile.

Max tugs me toward the front door, muttering, "So much for sweet and gentle."

Out in the truck, he cranks the key in the ignition. "Islands in the Stream" blares from the speakers. I wince. He waves his hand toward the stereo. "Go ahead."

I fiddle with the music while we drive north on I-5. When I can't find anything I like that won't send his head into a spin, I turn the radio off. "Quiet's better than Hank or Johnny or Merle."

"You shouldn't talk about the legends that way. I'll convert you to a country girl one of these days." He combs his fingers through my hair. "Happy Valentine's Day, by the way."

"Thanks, Holden. Back at ya."

"What'd you do this morning?"

"Made fondant."

"What the hell is fondant?"

"Heated powdered sugar and water, like Play-Doh for decorating cakes."

"Teach me how to make it someday?"

I laugh. "Okay, but I'm not sure you'll ever use the knowledge."

"Oh, I definitely won't, but you've educated yourself on all things football. The least I can do is get a handle on fondant. Despite my recent track record, I can be a pretty decent boyfriend. You'll see."

My heart skips a beat, but I keep my voice light as whipped cream. "Oh, you're my boyfriend now?"

He pulls his attention from the road to blink at me. "Uh, aren't I?"

"I guess? I wasn't sure we were doing the boyfriend-girlfriend thing."

"You don't want to?"

"No, I—"

"Because I can look somewhere else," he interrupts, reaching over to tweak my hair. "If you're not willing to step up to the plate, there's gotta be someone who is."

I roll my eyes. "You can be really idiotic."

"And you can be really dense. Are we on the same page?"

"Officially."

He lifts the center console out of the way. "Then get over here."

Blissfully, I scoot into the middle seat and rebuckle. I lean into him as I say, "In case you're unaware, our fellow freeway travelers probably think we're a couple of rednecks."

"I could give two shits," he says, taking my hand.

· · · ·

I'm glad I let Max plan our Seattle adventures. First activity on the itinerary? Forty-three seconds spent shooting five hundred twenty feet into the air.

In all the years I've lived in Washington, I've never been to the top of the Space Needle, so this first excursion is well received. Max grips my hand as the glass elevator rockets into the cloudless sky, and up on the observation deck, we walk a slow circle, pointing out landmarks: the Cascade Range, the downtown skyline, Mount Rainier, the Puget Sound, and the Olympic Mountains.

We stop walking when we're facing north. Though the sun's shining, it's freezing. The wind whips my hair into a snarl. I smooth it out of my face, shivering, and lean against the rail to gaze at Queen Anne Hill. A seaplane touches down on the sparkling waters of Lake Union while silent, toy-sized traffic zips about directly below. Farther in the distance lies the University of Washington, Max's first choice in institutes of higher education.

He wraps his arms around me, blocking me from the relentless wind, and rests his chin on my shoulder. Quietly, he looks out upon Seattle, then nuzzles his nose against my neck. "Are you gonna apply to the U next year?"

"Maybe as a fallback."

"Still got your eye on NYC, huh?"

My stomach drops. New York City. The International Culinary Institute. A lot like my parents' marital issues, talk of higher education and its challenges feels personal and embarrassing and just . . . off-limits. But I want to trust Max like he's starting to trust me. I want to be honest about what's good *and* bad. "I've kind of let New York go, actually."

"What? *Why?*"

I shrug, feigning indifference. "Too expensive."

"But the International Culinary Institute's your dream school."

"There's no money for it. Not after Meredith's fertility treatments. Not after Ally." I feel a blast of residual guilt; I spent a long time resenting my unborn sister for stealing culinary school from me, but the fact is, none of this is her fault. It's not Meredith's fault, or my dad's, either. It just is.

Max squeezes me close. I feel his sympathy, his solace, as plain as I see the sun's light. "Sorry, Jill," he says, and then, tentatively, he broaches the topic I've spent the last couple of weeks musing. "Couldn't you go to one of the culinary schools in Seattle?"

"I could. There are a few good ones. But I want to go to the *best* culinary school."

"There've gotta be scholarships, then. Loans, even, right?"

"I've looked into financial aid. I'm pretty sure I could get close to covering tuition with scholarships, but living expenses are astronomical, and I don't want to finish school with a mountain of debt. There's no way, Max. New York's out of my league."

"Then put it on hold. Go to school around here for a couple of years, then see where you're at."

I consider, leaning into him as I say, "That's . . . not a bad idea." I don't know why this hasn't occurred to me—attending a Seattle culinary school doesn't have to mean giving up on New York; I'd only be tabling it. "I could get my associate's locally," I say, thinking aloud. "I could keep working at True Brew while I live at home and save up. For a couple of years, I could focus on general culinary arts and the business side of restaurant ownership. When I get to New York, I could concentrate on pastry arts."

"By then," Max says, "you'll have made such a reputation for yourself, the International Culinary Institute will be begging you to study with them."

I smile; his faith is endearing. "It'd be nice to stay close to my family, at least for a while. I'd see Ally grow up a little. Plus," I say, letting uncertainty lower my voice, "I'd be near you."

His eyes flash, more warm pewter than cool silver. "Let's assume you do it—school here for a year or two, then you go to New York to finish. By the time you graduate, you're a baking superstar. What's next?"

"I'll get an apprenticeship somewhere fantastic, hopefully. I'd love to study under Ansel Badon or Jacquelyn Montfort. One day, I'll open a pâtisserie and spend my days baking. That's a long way off, though."

"Won't you miss me when you're trotting the globe, baking cookies and cakes for strange men?"

"Aww, Max. You know you're the only strange man I associate with. Besides, you'll be too busy tearing up the football field at the U to miss me."

He grunts, like that's the most ridiculous thing he's ever heard. "It's gonna be a while before I know if I'm going to UW. Besides, no matter how far down the line, living thousands of miles away from you is gonna blow."

I twist in his arms to see if his expression is as intense as his words and it is, which thrills and terrifies me equally. He's making big assumptions—life is unpredictable. I'm not trying to be cynical or negative or even doubtful, but after listening to Dad and Meredith tear into each other night after night, after seeing Bill cut down by a stroke nobody could ever have predicted . . . Shit happens, and I'm not so naive as to assume that now that I've got Max, I get to keep him forever.

"Hey," I say, placing my hand over his heart. I feel it beating through the layers of his shirt and jacket. "The future's so wide open. Who knows what it holds?"

He takes my face in his hands. His palms are hot against my windblown cheeks, his gaze hard as steel. "Jilly, you make life feel okay, even when it mostly sucks—you always have. It pisses me off that I've wasted time I could've spent with you, so God, don't make me worry that the future's not a sure thing. If you're not serious, tell me now, before I get in any deeper."

If his body language is any indication—tense and expectant, jaw tight, shoulders rigid—he's in pretty deep already. And I'm on emotional overload. I have to swallow before I can say, "I'm serious." A gust of wind carries my promise away. "I'm serious, Max," I repeat. "I'm as serious as you are."

I don't miss his exhale of relief as he dips his head so we're eye to eye. "Good."

He gives me a sweet smile, then kisses me, a kiss too intimate for the very public observation deck of the Space Needle—not that I'm complaining.

When we're sufficiently frozen, we ride back down the elevator and climb into the truck. With the heater on high, Max drives south, adjacent to Elliott Bay, and parks across the street from the waterfront. He takes my hand and we jog toward the water, where the air is crisp and briny. He stops in front of Pier 59. I read the sign above the weathered powder-blue building.

"Seattle Aquarium?"

"I thought it'd be fun."

He's freaking adorable, all flushed cheeks and hopeful smiles. I tug him through the entrance.

We spend the rest of the afternoon wandering the aquarium like little kids. We marvel at the giant Puget Sound octopus, peer at tiny sea horses and transparent jellyfish, watch playful otters splashing around, and point out puffins torpedoing through their pools. I laugh when Max stands next to a huge wooden cutout of a shark to measure his six feet, two inches, then squirm when he makes me poke at sea stars and anemones in the hands-on tide pools. We walk through the gift shop, where he buys Oliver a rubber version of the creepy octopus we saw, and I pick out a stuffed sea horse for Ally.

After, we sit on a bench in front of a huge wall of aquarium water contained behind glass so thick it distorts what's beyond: salmon, eels, and oddly, a scuba diver.

"Hungry?" I ask Max.

"Starving. What're we doing for dinner?"

"Wouldn't you like to know."

"Pizza?" he guesses, taking my hand and pulling me from the bench.

"You think my favorite restaurant in all of Seattle serves pizza?"

"Mexican?"

"Nope."

"Thai?"

"Max," I say, flashing the flirty I'm-so-innocent smile I learned from him. "You'll see when we get there."

He swats my butt. "Then let's move. I'm withering away."

We hoof it up the hill toward Pike Place Market. Darkness has fallen and it's bitter cold. He offers me his jacket; I feel a little silly accepting it, like a distressed damsel, but it's toasty and smells delightfully of him. I don't slip it off my shoulders until we've climbed a steep set of stairs that takes us to the entrance of a little restaurant. Its door is the color of sunlight.

"The Yellow Door?" Max says, reading the plaque.

"My dad and I used to come here all the time. It's the best—you'll see."

We're slightly underdressed, but the hostess is gracious, the restaurant cozy and familiar. Candles flicker and the aroma of smoky meat and bright citrus makes my mouth water. We're shown to a secluded table overlooking the darkened bay. Wineglasses sit in front of our places, along with a line of sparkling silverware. I skim the menu's *Chef's Specials* insert: *Seared Artisan Sonoma Foie Gras* and *Escargots à la Bordelaise*.

Under the table, Max nudges my ankle with his foot. When I look up, he winks. "Bunco was good to me, so I've got the check. Get whatever you want."

We decide on the tasting menu—that's what my dad and I used to share—and end up oohing and aahing our way through each course: sweet cream of carrot soup, *foie gras*, pan-seared salmon, and melt-in-your-mouth beef tenderloin with fingerling potatoes. Dessert, a velvety chocolate mousse, is delectable. By the time we've finished, I feel like I'll need a crane to lift me from my upholstered seat.

"You were right," Max says, looking over the bill. "That was really freaking good."

"I knew you'd like it. Also, will you please let me split that with you?"

He eyes me, offended. "I told you I've got it."

"But—"

"Jillian," he warns, "don't even. Treat me to ice cream next weekend, okay?"

Hardly a fair trade, but my stomach is pleasantly full and I'm gratifyingly content, so I give up my protest. When the bill's settled, we grab our aquarium bags and stand to leave. I smile up at Max. "Thanks for—"

He stops suddenly, pulling me back against his chest with a mumbled, "Uh-oh."

I look to him for explanation, and I'm thrown by his panicked expression. I follow his gaze to the lobby, my hands tingling with trepidation. There, a man checks in with the same hostess who seated us. His back is to us, but his confident stance and chestnut hair are alarmingly familiar.

Dad.

I notice his suit first—charcoal, expensive-looking, one I haven't seen before—and then the fact that he's unaccompanied. Of course he's unaccompanied; Meredith's home with Ally. But Dad wouldn't come to the Yellow Door on Valentine's Day by himself.

Dread tiptoes up my spine.

Max mutters through clenched teeth, like a ventriloquist, "What do you want to do?"

I am literally speechless.

"Jill—"

I yank him behind the back of the nearest booth, pulling him down until he's crouched beside me, until we look like two kids playing hide-and-seek in the world's most inappropriate venue.

"You've got to be joking," Max says in an undertone.

Nearby diners stare us inquisitively, but I don't care. "We can't let him see us."

"You want to crawl out of here?"

"No. I want to spy. Then, when he turns his back, I want to run."

Max doesn't consent, but he doesn't object, either. I suspect he's annoyed—worst ending to a date ever—but this is it. Tonight, I'm going to get to the bottom of my dad's disappearances.

Bracing my hand on the floor, I lean around the edge of the booth. Dad's still talking to the hostess, grinning broadly, gesturing toward the restroom—the location of his companion, if I had to guess. The enormous meal in my stomach gurgles like chocolate in a double boiler.

"Maybe it's a work thing," Max says, leaning forward to take a peek.

"Maybe," I say. Or maybe not.

Dad's on the move now, following the hostess, who carries two menus. They're headed right for us. I wrench my head back like a turtle tucking away from a predator. I hunker down next to Max, the two of us barely concealed, as the hostess says, "Will this table do?"

"It's perfect," Dad says. I sneak an upward glance: the back of his head moves closer, closer, and then he sinks down onto the bench and leans back against the seat Max and I are hiding behind. My heart's jumping around behind my ribs, trying to break free.

The hostess says, "Enjoy your meal, and happy Valentine's Day."

I've seen enough. Two menus and a Valentine's Day salute—he's on a date.

Max grabs my hand and whispers, "Let's go."

We circle around the perimeter of the restaurant, faces hidden, dodging waiters and waitresses as we make our escape. We don't slow until we're in the lobby, well out of sight. I'm panting, more from adrenaline than actual fatigue, and I'm so hot I'm light-headed. Max cradles a cool hand around the back of my neck and guides me to the exit. Down the steep staircase we go, and then we're standing in the bracing night air.

He exhales a big breath and says, "Holy. Shit."

"Indeed."

He touches my cheek. "You okay?"

"Tell me I'm not nuts to think something's going on."

He hesitates. "It was sort of sketchy."

"Sort of?"

"I really do think it could've been a work meeting."

"In Seattle? On Valentine's Day? At a restaurant that's supposed to be special to the two of us?"

"Maybe he's seeing a client who lives close by. And you said so yourself—he likes the Yellow Door, too."

"Or, maybe he was on a *date*. He kept looking at the bathroom. Did you notice that?"

"No, Sherlock, I sure didn't."

I know he's trying to nudge a smile out of me, but I'm in no mood for jokes. A gust of wind lifts my hair, and I shiver. "He's having an affair, Max."

He rubs his hands briskly over my arms. "Let's go to the truck. You're freezing."

"Oh! Your jacket! I left it with the hostess."

"I'll get it. You wait here."

"No. I'll get it."

"Jillian, let me. Don't torture yourself."

"I just . . . I need to know for sure. Besides, I'm not standing on this corner alone."

He surveys the darkened street. Down an alleyway, a man in layers of filthy clothing emerges from behind a Dumpster, pulling a wagon of worldly treasures behind him. Max grimaces. "I'll come up with you."

"The two of us will attract too much attention. Please, go get the truck. I'll be right back."

He looks torn, but then he lays a kiss on my cheek and jogs down the sidewalk in the direction of the parking lot. I hurry up the stairs to the Yellow Door.

Max's jacket hangs from the corner of the hostess's podium. She hands it to me. "I thought you might be back for this."

"Thanks so much," I say, keeping my voice low. I scan the faces in the glowing restaurant as I pull Max's jacket around my shoulders. Stranger, stranger, stranger . . .

They all go blurry, save one distinct and very significant man. What I see, the *only* thing I see, is my father. His smile is enchanting—he hasn't appeared so happy in months. He slides his hand across the table—free of the notepads and documents and pens that might indicate a work meeting—to cover his companion's.

Her back is to me, but I gather every observable detail, greedily stashing data for future analysis. Only the crown of her head is visible over the top of her tall seat, but I note her sunrise hair. A high-heeled shoe—black patent leather, pointy toe—peeking out from beneath the tablecloth. Her hand, small and manicured, turning over, opening, accepting my father's. Her fingers, wrapping around his palm.

My stomach heaves.

Dad looks up, right into my eyes. He stares for a second, like he's trying to reconcile my presence with the backdrop, and then his mouth forms a perfect circle of shock. He snatches his hand from the woman's, reeling backward, moving to stand.

I whirl around.

I run.

30

AX'S TRUCK IDLES AT THE CURB, ENGINE rumbling. When I throw the passenger door open, I find Patsy Cline's "Crazy" blasting from the stereo—a fitting soundtrack for the last few minutes.

"Go!" I say, and he does.

When we're safely on the freeway, I tell him everything.

"You have every right to be pissed," he says when I've finished.

"I'm not pissed."

"Then you're in shock."

I sit quietly, breathing in and out, watching the freeway fly by. My emotions sink and settle, silt in a creek bed. How *do* I feel? Dazed, certainly. Sad for Meredith, and sad for Ally. And I'm filled to bursting with hate—I can hardly think of anything but hate, hate, hate.

How could my dad be so selfish, and lie so blatantly? How could he jeopardize our family in the name of getting a piece? Because that's what's happening—he's sleeping with that woman, the woman with the rose-gold hair. There's not a doubt in my mind.

"Okay, maybe I'm pissed," I admit, "but I'm not going to freak out and scream and cry."

"That would be okay," Max says.

"I won't give him the satisfaction."

"Are you one hundred percent sure about what you saw?"

I turn to give him an incredulous look. "Yes. Yes, I am."

"Jilly . . . I'm really sorry."

I am too, I think, scooting across the seat to assume the position of redneck girlfriend. Max uses his free hand to rub my shoulders, and as his fingers knead away clusters of tension, I think about Bill. He's facing a lifetime of immobility and dependence, yet he's indomitable in spirit. He would *never* cheat on Marcy.

Why is my dad such an asshole?

Max exits the freeway. "Do you have any idea who she was?"

"I only saw her from behind, and at a distance. Young, old, pretty, hideous . . . who knows? She could've been a work associate. A friend of a friend. Someone he met pumping gas. Doesn't matter. All that matters is that he's screwing around on Meredith."

"Are you gonna tell her?"

I don't answer right away—I hadn't considered that breaking the bad news might fall on my shoulders. "God, I have no idea what to do. . . ."

"You can talk to my mom," he offers. "Or Zoe."

"Thanks, but I feel like Meredith should know before anyone else."

He nods and drives on. He doesn't head straight for our neighborhood. Instead, he cruises around town, twisting and turning up and down hills, touring neighborhoods and our quiet river road. He's stalling, which is fine with me. I have zero desire to be at home.

"Jill?" he says after a long space of silence. "Maybe I'm a jerk bringing this up now, but has it occurred to you that we're kind of doing the same thing your dad's doing?"

I sit back so I can see his face. "Having an extramarital affair? Not exactly."

"No, but I cheated on Becky with you, and I'm not proud of it. We've been sneaking around. Hiding out. Keeping secrets."

"Max—"

"No, hear me out. I go along with our little arrangement because it's what you want, but I don't like it. I've got enough going on with my family, and now you do, too." His words puncture my deceit-filled bubble. It sputters and hisses, disillusion leaking out, evaporating into the truck's artificially balmy air. I find myself listening, *really* listening.

"Keeping something this huge from my parents sucks," he says, gentle but persuasive. "What's the worst that'll happen if your dad finds out? He'll be mad, but who gives a shit? Better than holing up in my truck every time we want to hang out. Better than creeping around like we're doing something wrong."

It hits me hard, how unfair I've been.

"Okay," I say softly.

"Okay . . . what?"

"No more secrets."

He looks from the road to me, eyes wide with surprise. "Really?"

"Yes, really."

He pulls me toward him again, and I nestle beneath his arm, closing my eyes. I feel good about my decision; the more dishonesty I can expel from my life, the better.

The truck rumbles onward, eventually into our neighborhood. Max pulls into his driveway and kills the engine. I lift my head to look into his uncertain eyes.

"I thought you'd fallen asleep," he whispers, brushing my hair back. We glance at my house at the same time, a cloud of foreboding suspended over the truck. My dad's Durango's still gone, but all the same, I hate the thought of walking across the street.

"Do you have to go home?" Max asks as I say, "Can I stay with you awhile longer?"

He flashes me a smile, amusement and mischief and arrogance squished into one. "You can stay with me all night if you like."

It's late, and the Holdens' house is quiet as we make our way up the stairs. Bill and Marcy are likely in bed, and Ivy's probably celebrating single-girl status with Becky and a box of wine.

Max closes his bedroom door while I slip my shoes off and make myself comfortable on his bed. He turns and stalks toward me all threateningly, but I know better. His jaw drops when I laugh, and he charges the bed like he's on his way to the end zone. He hovers over me and kisses me, a hot, needy kiss that leaves me breathless. When it's over, his face is a fascinating mix of desire and restraint. He asks, "Do you want me to put on a movie?"

"Um, *no*. Not unless you want to."

"I wasn't sure if you'd feel like . . . you know. We can just hang out."

"Aren't you considerate?"

He smiles. "Only on my best days."

"Thanks, but I think too much when I'm just hanging out."

I pull him close and kiss him hard, and he quits being chivalrous and gallant and starts acting like the lustful teenage boy I need him to be. I sneak my hands under the hem of his button-down and the T-shirt he wears beneath. His skin is on fire, and smooth, like satin stretched over stone. I trail my hands up his torso, as far as I can within the confines of his shirts.

He sits up, suddenly, and yanks them both over his head.

I might be hyperventilating.

"Hey," he says, resting his palm on my cheek. "You okay?"

I nod, leaning into his hand.

He stretches out next to me and I reach for his arm, trailing the tips of my fingers over his skin. He's watching me, and his expression . . . It's awed and adoring and completely disarming. No one's ever looked at me the way he's looking at me now, and for a moment I'm overwhelmed by the intense physicality of my feelings for him. I've heard love talked about a million times, in a million different ways, but I've never imagined it would feel like this, so raw and powerful.

His hand wanders to my stomach. His fingertips drift under my shirt and trace circles over my skin, slowly, higher and higher. His touch is torture, and it's bliss. It makes me shiver, and wonder how far he'll go, and hope he'll never, ever stop. But then, like the gentleman he's been raised to be, he smooths the hem of my shirt down. "I won't push."

"I know."

He pulls me against him, until we're a lace of limbs.

We lay perfectly still for what might be the very best minutes of our day.

31

MY SUNDAY MORNING TRUE BREW SHIFT IS winding down when my dad's Durango pulls up to the window. I haven't spoken to him—haven't even seen him—since he spotted me at the Yellow Door last night. I'd prefer to keep it that way, but Kyle's wiping down café tables and chatting up customers, and I'm left with no choice but to slide the window open.

"What can I get for you?" I ask politely, as if he's a stranger.

He shifts the Durango into park, staring crossly through the open window. "My usual cappuccino, and a minute to talk to you."

I splash milk into a pitcher and set it to steam. "What about?"

"For starters, I'd like to know what you were doing in Seattle last night."

"Yeah? Ditto."

"This isn't a game, Jillian. You'd better not have been with the Holden kid. I thought I made my feelings clear."

I jam a loaded portafilter into the machine. My anger is scalding, like water rushing through ground espresso. I look him square in the eye. "I thought I'd made *my* feelings clear."

He emits a heavy sigh. "I'd appreciate it if you'd stop acting like a child."

"And I'd appreciate it if you'd stop acting like an *adulterer.*" The words are out before I register thinking them, spoken in an acidic tone that makes him wince. I glare, merciless. "You can't deny it, can you? Last night, you were with her."

"I don't know what you think you saw—"

"I saw *you*, with another woman, smiling and laughing. You were *holding her hand*. God, Dad. I'm not stupid. You're cheating on Meredith!"

His righteousness crumples as he looks at his lap. I slap a lid on his cappuccino and hold it out the window, waiting for him to take it. He doesn't, and we're left at an impasse; me, pulsating with rage, my arm suspended in the morning air, and my dad, hanging his head. Behind me, Kyle whistles the chorus of Michael Jackson's "Man in the Mirror" as he completes the midday cleanup duties.

"It's over," Dad says quietly.

I draw my arm and his cappuccino inside. "How convenient."

"Really. I ended it last night."

"On Valentine's Day?"

"That's right. I won't see her again."

"Who is she?"

"That's not important."

"Were you with her the night Ally was born?"

"That's not important, either."

I roll my eyes. "I should've known you'd be incapable of honesty."

He fixes a steady stare on me. "I'm not sure you're one to judge."

I refuse to let him point his flawed finger at me. "This is what happened with my mother, isn't it? You guys had a baby—*me*—and your wedding vows didn't matter anymore. It's no wonder she left. How do you think Meredith's going to react?"

"You're going to tell her?" he says, and his surprise—his alarm—bowls me over.

"*You're* going to tell her."

He shakes his head. "I can't."

"God, Dad! She deserves to know!"

"But it's done. I swear to God it is. Please, Jillian. This will ruin her."

"Like it ruined Beth?"

He flinches, but doesn't contradict me.

I've never missed my mother—I don't know her enough to miss her—but I've missed the *idea* of a mother, not to mention all the things I imagine they do for their daughters: French braids before school and warm cookies after, Saturday afternoon shopping trips and homemade chicken soup during flu season. I've felt sharp stabs of envy watching silent smiles pass between Marcy and her girls, and I spent years holding Meredith at arm's length because she tried too hard to fill a colossal hole.

Dad says, "Is that what you want? Meredith to move out? She'll take Ally with her."

My heart plummets—that's the *last* thing I want.

He senses my weakness and seizes control. "It's *over*. Let me work things out with Meredith. Let Ally grow up in a house with a mom and a dad and a big sister."

"You're not being fair," I say, but I'm wavering. Ally's the innocent party in all this; I spent a lot of my childhood with one parent when I would've liked two. How can I force the same future on her?

"Jillian," Dad says, poised and stolid. "I'll make things right with

Mer, and I'll do everything in my power to help you pay for the International Culinary Institute next year. Now, please. Let me live my life, and I'll let you live yours."

I'm tempted to test that last declaration, to flat-out confirm his suspicion that I was with Max in Seattle last night, to tell him Max and I are together, and that I love him more than cookies, cakes, and cobblers combined, but I'm not about to let my father exploit me in the name of keeping his affair a secret. Meredith doesn't deserve that, and neither does Max.

My heart aches. Dad and I are traveling parallel courses and I can't imagine our paths intersecting again, but for now, all I want is stability. For Ally. For Meredith. And for me. If Dad's telling the truth, if he ended things with that *woman*, and if he's serious about getting back on track with Mer, then maybe we can start fresh. Maybe everything'll work out, like he said.

"It's really over?"

He nods gravely. "Yes."

"I still think you should tell Meredith."

"Jill, that'll only build new problems on top of the ones we already have."

"But you'll fix things?" I ask, my voice high, childlike in its desperation. "You'll make everything at home right again?"

"I'll do my best. For you and for Ally."

I thrust his cappuccino through the window. "Fine. Now go."

. . . .

I spend what remains of Sunday in the kitchen, baking my favorite quick breads. I can't stop thinking about my conversation with my dad; hindsight can be a real bitch. I should've demanded he tell me who he's been seeing. I should've insisted he tell Meredith. I should've come clean about Max and me. Instead, I did everything wrong for fear of challenging the status quo, which was so stupid.

The status quo sucks.

Before dinner, Max calls. "How're things?" he asks, and even though he's just across the street, he feels miles away.

"They've been better." I tell him about this morning: my dad's confession, and my concession on the Meredith issue. I describe how cheap, how *dirty*, surrender feels. My throat tightens, squeezing my voice like frosting through a piping bag, and it takes incredible focus to keep my emotions in check.

Max says all the right things, warm and comforting, until: "You told him, though? About you and me?"

"I—uh . . ."

"Jill, I thought we agreed."

"I know, but this morning was just . . . not a good time."

"There's never gonna be a good time. You know that, right? You've just gotta pull the trigger."

"I *can't* pull the trigger—not yet. I can't believe you're pushing me on this."

"And I can't believe you went back on your word."

"My *word* came before I had a frank conversation with my father about his infidelity. I'll keep my word, Max. Obviously I will. But it's not going to happen while my dad and Meredith are in the midst of a marital meltdown. Can't you just be patient?"

He sighs, an arduous sound that makes me feel like I'm suffocating.

"I'm sorry," I say, regretting the sharp way I spoke. God, this day . . . I wish we could reclaim the impossibly perfect moments we spent on his bed last night. "I'll tell him, okay? I swear I will."

"Cool," he says, detached. "I guess I'll see you tomorrow."

And then he hangs up.

By the time the sun sets, I've got double loaves of apple spice, chocolate chip banana, and zucchini, an empty flour canister, and a heavy heart.

32

ONDAY MORNING, I SIT ON OUR LIVING ROOM couch with my school bag and a saran-wrapped loaf of chocolate chip banana, waiting. I might not be ready for a grand gesture, but after a night spent twisting and turning, racking my brain for a way to fix things with Max, I'm certain I can pull off a medium gesture. I hope it'll be enough.

"Do you need to take my car today?" Meredith asks, surprising me. She's standing under the living room's archway, where a sprig of mistletoe once hung, and she's holding Ally, who's racked out—naturally, because no one else in the house is currently asleep. Mer's wearing jeans and an emerald sweater, and she looks pretty in the morning light.

"No, thanks. Max will take me. I'm just waiting for Ivy to leave before I head over. I've got to talk to Bill and Marcy, and I don't want her skulking around, acting like a she-devil."

Meredith smiles. "She's not so bad, is she?"

"Oh, she's pretty bad." I say this lightly, like it doesn't bother me that Ivy takes Becky's side in battles I don't even want to be a part of, but it does. It bothers me a lot, because even though she and I have never shared a bond like the one I have with her brother, I assumed she cared in her own aloof way.

"What do you need to talk to Bill and Marcy about?"

"Max and me."

She smiles. "Going public, finally?"

"To a select few."

"I'm glad. Max obviously adores you."

"But Dad . . ."

Meredith rolls her eyes, folding the hem of Ally's blanket under. "Your dad's hardly an authority on character these days." She presses her lips together, then draws a breath. "I'm sorry. That was uncalled for."

"No," I tell her. "It really wasn't."

Our shared gaze holds. She looks both mystified and melancholy, like she's trying to figure out how her life reached this juncture while at the same time yearning to move beyond it.

"I'm going to lay this girl down." she says, squinting at Ally. "Have a good day, okay?"

I nod. I'd return the sentiment, but I suspect the words will sound hollow; from what I can tell, Meredith's good days have been few and far between lately. Dad may have ended it with the Other Woman, but he's got a long way to go if he's going to make the last several months up to his wife.

Through the rain-streaked window, I catch sight of Ivy walking briskly down the Holdens' driveway, umbrella overhead. As soon as she backs her car out and heads for school, I spring from my seat and sling my bag over my shoulder. Then I head into the rain, hustling across the sodden lawn, shielding my hair and my bread as best I can.

At the Holdens' front door, I give a double knock and slip inside, wiping my wet shoes on the woven mat before making my way to the kitchen, where Marcy and Bill are seated at the table. She's got a cup of coffee, and there's a protein shake with a thick plastic straw sitting in front of him.

"Jillian!" Marcy says, patting the bench beside her. "What a nice surprise. Come sit."

Leaving my bag on the floor by the fridge, I pull a knife from the butcher block and carry my loaf to the table. "I brought breakfast," I say, taking the seat Marcy offered.

She unwraps the banana bread and inhales. "Smells amazing," she says, holding the loaf out to Bill. He sniffs, and smiles his approval. "Coffee?" she says, taking the knife and slicing the bread into even pieces, which she places on napkins and divvies out.

"No, thanks. Max is still upstairs?"

She nods, helping Bill with a bite. "He should be down in a few minutes. You need a ride, sweetie?"

"I do, actually, but that's not the reason I'm here. I kind of need to talk to you guys."

Marcy brushes crumbs from her fingertips and folds her hands. I've got her full attention—Bill's, too—and I'm nervous. I'm trying to remember why I thought this was a good idea when the conversation Max and I had last night bounces through my head: his dismay, his thousand-pound sigh, his lack of farewell.

Of all the people in my life, he's the last I want to disappoint.

"So," I say, wishing I'd accepted that offer of coffee after all. "You might've noticed that Max and I have been hanging out a lot lately. For a while we were just friends, but then we realized it was more than that, and now . . ."

Bill's nodding. Marcy's smiling auspiciously. "Now, *what*?"

God. This is awkward.

I imagine grabbing the edge of a Band-Aid and tearing it clean off. It'll be painful for a half second, but that'll subside, and even though the cut underneath might not be entirely healed, it'll be on its way.

"Now we're together," I say, and suddenly I'm on roller skates, barreling downhill, unable to stop or even slow down. "I like him. He likes me, too. And it's good between us—I really think so. We were worried about telling you—no, *I* was worried about telling you—but I'm not even sure why, now, except we just want you to be happy for us. Because my dad, well, he hasn't been himself lately, and he hasn't been very supportive. He has his reasons, but they're stupid, and I just really wish I could be honest with him." I pause, catch a breath, and tack on a question. "Kind of like I can be honest with you?"

Marcy's got a hand pressed to her heart. "Of *course* you can be honest with us."

I glance at Bill and find him beaming. I remember his years-ago prediction about his son and me, our probable future together. I smile, too.

"So, it's okay? Max and me?"

Bill's bobbing his head and Marcy's wrapping me in a hug and I'm getting a little teary myself. "He's been better, you know," she murmurs, pressing her cheek to mine. "Happier. I hoped it was your presence. Your influence."

"It's not, though," I tell her. "He needed time, is all."

She nods, pulling back as heavy footsteps thud down the stairs. Max plows into the kitchen, pulling up short when he sees me at the table with his parents. "What's up?" he asks.

"I brought you breakfast," I say, pointing at the sliced loaf. "Come sit?"

He does, straddling the bench adjacent to me. He helps himself to a piece of bread, taking an unthinkable boy-sized bite. After he's chewed and swallowed and complimented my baking, I lean in to kiss his cheek. "Good morning, by the way."

His eyes go wide as he looks from his parents, who are grinning conspiratorially, to me. It's fun to watch as realization dawns on him. "Wait—you told them?"

I shrug. "That's okay, right?"

He hooks his arm around my neck and pulls me into his chest. I'm laughing when he says, "You did good, Jilly."

We spend a little longer with his parents, eating banana bread and filling them in on the highlights of our day in Seattle. Marcy's practically oozing happiness, and it's been a long time since I've seen Bill so enlivened. He's not observing our conversation; he's participating in all the ways he can. Max keeps glancing at him, smiling slightly, almost bashfully, then looking away. *I'm trying—I swear I am*, he said the night we went for ice cream. I can see that he is. I can see that he *wants* to.

The bond he and Bill shared was interrupted—never broken.

Slowly, carefully, it's being restored.

· · · ·

When we arrive at school, Max and I make our way through the rain-drenched quad and into the locker bay. Our shoes squeal against the linoleum as we maneuver through the crowd. We stop at his locker first, where he collects books for chem and civics, then head down the corridor to my locker. After I've gathered my own books, I face him, thinking about how good, how *normal*, it is to slog through the mundaneness of preparing for classes with this boy who makes me feel like a colony of butterflies have taken up residence in my stomach.

When he reaches for me, though, I recall the swift, searing pain of Becky's shoulder clashing with mine, demeaning as the day it happened. It's instinctual, the way I sidestep his touch. It hurts him, I know it does, because his hand sinks to his side and his face crumples, and all the good I did with his parents this morning is demolished by one impetuous slip.

"We should be careful," I say. "That's all."

As if on cue, Becky emerges from the crowd, copper curls bobbing as she struts in our direction. She stops in front of me, *beside* Max. Her green eyes roam his face as she glides a possessive hand along his arm. He quickly shrugs her off, but the red-hot bitterness I feel seeing her touch my boyfriend is visceral; I want to knock her down.

"I miss you," she says to Max, softly, like no one's around but the two of them.

He moves to my side, slinging an arm over my shoulder, and despite my misgivings, I lean into him. "You haven't said good morning to Jill," he tells her.

She looks at me like I'm curbside trash. "There's a reason for that."

"Get over it, Beck. She had nothing to do with what happened between you and me."

"Please. We'd still be together if she would've stayed on her side of the street."

"Bullshit," he says without malice, like he's just stating a fact.

"Who does that anyway?" Becky barrels on. "Breaks a couple up because she can't get over her childhood crush?"

Max shakes his head. "You and me were done long before Jill and I started hanging out."

"We were together when she kissed you."

Feeling ballsy and aggressive and a little out of control, I step forward. "*He* kissed *me*."

She crosses her arms, not-so-subtly flaunting her chest. "Just like he begged you to let him go to your parents' stupid party, and forced you to cuddle up next to him while you guys watched that asinine movie? You've orchestrated this whole thing because you're jealous—because you don't have a life of your own."

I clench my hands into fists, my fingernails digging into my palms. I want to shove her so bad—I'm desperate to dehumanize her the way she did me that day on the quad—but I refuse to stoop to her level. "I have a life," I say, quiet and controlled. "And I wish you'd stay out of it."

"I can't, because my ex—my best friend's brother—trails you like a puppy." She leans forward, sticking her nose in my face like a bona fide bully. "I'll always be around," she says, "a reminder of what you did. What you *ruined*."

"Becky," Max says, a low warning. "Shut up."

She turns on him. "What? You thought I'd disappear so you could have a happily ever after with your trampy neighbor? You thought it'd be that easy?"

"I thought you were better than *this*," he says, looking pointedly at the audience we've attracted. Dozens of people have stopped to observe us, two cats wrestling over a tom. I'm not this girl; I've *never* wanted to be this girl. I step back, using Max's height to shield myself from their stares. Callously, he says, "Get the hell out of here, Becky."

As the warning bell trills, I spin around, intent on making an overdue escape, but Max catches my hand. I pause, but I don't turn to face him. I don't want him to see how my cheeks burn, how my lip trembles, how utterly humiliated I am. I wait, staring unseeingly at the floor, clutching his hand, bound to him in all the ways that count as our classmates reanimate, hustling to get to class before the final bell.

When the hallway has mostly cleared out, Max twirls me around and pulls me close.

"She's mad at me," he says. "Don't let her get to you."

"Do you see, though? Why I don't want to make a big deal about us at school?"

"Jill, it's not like things can get any worse."

I'd like to tell him about Becky knocking into me because, yes, things *can* get worse, but I don't want to trigger his anger—not over this, something I should be able to handle on my own. "If I ever see her touch you again," I tell him, "I'll have to hurt her."

His eyes take on a devilish gleam, and he walks me back, until I'm leaning against the cold metal of my locker. He turns his hat around so its bill is out of the way, and I grip the hem of his jacket, tugging him closer, until his mouth is inches from mine. "I like when you get all fiery," he says.

"Oh, I bet you do."

The tardy bell rings. The hallway's empty but for us. I should be in French.

Max places a hand on the locker next to my head and moves closer. He tucks a leg between mine, pressing his body against the length of me. I feel him inhale, slow and shallow. He skims his nose along that place where my collarbone meets my throat, and heat rushes up my neck. God. When did the hallway get so warm? He brushes the side of my face with his prickly cheek, touching his lips to my ear, lingering a moment before easing back. His cinnamon exhale fans my skin. "I'm dying to kiss you."

My breath hitches. "Then maybe you should."

He closes the space between us, but at the last second, bluffs and pecks the tip of my nose. "No more kisses for you—not until you're cool with doing it out in the open, in front of anyone who cares to watch."

I gasp. "Max Holden, you are the worst kind of mean!"

He takes off down the hall, turning once to look back at me. He's smiling, but his voice has a serious edge, and it reverberates in the deserted corridor. "That's the deal, Jillian Eldridge."

33

I DON'T CARE FOR MAX'S NO-MORE-KISSES decree, or the way his mood declines as the week drags on.

After school on Tuesday, we drive to the river and park in our spot. He's distant, even while using the flash cards I made to quiz me on my bio vocabulary. Late Wednesday night, he knocks softly on my window, but when I let him in, he's surly and restless. He stays thirty minutes before leaving the way he came. Thursday, he goes to a midnight movie premiere with the guys; he doesn't text before he leaves or after he gets home. I'm not so needy that I require his rapt attention at all hours, but this behavior's so different from how he's been since we got together. . . . I feel like I'm being punished.

Friday, I still haven't spoken to my dad about Max and me. He's hardly been home, is part of the reason, but mostly I'm reluctant to slap more angst on the messiness that is my family. I haven't seen him put one iota of effort into fixing things with Meredith, like he promised, and on the few occasions he and I have shared space, he's barely been able to look me in the eye.

Max doesn't get it, though. The well of points I earned talking to Bill and Marcy has run dry, and I end up having to take Meredith's car to school because he left early to fit in a workout with Kyle before first period.

His fortitude is one part impressive, two parts aggravating.

I suffer through my classes, stewing instead of absorbing the material.

I'm feeling sorry for myself as I navigate the halls after the final bell, wishing Max would materialize. And then he does—the first time I've seen him all day. His eyes meet mine, and with a nod of his head, he summons me to a recess beneath the stairwell. I make my way toward him and slip into the nook.

"What are you doing tonight?" he asks without preamble, the underlying cord of tension in his voice hard to miss.

"Kyle and Leah convinced me to go to Leo's party. Are you going?"

"Planning on it." And then he asks the question he's asked every afternoon for the duration of this week: "Talk to your dad yet?"

"Max—" I begin, but he cuts me off.

"Look, Jill. I'm trying to be patient, like you asked. I played along with your game at the Yellow Door. I've given you space at school. I've crawled through your window instead of walking through the front door like an actual human being. All week I've waited, hoping you'd follow through, hoping you'd own up, because I've gotta tell you: The way you're handling this sucks."

"But I told your parents. And Meredith knows."

"Yet here we are, arguing in an alcove because you refuse to tell the person who matters most. Your dad's this huge part of your life.

He's got his reasons for not liking me, and you're giving them weight. You're turning me into the villain he thinks I am."

"It's just such a bad time." Stupid—I know as soon as the words leave my mouth.

Max throws up his hands. "Jesus, Jillian, you keep making excuses to let yourself off the hook. That's probably the same thing your dad did every time he lied to Meredith and climbed into bed with his girlfriend."

He might as well have socked me in the gut; oxygen rushes from my lungs, leaving me empty. I'd forgotten how utterly excruciating fighting with Max Holden can be.

"That's a terrible thing to say," I tell him quietly.

His gaze shifts, like the sight of me leaves him cold—a heart-breaking thought. His scowl is a brutal reminder of how he used to be, before we were us.

"Please, Max. Tell me how to fix this."

He bristles. "You know how to fix it."

I reach for his hand. My fingers skim the band of his father's watch, working their way into his tightened fist. When our palms align, the contact—my skin on his—is unhinging. A dizzying sensation takes me, like the undertow that would've dragged me under at the beach a few years ago, had it not been for him. All I can focus on is the sudden, stomach-churning realization that I could lose him over my unwilling-ness to openly defy my dad, who's raised me lovingly but disappointed me unequivocally.

Max pulls his hand away, burying it in the pocket of his sweatshirt. I'm at a loss, and I'm agitated, and I'm scheduled for a closing shift at True Brew. It's almost comical, the idea of serving coffee and conversa-tion when my life's so screwed up.

"I need to get to work," I tell him.

His eyes find mine, immobilizing me with their deep discontentment. "Before you go . . ." He hesitates, uncertainty slogging across his face before he says, "I want normal, you know? And I'm looking for it with you." He steps nearer, bringing his evergreen scent with him, and I wonder when he'll he grow tired of having this discussion. He clutches my waist and pulls me against him, so I can't help but look at him and feel him and breathe him in. He's strong enough to hold me in this space forever, if he wants to, but I'm relaxing in his arms, drowning in his sad, sad eyes. "I want you, Jill," he murmurs, "but I don't understand why you'd choose lying over the truth. Over *me*."

He squeezes me to him, burying his face in my hair. My arms wind instinctively around his neck. Warmth blooms in my chest, trickling through my arms and into my hands, all the way to the tips of my fingers. He hasn't initiated contact for days, and I can't help but think . . .

This feels like a good-bye.

I have to fix this. My dad's been there for me from the very beginning, but it's Max who I can't live without.

The realization sends my head spinning, as if the earth is tilting on its axis. I shiver.

He pulls back, eyeing me warily.

"I'm sorry," I tell him, blinking back tears. "I'm so sorry. I'll talk to my dad. I'll go to his office after work, before I come to Leo's. I'll tell him about us."

"Really?"

"Really, Max. I'm done with secrets."

He takes my face in his hands and kisses me, a long press of his mouth to mine. The tears that were tickling my throat a moment ago recede. I've missed this; I've missed *him*. When he pulls back, he's wearing a hint of a smile, and I feel better than I have all week.

He strokes his calloused hands down my neck, his thumbs resting atop my pulse points, the heat of his palms bleeding into my skin. He presses a kiss to my forehead, and thanks to his slight movement, I catch sight of Ivy over his shoulder.

She's standing ten feet away, watching us from beneath the fringe of her bangs. Her granite gaze meets mine. For an excruciating second, I think she's going to confront us—confront *me*—but then her face unfurls, opening in comprehension, in a way I've never seen. It only lasts a second, our shared stare, and then she's gathering her emotions and stowing them away, scurrying down the nearly empty hallway.

To find Becky, I suppose. To tell her everything.

I don't even care.

Max becomes my center again, his stormy eyes, his warm palms, the persistent thudding of his heart against my ribs. He's my quiet place, my well of happiness.

I reach up to cover his hands with mine. "Tonight, Max. I'll tell my dad everything."

. . . .

The coffee shop is quiet when I walk in. Kyle's mom, who looks up only briefly to smile in greeting, is counting out her cash drawer. Kyle's restocking the small front refrigerator with dairy products. He doesn't turn around as I tie on my apron and apologize for being a few minutes late. It isn't until his mom's headed out the door that he kicks the fridge closed and pivots to face me. He puts his hands on his hips and widens his stance, the way he does when he addresses his teammates on the football field. "You're making Max miserable."

"You talked to him?"

"I've been talking to him all week." He pulls a broom out of the utility closet and whips it around our workspace. "You're not being fair. Everyone has shit they keep quiet, but I thought you were beyond senseless drama." He coaxes a pile of coffee grounds and dust bunnies into a dustpan. "I don't know how much longer he's gonna put up with you."

I'm coming apart at the seams. My shift's over in a couple of hours, and soon I'll be face-to-face with my dad, admitting that I've done exactly what he told me to avoid, confessing that I've lied for months. He's going to be *so* pissed, and who knows how he'll cope? He could yell. He could threaten. He could pick a fight with Meredith.

Or he could call the Other Woman.

Bleakness sloshes over me. Kyle pushes the broom back into the closet, then comes my way, reaching out to steady me as I wobble on Jell-O legs.

"Jesus, Jill. What is it?"

I blurt out, "My dad's been cheating on Meredith."

He shakes his flaxen hair out of his face. His eyes are wide as pie plates. "Oh, shit."

"She doesn't know—not for sure—but still. Things at home are kind of awful."

"I guess," he says. "I'm really sorry, Jelly Bean. Wish I would've known."

"Doesn't matter—it's no excuse for how unfair I've been to Max."

He wraps an arm around me. "Why didn't you tell me about your parents?"

"I don't know. It's not fun-to-share news. I didn't want to bug you with my problems."

"That's bananas. The only thing you do that bugs me is hold your cards close. I want you to tell me what's going on in your world. The good *and* the bad. That's what friends do—confide, and support each other when things get rough."

"In that case, there's more," I say, because it's clear now: I need to be straightforward with the people I care about. I need to lean on them in the same ways I expect them to lean on me. And so, I tell Kyle, "I'm not going to the International Culinary Institute after I graduate. There's no money for it. Meredith and her fertility treatments, the pregnancy, the baby . . . My school money paid for other things. More important things." Saying this—meaning it sincerely—is like breaking the surface after being underwater too long. "But don't worry—my True Brew paychecks will get me to New York eventually."

Kyle kisses my cheek. "I have no doubt."

A couple comes through the shop door, pushing a toddler in a stroller. She whines, straining against the buckle that keeps her seated while her parents stand opposite the counter, perusing the menu board like they don't hear their child squealing. Kyle gives me an *oh, hell* eye roll, and despite the general crappiness of today, I smile.

"After work," I tell him over the kid's yowls, "I'm going to set things straight with my dad, and then when I get to Leo's, I'm going to find Max, and everything will be perfect."

34

KYLE SENDS ME ON MY WAY EARLY, promising to take care of closing duties so I'll have plenty of time to talk to my dad. The evening's dark, appropriate in its dreariness. It's not far from True Brew to Dad's office, and I have only a few minutes to rehearse my confession before I've arrived. Drawing a deep breath, I kill the engine and climb out of the car, giving myself zero time to rethink my reason for being here.

This is it—time to take control of my life.

I cross my arms as I hurry toward the office. I let myself into the reception area, expecting to see Natalie. She's not at her desk, though, and I'm not sure why; business hours aren't over for another thirty minutes. Also weird: The heavy oak door leading to Dad's personal office is closed.

I walk a slow circle around the small space. The air's thick with perfume, heavier and muskier than Meredith's signature scent, but oddly familiar. Trying to place it, I step up to Natalie's workspace. On her desk, there's a blotter covered in doodles (butterflies and hearts and stars—how trite) and a tube of lipstick (deep, deep red—I've never seen her in anything else), but otherwise there are no personal touches. No pictures of family or boyfriends or pets, no day planner, no potted plants or dish of candy. It hits me then, how little I know of Dad's perky blond secretary, this girl who fetches his cappuccinos, and who's also really pretty.

What if . . . ?

No. Natalie's only a few years older than me, and my dad's not a secretary-screwing cliché. I'm shaking that thought right out of my head when I hear laughter coming from behind his office door: a coy, feminine giggle, and a deeper chuckle.

My stomach lurches.

I stand statue-still, listening to the rhythmic pounding of blood in my ears and the voices, his and hers, murmurs drenched in bliss and beatitude. I think back to Valentine's Day and the Yellow Door. The woman Dad was with had daybreak hair, peachy blond, a lot like Natalie's.

Comprehension hits me like a football to the face—she's not at her desk because she's with him, behind the closed door of his office.

Dad vowed to work things out with Meredith. He promised Ally would grow up in a house with two parents. He *swore* the affair was over.

What a liar.

I fight my immediate impulse to shove the office door open, only because the thought of what I might interrupt disgusts me. I will be a grown-up about this—somebody has to. But as I step forward, raising my hand to knock on the tall oak door, my phone comes alive with a text, the silly, very loud banjo riff Max programmed as a joke.

The giggling in Dad's office screeches to a halt. In fact, the entire building has gone eerily quiet. They've heard my phone. They're onto me, just as I'm onto them.

My voice shatters the quiet. "Dad? I need to speak with you."

After a moment of shuffling and frantic utterances, the door swings open. Bile ascends my throat as my already-queasy stomach makes the leap to full-fledged nausea because . . .

It's not Natalie who stands beside my father—it's Mrs. Tate. Her strawberry-blond hair's tousled and her lipstick's smudged—smudged across my father's mouth. God. I can hardly look at him. His hair appears windblown, his tie's been removed, his shirt collar unbuttoned, and his expression is a landscape of dread.

Robin Tate: hospice nurse, police officer's wife . . . *mistress*.

She comes to our house to drink coffee and gossip. She plays Bunco in our basement. After Ally was born, she helped Marcy tie those damn balloons to our shrubs. She and her *husband* brought a freaking casserole.

She's Meredith's friend.

The first thing out of Dad's mouth is the last thing I want to hear. "Jillian, this isn't what it looks like."

"Don't lie to me." My voice is steady, restrained, my anger barely eclipsed by grief. "It's *exactly* what it looks like."

Mrs. Tate's eyes are puddles. She looks at my dad like she's a helpless little girl instead of a middle-aged, *married* woman. Like it's his job to bail her out. How dare she turn to him for reassurance? I'm the one who needs reassuring. I'm the only person in this room who has a right to ask Jake Eldridge for anything.

My hurt spills out in a frustrated cry. "How *could* you?"

"It just happened!" Mrs. Tate says, and I'm struck momentarily speechless by how readily she's confessed to shattering a family.

"It just happened?" I repeat. "You admit it? You two-faced home wrecker."

My dad steps forward. "Jillian—"

"Don't! You don't get to parent me. You said it was over. You *swore* it was over!"

His posture sags, and he presses his lips together. The simple show of weakness sickens me. "How?" I ask. "When? *Why?*"

"I don't think you want the details," Mrs. Tate says. My dad reaches out to give her arm a warning touch, but jerks his hand back when he remembers himself—when he remembers *me*.

"I guess I already know the whens," I say. "Valentine's Day. Ally's birthday. Every late night, every lengthy Saturday. How long have you been lying to everyone?"

They glance guiltily at each other.

"Since just before Christmas," Dad says. He lets his confession fester for a moment before adding, "Life is short, Jillian. I don't expect you to understand my choices."

I snort. "Good, because I don't. Choosing to cheat with the neighbor—*your wife's friend*—will never, ever make sense to me."

Mrs. Tate says, "We care about each other."

It's infuriating, the pointed manner in which she speaks, the way she emphasizes her syllables like she's teaching me a lesson. It pisses me off, and I'm in her face before I process the movement. "You're a bitch!"

Panic flashes in her eyes, but she's not without a retort. "And you're a child."

Dad shoves an arm between us. "Jillian, stop it. Robin, for God's sake. Shut up!"

I blink, trying to clear a wave of vertigo; this whole exchange is so surreal. "Meredith knows you're having an affair," I tell my dad. I pause to glare at Mrs. Tate—*Robin*. "She might not know that *you're* involved, but she knows something's wrong."

Dad takes a step forward, like he might want to join my team. Or, at the very least, use me as an ally. "Jillian, are you going to tell her?"

I pause, because in all my fury and resentment and sorrow, it hasn't dawned on me that, yet again, the responsibility of passing on this news will fall to me.

I whisper, "I have to."

"God, Jill. Don't. Please let me handle it."

He won't. He's not reliable, and he's not honorable. He's a liar and a fool, and I can't fathom a day when I'll see him as anything but. My throat constricts as I mourn the decent man I used to idolize. I stare at my father until my eyes flood with tears. "You've broken us—*ruined* us—and I will *never* forgive you."

I rush through the door, out of the office, into rain that pelts my face, mingling with the tears that stream down my cheeks.

35

I DRIVE, UNAWARE OF MY SURROUNDINGS AND the passage of time—until I notice the moon overhead. I pull into a 7-Eleven parking lot. I'm thirty miles from McAlder, nearly out of gas, and I have no recollection of my time on the road. The realization is sobering.

I sit in Meredith's car, collecting my bearings while I watch two aging hippies emerge from a beat-up station wagon with a travel trailer hitched to its bumper. He has long, graying hair and a fringed leather jacket. She's in Birkenstocks and a patched peasant skirt, even though it's sleeting and blustery. He smiles and takes her hand, and they walk into the convenience store. I imagine they're headed south to some commune in the California desert, where they'll spend their nights making music around a big bonfire, then crawl into their trailer to keep each other warm until the sun peeks over the horizon.

I could live that life; compared to my current situation, it sounds lovely.

Okay, no. I can't hitch a ride to California; I can't run away. I need a calming presence. Someone capable of balanced advice. Someone who'll tell me everything's going to be okay.

I need Max.

Instead, I call Kyle. I thank him for covering for me at work, and then I tell him about Dad and Mrs. Tate. He's horrified, and incredibly sympathetic. I ask him to be sure Max stays at Leo's until I get there.

I fill the Saturn's gas tank and head for McAlder. I drive carefully, watching for pedestrians and merging vehicles and construction zones. I'm able to recall the entire trip when I pull into Leo's neighborhood—a small victory.

The street's lined with cars, and I'm forced to park halfway down the block. I lock the car and hurry toward the house, which shines like a beacon of high school debauchery.

As I get closer, I see a few of my classmates spilling witlessly from the front door, stumbling in the general direction of the driveway. Kyle is manning the porch—unofficially, if the keg cup he holds is any indication. He wraps me in a hug, sloshing a dribble of cold beer down my back. "You okay, Jelly Bean?"

I nod. I'm in coffee-spattered jeans and a True Brew T-shirt, my hair is rain-frizzed, and I've cried my makeup off. I'm at the kind of party I usually avoid—drunken hordes of people with wanton objectives moving in time to a booming bass beat—but now that I'm with Kyle and in Max's vicinity, I feel grounded.

"I saw him in the kitchen a few minutes ago," Kyle says. "Want me to go with you?"

I nod, then follow him through the mob, dodging splashes of foamy beer while attempting to keep up with the choppy, whistled strains of "Don't Worry, Be Happy." Kyle's equilibrium doesn't seem to be much better than mine, but at least he can claim drunkenness.

We find Leah in the living room, and she makes our duo a trio. She looks like she just stepped out of a magazine—artfully distressed jeans, a tank with a beaded neckline—and she's sipping from a bottle of hard cider. "I'm trying to find Jesse," she shouts over the music. "He's probably with Max!"

I nod as she loops her arm through mine, and we resume our trek through the house.

As we near the kitchen, my footsteps grow heavy, like I'm trudging through marshland, and a fit of nerves nearly swallows me. Despite the bombshell that detonated at Dad's office, I haven't forgotten why I went there in the first place. Thanks to the confusion and accusations and anger, I never did get my news about Max out. I know that'll be the first question he asks; he doesn't know any better.

I'm trying to figure out how to tell him that, yet again, I've failed in the full disclosure department, when a heeled boot juts out in front of me, catching the toe of my shoe. I pitch forward in this hideous, slow-motion stagger, bumping innumerable bystanders, nearly taking Leah down with me. By some keg-party miracle, I'm able to grab the back of Kyle's sweatshirt, saving us from a face-plant on the sticky floor.

He and Leah help me recover, and as soon as I'm stable, I whirl around.

Becky. Her penny-colored hair is slicked into a ponytail so severe she looks like the victim of an unfortunate face-lift, and she's got a hand braced on her hip. "Have a nice trip?" she asks, snickering like she didn't just sputter the most juvenile inquiry ever.

"What is *wrong* with you?" I ask, taking a belligerent step toward her.

"You broke Max and me up. I told you I wouldn't let you forget."

"I didn't break you and Max up; he left you. He left you because you're the *worst*." In my periphery, I spot Ivy coming to stand behind Becky, propping her up like a buttress, but I don't care. I've kept quiet too long, and now that I've given the valve a twist, the words I should've said weeks ago come streaming out. "Even if Max and I hadn't ended up together, he'd still be better off because he'd be free of *you*." Behind me, Kyle and Leah break into applause, the sound like gasoline to a flickering flame. With more vitriol than I knew I had in me, I snarl, "Screw you, Becky."

She juts her chin out. "If you think you can compete with me—"

"I can't," I say, "and I don't want to. You're nothing. *Nothing*."

I'm turning to walk away, to rejoin my friends, when Ivy bounds forward. She grabs my hand and pulls me back and for a horrific moment, I wonder if she's going to hit me. But her glower loosens, her whole face melting into an expression like understanding—like the one she wore in the hallway at school this afternoon as she watched Max and me talking. She reminds me so much of Marcy as she leans forward to speak into my ear. "This is done. No more. I'll handle Becky—she won't bother you again. Just . . . don't break my brother's heart, okay?"

"Ivy, I would never."

She drops my hand but holds my gaze, and a silent promise passes between us. We might never be friends, but this . . . This feels like it could be enough.

She disappears into the crowd, dragging Becky behind her.

Kyle, Leah, and I head toward the kitchen. "You and Max, huh?" she says as we battle the mob. She grins and holds her cider bottle up like, *Cheers!* "I wish I could say I'm surprised."

And I wish I could share her blind enthusiasm, but we've rounded a corner and there he is, in jeans and a white T-shirt. His hair's a disaster, surging skyward in every direction. He's standing with Jesse and Leo, and he's clutching a keg cup.

Of course.

His wild eyes trap me in a silent question.

I'm frozen, torn between running from him and what'll likely be another argument, and running *to* him, finding assurance in his presence. When I don't make a move in either direction, animosity marches across his face.

"There he is," Leah says, like I can't see what's right in front of me.

"Yeah. I need a minute."

Max raises a challenging eyebrow. I swear to God, my feet have turned to lead.

"He doesn't look very happ-y," Kyle singsongs.

"You're not help-ing," I sing back.

He places a hand on my back and shoves. At the same time, Max slams his cup down, slopping liquid onto the counter, and takes a step toward me. I'm standing in front of my boyfriend, who's flushed and so obviously frustrated, and I have no idea what to do. Leah and Kyle appear apprehensive, while Leo and Jesse survey the scene with fuzzy bewilderment. I wonder how much they've had to drink. I wonder how much *Max* has had to drink.

"Nice of you to join me," he says, loud enough to be heard through-out the bustling kitchen.

"Nice of you to get wasted before I showed up."

"I'm *not* wasted."

I might believe him. I can see now that the liquid in his cup is clear, and he's not swaying or stumbling. His eyes aren't glazed or red, like his friends'.

"I need to talk to you," I say, glancing at our audience. "Can we go outside?"

"Outside," he repeats, lofty and condescending. "Figures."

He stomps out of the kitchen, and I crash into half of McAlder

High's student body trying to keep up. Finally, we slip out the front door and into the night. The rain has stopped, but the cloud cover remains, leaving the air dense and damp.

Max is halfway across Leo's soggy lawn when I catch up. I grab his arm, and he skids on the slick grass, reeling around. "You didn't tell him, did you?"

"No, but—"

"Jesus, Jillian. Not six hours ago you promised you would!"

"Are you drunk?" I ask. I don't think he is, not anymore, but I'm half hoping he'll tell me yes anyway, so I can pin his anger on beer instead of myself.

His hands clench, his expression incendiary. If there was a wall nearby, I'm pretty sure he'd put a fist through it. "No, but it's nice to know that's your immediate assumption."

"It's not like you have the best track record, Max."

"Oh, and you're so fucking perfect."

I will myself to hold his gaze, to maintain an assertive posture on the saturated lawn, though he's never made me feel so small.

When he speaks again, his tone is flat, explanatory. "I poured a beer when I got here. Is that what you want to hear? Would you believe me if I told you I couldn't finish it? I was too busy thinking about football and my family and *you*—how I want to be good enough for you. I dumped it down the drain."

"Max—"

"Because that's what it is, isn't it? I'm *not* good enough. All that shit your dad fed you about me being trouble—you swallowed it. I've been busting my ass to get my act together, to prove I'm not a screwup, but you're ashamed."

"That's not true!"

"Then what? You just like having me by the balls?"

"Max, *no*." It's a tiny, timid word, but it's all I've got. He's thought this through. He believes what he's saying. How is that even possible?

"I see how it is," he says. "You made a choice, and it's not me." His hand is on my shoulder, a consoling pat. Gently, he adds, "It's okay."

I bat him away, sick of being interrupted, talked down to as if I'm too meek for hard truths. My heart hardens, crystallizing like candied ginger, and I throw up my hands. "Nothing is okay! That's what I've been trying to tell you, if you'd just listen!"

He stares, stunned, because for all I've tried to numb myself to tonight's events, I'm crying. I'm *sobbing*. Max's surprise gives way to concern, and he grasps my arms, his eyes narrowed in confusion. "I'm listening now," he says. "What happened?"

"My dad. I went to talk to him, but he wasn't alone. . . . I found him in his office with *her*, and I just—I couldn't get out of there fast enough."

Max runs his hands up and down my arms. "Shit, Jill. Who?"

"Mrs. Tate."

He blows out a heavy breath. "Jesus."

"Sucks, right? And to top it off, your ex more or less assaulted me when I got here, which was icing on the freaking cake. So, yeah. My dad's sleeping with Robin Tate. He's an asshole and he's tearing my family apart and today has been absolute shit, so excuse me if I didn't get around to making a grand announcement about you and me."

"I didn't realize—"

"Of course you didn't," I say, shaking free of him. My throat feels as if it's coated in pastry flour, and I swallow before barreling on. "You didn't even give me a chance to explain. God, Max! You think I'm some snob who's shuttering you away because you're not good enough? How many chances have I given you over the last few months? How many times have I listened to you vent? How many times have I eased you off the ledge? Why would I bother if I thought you were less-than? I care about you so much, and it breaks my heart to know you might not feel the same."

"Jilly . . ." But he doesn't finish.

Good, because there's nothing left to say.

I'm backing away as he scours his face with his hands, looking so dejected I can't believe he's still on his feet. I've seen varying degrees of this expression too many times, and while it shreds me, I don't have the strength to help him recover. Not tonight.

I leave him to stand alone on the dark lawn.

36

*A*T HOME, I PACE MY ROOM.

My dad's yet to show; it sickens me to think he might've stayed with Mrs. Tate even after our confrontation. Poor Meredith must be bored, because she's knocked on my door a dozen times, wondering aloud if I'm okay, if I need anything, if I'd like some company.

I know I need to talk to her, and I'm going to, but . . . not now.

Feeling alone and agitated and abashed, I wash my face and brush my teeth, then dress for bed in sleep shorts and the McAlder football T-shirt I snatched from Max last weekend. It's threadbare and faded, but it smells like him.

Regret's gnawing a hole through my stomach. I feel terrible about our fight, the events that sparked it, my suggestion that he doesn't care.

I *know* he cares; I just worry that for us, caring might not be enough.

I'm seconds from falling into a restless sleep when an urgent rapping rattles my window, startling me out of bed. I stumble across my dark room and yank the curtains open. Max is standing in the side yard. His eyes meet mine, their sadness so exposed and acute, I feel it instantly, intensely, a knife of sorrow straight to the chest.

Being next to him is at once a basic, physical need, as crucial as oxygen.

I throw the window open. He puts his hands on the sill and hoists himself through, then pulls me to him. His lips touch my hair, my cheeks, my throat, a flurry of butterfly kisses. He's clinging to me, shaking, his raspy breaths skimming my skin. I haven't seen him this upset in months, since the night after Bill's stroke. I'd tried to console him, a naive attempt at erasing his pain, but he brushed me off and went to Becky's, where he drank himself stupid. Later, after she dropped him off at home, he got sick in his dad's immaculately pruned hedges.

Tonight, he could've drowned his sadness in booze. Instead, he came to me.

I press my palms to his chest and lean back to look at him. He wipes his hands roughly over his face. I follow their path with my own, and find his bristly cheeks faintly damp. What's left of my anger dies like a smothered flame. "Talk to me?" I whisper.

His eyes shine like silver coins. "How can you think I don't care?" he says, holding my hand flat to his chest, atop his racing heart. "I care so much it hurts, right here, all the time."

And then he's kissing me, rashly, feverishly, insistently.

We stumble across my room until we're a knot of limbs before my bed. He kicks off his shoes and falls onto my mattress, pulling me down beside him. Our kisses build, deep and eager, until he breaks away to pull his shirt off. I run my hands along the plane of his stomach, and across his strong shoulders. He hovers above me, working my top up and over my head, and I arch my back to help. His touch, his muffled sounds, the way his skin tastes equally salty and sweet—he's all I can think about, all I can focus on.

I find the button of his jeans and fumble to open it. Rational thought is an elusive thing, but when he inhales a sharp breath and rolls away, I know I've done something wrong.

"Jilly, no," he says, catching my expression in the weak light. His chest rises and falls in time to my nervous heartbeats. "It's just—we shouldn't. Not like this."

I sit up, my face hot with the wretched sting of rejection. Suddenly very aware of my toplessness, I turn away and grope for my shirt, then yank it over my head.

Max sits up, too, behind me, freeing my hair from the collar of my top before pulling his own shirt on. "It's not like I don't want to," he says.

I feel like I'm sitting under a broiler. I focus on my comforter, the carpet, the cookbooks cluttering my desk—anywhere but him. "It's okay," I mumble. "I get it."

He runs his hand down my back, kisses my shoulder. Softly, he says, "I love you. You know that, right?"

My bedroom is a watercolor of streaks and smears. I've wanted to hear him say those words since I realized how deep my own feelings run. "Then why . . . ?"

"Because I don't want it to happen after a fight. I don't want it to happen because I'm being impulsive, or because you're trying too hard to right wrongs. I don't want it to be careless."

"Is that what you think I do? Try too hard to right wrongs?"

"It's one of my favorite things about you," he says, and there's a buoyancy to his voice that tells me he means it. "But I think we're both gonna have to learn to deal with shittiness. I don't think we'll have much luck avoiding it."

I swivel around to face him. "I love you, too, Max. Of course I do."

He waits a tentative beat before saying, "But?"

"But . . . are you sure?"

"Am I *sure*?"

"I mean, it hasn't exactly been easy between us. Are you sure this is what you want?"

He scoots forward to sit beside me. "Jilly, I can't lose you—not because of what happened tonight, not because of Becky or your dad, not because we may end up in different time zones one day." He captures my gaze; his eyes blaze with resolve and, at the same time, longing. "I want to be with you, now and next year and after, for as long as we're happy."

He pulls me into a hug, and I bury my face in the warm place between his shoulder and his neck. His pulse thrums an unfaltering beat and for the first time in hours . . .

I breathe.

. . . .

He offers to leave through the window, but I won't let him. "The window is sneaky."

"But what if your dad's home? What if he sees us headed for the door?"

"He won't be able to say a word, because he'll be choking on hypocrisy."

"Jill—"

"Max," I say, taking his hand and leading him down the hallway. "If he doesn't find out tonight, he'll find out tomorrow. What was that you said about dealing with shittiness?"

Quietly, he laughs.

When we reach the door, I hesitate, standing woodenly with my hand wrapped around the knob. Saying good-bye, watching him walk across the street, gearing up to brave my messy, messy family . . .

Max brackets my face with his hands and says, "I'm sorry I acted like a dick when I should've been there for you. I'm sorry your dad's made such a disaster of things. And I'm sorry Becky's been screwing with you—that's not gonna happen anymore." He stoops down and kisses me, sweet and tender. "From now on, things are gonna be better."

"Promise?"

"Promise." He nudges my hand from the knob and opens the door, stepping past me. He touches me once more, a warm hand on the back of my neck, a reassuring squeeze. "You and me, Jilly."

37

I FIND MEREDITH IN HER BED, CLUTCHING a mug of tea. A book lies open across her lap, but she's staring up at the ceiling, her expression so mournful my breath falters.

"Mer?" I say, stepping through the threshold. This was my dad's bedroom first, his alone for several years, a space draped in dark textiles with geometric shapes, the air rich with soap and cotton and polished wood. Then it was their bedroom, masculine linens traded for light, delicate fabrics, her perfume mingling with his familiar cologne. Now, the space is wholly Meredith's. Her clothes lay discarded across the chaise. Her makeup clutters the dresser's smooth surface. Her romance novels stand in towers on both nightstands. My dad still sleeps at this home of ours, but it's clear he mentally moved out months ago.

Meredith's empty stare finds me. "Jill? Are you all right?"

"I've been better."

She pats the mattress, and I climb up. "Did something happen with Max?"

"A lot of things happened with Max, actually, but we're okay now."

"New relationships always have their kinks."

She passes me her tea, and I take a sip. It's lukewarm and very sweet, comforting. I swallow and inhale a deep breath before saying, "Meredith, there's something I have to tell you." I pause, lost for words. How do you tell a woman she's been betrayed by the person she loves most, her husband, the father of her new baby? I'm going to break her heart, wreck her dreams, shatter this life she knows so well. But . . . *no*. It's Dad who's ruined everything. I try again. "Mer, my dad . . . There's someone else. It's been going on for a while, and I'm so sorry I didn't tell you sooner. He asked me not to. He promised it was over. But . . . it's not."

"I know," she says.

"You do?"

"He called."

"He *did*? I mean . . ." I tuck my legs beneath me, balancing her mug of tea on my knee. "What did he say?"

"He told me about Robin," she says evenly.

"Mer, I'm so sorry. I can't believe he's done this to you."

"To us," she corrects, linking her arm through mine. "I've felt something wasn't right for a long time, but I blamed Bill's stroke and the pregnancy and then Ally herself. I let myself believe our problems would disappear if I spent enough time wishing them away. I didn't know Robin was involved—I'm not sure that piece of the puzzle has registered, if I can be honest—but I knew your father was unhappy, and I suspected he was seeking happiness elsewhere."

I think about Max, how he sought happiness with me while he was with Becky. Even though I knew cheating was fundamentally wrong, I still took part. Is what Max and I did behind Becky's back any different from what Dad and Mrs. Tate did behind Meredith's? Does genuine emotion pardon unfaithfulness?

"He had no right to do what he did," I tell Meredith.

"No, he didn't. And he had no right to involve you. I'm so sorry he put you in such a terrible position." A tear trails down her cheek, and she dabs it with the cuff of her robe. "It's best all this came out, though. I'm not interested in being married to a man who strays."

"But Ally . . ."

Her face twists. "Ally will be okay. She's got me. She's got a big sister who cares."

"And the worst father ever." The stark truth leaves a sour taste on my tongue. Any allegiance I felt toward my dad went up in flames with his integrity.

Meredith sighs, a conflicted sound. "This will blow over someday. Don't hate your dad because of it." She kisses the top of my head, a motherly gesture that fills me with fondness. "Now, tell me what happened with Max."

I fill her in on the secret I convinced Max to help me keep, and how I made him feel—inadequate. I tell her about Becky's harassment, and how even though I hate that girl with a fiery passion, I can't kick the guilt I feel regarding the demise of her relationship with Max. Meredith listens thoughtfully, without comment, until I say, "I'm just like my dad."

"No, Jill, you're not. You made mistakes, but your intentions were admirable."

"Do you think that matters?"

"In your case, yes. Your regret's so obvious."

"I'm not sure regret absolves bad choices."

"Maybe not, but it helps you grow. And when it's genuine, it lets the people you wronged know that, deep down, you care."

She's not talking about me anymore; she's talking about Dad, and the hurt saturating her voice makes my chest feel as though it's splitting open. God, did he express regret when he called earlier? I mean, I'm pretty sure it'd be too little, too late, but I hope he showed Meredith more remorse than he showed me. A thousand apologies won't make up for what he's done, but a little contrition might be *something*.

"I'm so sorry, Mer. I wish there was something I could say that'd fix this." But there isn't—all I can offer is my support and my love and, maybe, my treats. I nudge her. "Tomorrow morning, I'm going to bake us something decadent, something buttery, full of chocolate and sugar, and you and I are going to eat every bite of it."

She gives me a sad smile. "I can't think of a better way to spend the day."

. . . .

Except the next morning, when I burst into the kitchen ready for a day of cheering Meredith up with my most mouthwatering confections, I find my dad sitting at the breakfast bar. He's wearing yesterday's suit—so he didn't come home last night—and he's sipping coffee from the World's Best Dad mug I gave him for Christmas a decade ago.

The irony.

Meredith's sitting on the stool adjacent to his; I imagine a gulf of tempestuous water between them. She appears bedraggled, like she hasn't slept a second, and she's holding the mug we shared last night. I wonder if she's washed it, or even bothered to refresh her tea. I wouldn't be surprised if she's nursing the cold dregs she steeped eight hours ago.

"Morning, Jill," she says, a little too merry, a put-on in an effort to reassure me, I think. At first, it rankles. Like, *Oh, hey, Meredith's her usual chipper self? Maybe this whole broken-home thing won't be so bad after all.* But then I realize her false cheer's more for her benefit than mine.

Sometimes, faking it's the only way to survive.

"Jillian," Dad says, an acknowledgment that's infuriating in its austerity.

I ignore him in favor of pouring myself a cup of coffee. It's the good stuff, rich and bold. My mouth is dry as burnt toast, and my hands shake as I add heaps of sugar and a generous splash of milk, then take a timid sip. Incredibly, it helps.

I stand across the counter from where my parents sit. Neither of them has said a word beyond their greetings, but it's clear they were talking before I came into the room. Dad's got the shreds of what was once a napkin sitting in front of him. Meredith must've used the last of her energy when she said good morning, because she's leaning against the countertop now, eyes unfocused.

"Where's Ally?" I ask.

"With Marcy," Dad says. "She offered to babysit while we . . . sort things out."

My sister's with the Holdens—with Max, Marcy, and Bill, maybe even Brett, Zoe, Oliver, and Ivy. She's probably snoozing while they feast on french toast, carrying on the way they do. Lucky Ally. I swirl my coffee in its mug, then clear my throat. "So . . . have you?"

"Have we what?" Mer asks, zombielike.

"Sorted things out?"

"It's not that easy," Dad says.

"I never thought it'd be easy. In fact, I imagine it's going to be really hard. On all of us."

He expels a mighty sigh. "I know you're upset."

"I'm more than upset—I'm *crushed*."

He looks away. "You're seventeen, Jillian. I won't explain my motives to you."

"God, please don't. There's nothing you can say that'll make me understand what you've done or why you've done it. Seventeen or not, I know what love is: hard work and sacrifice, common ground and compromise. I know that love is the same as giving someone your heart, and trusting them to cherish it, to hold it like it's made of blown sugar. I know about love, Dad. Max showed me."

He says nothing.

"He and I are together," I go on. "Without him, last night would've been—" There's a sob climbing my throat, keeping me from finishing my thought.

"Last night would have been unbearable," Dad finishes, and finally, *finally*, his voice roughens with penitence. "I'm sorry, Jill. I shouldn't have let you drive away. I shouldn't have let you think talking to Meredith was your responsibility. Much as I hate to admit it, I shouldn't have let you believe you needed to lie about Max. And I shouldn't be saying these things now, when it seems like I've got no other choice, but I mean them." He stops to survey me, part hopeful, part fearful. When I don't respond, he goes on. "I've got a lot of rebuilding to do in the way of your trust. I hope, one day, I'll be able to earn it back."

My eyes well with tears, again, because apparently I'm going to do more crying this weekend than I've done all my life. "I hope so, too," I tell him.

"Your father's going to leave," Meredith says, apologetically, like the surprise of this news might be too much for me to bear. "At least for now."

"There's an extended-stay hotel not too far from here," Dad says, "and there's a place for you there, with me."

"I—uh . . ." I can hardly breathe. It never occurred to me that *I'd* have to go away. Mer and Ally, my bedroom and the kitchen I adore, the Holdens—*Max*—across the street. I know the extended-stay Dad's talking about; it's a few miles down the highway, but it might as well be on Jupiter. I don't want to leave home.

"Or," Meredith says stretching to cover my hand with hers, "you can stay here with your sister and me. Your dad and I agreed—this house was yours long before it was mine, and more than that, I'd be happy to have your company. Ally would, too."

It would've been enough for her to offer out of obligation, but to know that she wants me to stay, she values our relationship enough to invite me to live with her sans Dad . . .

It'll hurt him if I choose to stay with Meredith. He stuck with me after Beth left, made sacrifices and compromises, showed me a version of the love I went on about a few minutes ago. He cares about me, I know he does, and it's possible he needs me, too.

I recall what Max said last night, about me trying too hard to right wrongs; it's not up to me to fix my father. My focus has to be on high school, and my job, and saving money. I'm going to settle on a local culinary school, one that rivals the International Culinary Institute, and then, eventually, I'm going to chase my Grand Diplôme of Professional Pastry Arts. I'm going to be present for Ally, and to do my best to be a kick-ass big sister. I'm going to concentrate on my relationships, all of them, but I'm not going to move to a hotel just to maintain a false sense of peace with my dad.

I meet his gaze. "I'd like to stay with Meredith."

38

HANGING OUT WITH MEREDITH AND MY SISTER turns out to be therapeutic. Mer's become something of a friend, and in the two weeks since my dad moved into a room at the extended-stay, we've spent a lot of nights talking our way through trays of warm chocolate chip cookies. Ally can lift her head now, and when she sees me, she smiles a gummy smile that makes my heart feel like it might burst.

I've decided on the Seattle Culinary Academy as the strongest contender for the first couple of years of my culinary education, and I've spent an inordinate amount of time baking, learning, practicing. Mer pretends to be displeased—I'm not helping her lose the last of the baby weight!—but she rarely leaves me alone when I'm in the kitchen. I think she's found comfort in my pastries, and in the act of creating her own. The other day, I shared my tried-and-true crust recipe with her, and she managed to fashion a passable lattice to top her cherry pie.

I've seen my dad only twice since he moved out, lunches initiated by him. They were quiet meetings, punctuated by the scrapes of silver against china and a lot of uncomfortable *ahem*s.

He's not seeing Mrs. Tate anymore, he claims, but it's hard to take his word at face value. He hasn't mentioned Max. I know he takes exception to the two of us together, though I think his objection comes more from principle than anything else. I went behind his back to spend time with the boy he told me to stay away from. He must have a Fatherhood Handbook tucked away somewhere, and it must advise him to remain quietly pissed for some predetermined number of days.

His disapproval doesn't bother me.

Tonight, I give Ally a bath, then volunteer to rock her to sleep. After I lay her in her crib, I find Meredith and Marcy scrapbooking at the kitchen table. This is a new hobby, one Mer jumped into to fill time not monopolized by the baby. I'm glad Marcy's joining in, though like me, her creativity comes more in the way of butter, sugar, and good chocolate than stickers, card stock, and fancy scissors.

I make a pot of coffee, fill three mugs, and join them. Glossy photographs litter the table, along with dozens of sticker sheets, printed pastel paper, and strips of waxy paper covered in glue dots, a miracle of scrapbooking I've only recently learned about. "What are you working on?" I ask, setting their mugs a safe distance from the memories.

"Ally's baby book. This page is dedicated to her first time in the bathtub." Meredith picks up a photo and passes it to me. I smile at the image: Ally sitting in a mesh bath seat, rosy pink and wailing, hair covered in sudsy shampoo.

"She's just the cutest thing," Marcy says, thumbing through her own stack of photos.

"Can I help?"

"Sure," Mer says, scanning the table for a suitable task, obviously trying to figure out where I'll do the least damage. She selects a few pictures, a celadon sheet of card stock, and a strip of glue dots. "You can glue these pictures to card stock, then cut them out. Leave about a quarter-inch of green border."

I study the example she holds up. I'm pretty sure I can reproduce it.

The pictures she's given me are of Ally's first full day of life. I recall it with perfect clarity. The tension incited by Dad's stunt contrasted with the immediate-yet-unforeseen love I felt for my baby sister. There's a picture of me holding her stiffly, then one each of Dad and Meredith snuggling her close. I flip to the next picture and find Ally in Marcy's arms. I stare at the photograph a beat too long, overcome by a rush of memories.

The final photograph in the pile steals my breath. It's the one I took of Max holding Ally like a little football—the moment I realized I was in love with him.

"You okay, sweetie?" Marcy asks, leaning in for a look at the picture I'm holding.

I pass it to her. She grins, then shows Meredith.

"That was a good day," Mer says.

"That was a *crazy* day."

"Max was such a grouch on the way home from the hospital," Marcy says, handing the picture back to me. "I had a feeling something had happened between the two of you, and Jill, I can't tell you how hard I hoped it'd work out."

I sip from my mug to hide a smile.

"You should've seen the two of them on Valentine's Day, before they left for Seattle. I caught them smooching in the hallway—"

I choke on coffee and laughter. "Meredith!"

She shrugs. "It's true."

I'm flushing raspberry-red when my phone chimes. I find a text from Max: *I miss you.*

I hear his words as much as read them, whispered low and gravelly, his breath moving tendrils of my hair, tickling my neck. I grin at my phone.

"Max?" Meredith asks, slapping pink teddy bear stickers to the layout she's working on.

"Tell him to come over," Marcy says.

I tap out a response: *I'd ask you to come over, but there's a whole lot of crafting going on around here.*

His reply comes quickly: *Meet me outside?*

"So, I think I'm going to take a break," I say, pushing card stock and photographs in Meredith's direction. "I'll be back . . . eventually."

She and Marcy wave me off with wily smiles. I doubt my scrapbooking skills will be missed.

I swing by my bedroom to slip on shoes and grab a jacket before dashing for the front door, fueled by the burst of excitement I always feel when I'm moments from seeing Max. It's something like the tingly zip that comes with sucking on a lemon drop, that moment when the bright, sweet-tart flavor finds its way under my tongue.

He's waiting in the middle of the street, and when he sees me racing toward him, his face becomes an explosion of happiness. I don't stop running until we collide, until his arms circle around my waist to hug me closely, warmly, completely; my feet dangle over the pavement.

An eternity passes before he loosens his hold. I slide down his body until my shoes find solid ground, then tip my head to look up at him. He's glowing in the golden light of the streetlamps, and I feel it, too— *illuminated*—because he's Max and I'm Jillian, and my life is so much better because he's a part of it.

"Love you, Holden."

He flashes me the grin I adore, the one that makes my heart flutter and my cheeks flush and my insides dissolve like sugar in simmering water. The grin that's all mine.

He kisses me. "Love you, too, Jilly."

ACKNOWLEDGMENTS

A bazillion people have helped me throughout the writing, revising, and publication of *Kissing Max Holden*. That might sound hyperbolic, but it's truly the way I feel. This novel has been very much a team effort, and I'm endlessly grateful to every single person who has had a hand in its journey from idea to book.

Holly West and Lauren Scobell, that November 2015 phone call changed my life. I can't thank you enough for your combined expertise, creativity, and warmth. Holly, *Kissing Max Holden* is a thousand times stronger because of your insight. Lauren, thank you for loving Max as much as I do.

Jean Feiwel, thank you for taking the genius idea of a crowd-sourced YA imprint and turning it into a reality. Because of you, I get to call myself an author—what a gift! Swoon Readers, without your ratings and your lovely, lovely comments, Jilly and Max might still belong to me alone. I'm thrilled to share them with you now.

Kelsey Marrujo, thank you for sharing your knowledge of all things publicity. My book and I are better because of you. Ashley Woodfolk, thank you for championing *Kissing Max Holden* from day one. I can't wait to read your debut! Valerie Shea and Starr Baer, thank you for your copy-editing prowess. You've made me look much more grammatically adept than I actually am. Emily Settle, thank you for graciously answering my many (many!) questions, and for your awesomeness in the way of organization and coordination. Rebecca Syracuse, thank you for the beautiful cover. It's everything I've ever dreamed of. Kat Brzozowski, thank you for your kindness, and your guidance in the year leading up to *Kissing Max Holden*'s release. I couldn't have done it without you! And to everyone else at Swoon Reads who helped bring this book to life, I am grateful.

Victoria Marini, thank you for your always excellent feedback. Thank you for the countless hours of unsung work. Thank you for your honesty and your humor. But mostly, thank you for believing in me.

My little writing tribe, I am so lucky to have you. Alison Miller, my wonderful friend, thank you for the e-mail exchanges, the unwavering support, and the many, many, *many* critiques. This book is what it is in large part because of you. Temre Beltz, I'm so glad we decided to swap manuscripts all those years ago! You inspire me, not only with your enchanting stories and gorgeous writing, but with your generous heart. Riley Edgewood, thank you for the lunches, the retreats, the accountability, and the savvy marketing advice. You push me to be better, while simultaneously making me feel like the best. Elodie Nowodazkij, who would've thought the French girl I once traded blog comments with would one day be a real-life friend? Thank you for your brilliant suggestions and boundless enthusiasm, and for genuinely believing this would happen. You were right!

Jessica Love, Tracey Neithercott, Jaime Morrow, Christa Desir, and Erin Bowman, thank you for offering invaluable feedback on *Kissing Max Holden* at varying points along its path to publication. Because of each of you, this story is deeper, smarter, funnier, and swoonier (I'm certain that's a word!). Additionally, enormous gratitude to Lola, Amanda, Jolene, Kate, Liz, Taryn, Danielle, Kari, Laurina, and Heather, who've all taken the time to read my work and provide critiques over the years. Someday I will bake cookies for you all!

To my fellow Swoon Authors: You have been enormously welcoming and overwhelmingly kind, and I'm honored to be a part of the Swoon Family. To my Swanky 17s: I can't imagine doing this debut thing without each of you. Thank you for the pep talks, the laughs, and the commiseration. Our year is finally here! And to the YA community: Thank you for making me feel like a real writer, like one of you, even in the very beginning.

Mom and Dad, thank you for indulging my love of reading, for buying me limitless paperbacks, and for stressing the importance of education. Mom, there's no one I'd rather chat books with. Dad, your quiet pride means the world to me. I love you both so much! Mike and Zach, thanks for providing plenty of fodder for my fictional familial relationships. Growing up with you guys was a wild ride, and tons of fun. I'm fortunate to call you brothers, as well as friends.

Bev and Phil, I'm grateful for your constant love and support. I couldn't have written a better pair of in-laws. And to the rest of my family—Michele, Gabe, Teddy, Thomas, Andy, Danielle, Grant, Reid, Caroline, Sam, Kacie, and Grandpa—thank you for your excitement regarding my writing, and especially *Kissing Max Holden*. You're the best!

Matt, I borrowed Max's best traits from you. Thank you for being the sort of husband who is enormously inspiring and infinitely patient. Thank you for knowing exactly how to cheer me up. Thank you for reading drafts, letting me drone on about all things publishing, fielding my random football questions, and suggesting pizza when I'm in the weeds. I'm so lucky, getting to live this life with you. You are my happily ever after.

Claire Bear, you were just two years old when I wrote the beginnings of what would eventually become *Kissing Max Holden*. You're days from ten as it finally (finally!) makes its way into the world. You've been by my side for every word, every chapter, every revised draft, every query, every rejection, and every celebration. You've helped me name characters, you've drawn cover mock-ups, and you've surrendered birthday wishes to this dream of mine. You never lost hope, so neither did I. This one's for you, baby girl.

FEELING BOOKISH?

Turn the page for some

Swoonworthy EXTRAS

JILLY'S *BEST* CHOCOLATE CHIP COOKIES

1½ CUPS (THREE STICKS) BUTTER

1½ CUPS BROWN SUGAR

½ CUP SUGAR

2 EGGS

1½ TABLESPOONS VANILLA EXTRACT

4 CUPS ALL-PURPOSE FLOUR

4 TEASPOONS CORNSTARCH

2 TEASPOONS BAKING SODA

1 TEASPOON SALT

2 CUPS SEMISWEET CHOCOLATE CHIPS

Preheat oven to 350 degrees. Cream butter and both sugars until fluffy. Add eggs and vanilla extract, then blend. In a separate bowl, combine flour, cornstarch, baking soda, and salt. Add in halves to butter/sugar mixture. Stir well. Mix in chocolate chips. Line two baking sheets with aluminum foil and drop cookie dough in generous tablespoon-size scoops, leaving two inches of space around each cookie. Bake for 10–12 minutes, watching for golden-brown edges. Don't overbake—the finished cookies should be soft and fluffy. Cool on a wire rack.

MAX'S FAVORITE
DARK-CHOCOLATE-CHUNK BROWNIES

1 TABLESPOON VANILLA EXTRACT

1½ TEASPOONS DARK-ROAST INSTANT COFFEE

1 CUP (TWO STICKS) BUTTER

2¼ CUPS SUGAR

¾ CUP UNSWEETENED COCOA POWDER

½ CUP UNSWEETENED DARK COCOA POWDER

1 TEASPOON SALT

1 TEASPOON BAKING POWDER

1½ CUPS FLOUR

4 EGGS

1½ CUPS (TWO LARGE BARS, CUT UP) DARK-CHOCOLATE CHUNKS

Preheat oven to 350 degrees. Grease a 9" x 13" glass baking dish. In a small bowl, let instant coffee dissolve in the vanilla extract. In a medium saucepan, melt the butter. Add sugar and the vanilla extract/coffee mixture to the pan. Stir, then cook over low heat for 2–3 minutes. In a mixing bowl, combine both cocoas, salt, baking powder, and flour. Stir in sugar/butter mixture. Add eggs and mix well. The batter will be very rich and thick. Stir in the dark-chocolate chunks. Spread batter in the greased 9" x 13" dish and cook for 30–35 minutes, using a toothpick to check for doneness.

A COFFEE DATE

BETWEEN AUTHOR KATY UPPERMAN
AND HER EDITOR, HOLLY WEST

Holly West (HW): What was the first romance novel you ever read?

Katy Upperman (KU): I don't think Caroline B. Cooney's *The Face on the Milk Carton* is technically a romance novel, but I read it when I was about thirteen and while the mystery behind why Janie's face appeared on that milk carton initially intrigued me, I was mostly consumed by her romance with boy-next-door Reeve. When he kisses her in the leaf pile? When he feeds her cake? My first instances of literary swoon.

HW: Who is your OTP, your favorite fictional couple?

KU: Westley and Buttercup from *The Princess Bride*. Their love is so intense, but they're playful with each other, too. There's this bit of dialogue that Westley says to Buttercup: "Do I love you? My God, if your love were a grain of sand, mine would be a universe of beaches," and it just gets me every time.

HW: *The Princess Bride* is possibly my favorite movie ever! Do you have any hobbies? Other than writing, of course, since writing doesn't count as a hobby when you are a published author.

KU: Baking! I started researching recipes while drafting *Kissing Max Holden* several years ago, and I still make at least one treat a week. I also love yoga; I've been known to make a quilt here and there; and I take lots of hikes and kayaking trips with my family. And reading. Of course reading!

HW: Jillian likes to compare people to desserts. What dessert would you be?

KU: I hope I'd be a chocolate chip cookie, because they're sweet and classic, and I think they come across as friendly and accessible. (Can a cookie be friendly and accessible . . . ? I think so.)

HW: Chocolate chip cookies are definitely friendly. And my favorite question: If you were a superhero, what would your superpower be?

KU: I feel like I should say something altruistic, like the power to heal, which would totally be great. But really, I'd love to be able to read at lightning-fast speeds. Or write books at lightning-fast speeds! Also, it would be amazing to be able to breathe underwater.

HW: How did you first learn about Swoon Reads?

KU: Social media. As soon as I heard about how Swoon Reads works, I did some research on books the imprint was publishing. I also followed the Swoon blog, which turned out to be a wealth of information. During that time, I was polishing *Kissing Max Holden*, trying to rally the courage to submit it.

HW: What made you decide to post your manuscript?

KU: The Swoon Reads site immediately felt like a place where writers are supported and encouraged, and I was drawn to its positive energy. I think it's so cool that Swoon Reads focuses on romance novels, because they're my favorite sorts of books to read and write—I can't imagine drafting a story without plenty of kissing. As I learned more about Swoon Reads and its selected titles, I came to realize that *Kissing Max Holden* would fit in well among them. It's a book about relationships of all sorts, but at its core, it's a love story. So, I submitted it!

HW: What was your experience like on the site before you were chosen?

KU: Awesome. What I said before about the site feeling positive and encouraging? It's been that way all along. I got lots of thoughtful feedback from Swoon readers, and I truly felt as though people were cheering Jill and Max (and me!) on.

HW: Once you were chosen, who was the first person you told and how did you celebrate?

KU: I told my daughter first, and she was thrilled. I called my husband just after, and then my parents. The whole thing felt very surreal (it still does!). We celebrated with dinner out, which was perfect.

HW: When did you realize you wanted to be a writer?

KU: Later than many, I think. I was a teacher until my daughter was born in 2007. I loved staying home with her, but I was also in need of a creative outlet. I started writing seriously in 2008 (YA before I realized YA was an actual thing) and I never looked back.

HW: Do you have any writing rituals?

KU: I do—I think I might be a little high-maintenance, actually. I always sit in the same corner of the couch. I do best in complete silence. I drink coffee with frothed creamer pretty much all day. I like when our dog and cat are nearby; they're like furry little cheerleaders. And when the words just aren't flowing, I resort to Jelly Bellies.

HW: Where did the idea for this book start?

KU: I wish I had a succinct answer for this question. I suppose it started with my love of romance and my fascination with friends-turned-sweethearts. *Kissing Max Holden* is a mash-up of things I love: baking, country music, the Pacific Northwest, football, coffee, kissing, and complicated relationships of all sorts. It started with Jill and Max, and the story sort of grew up around them.

HW: Do you ever get writer's block? How do you get back on track?

KU: I do. Usually, it happens when the story I'm working on has somehow derailed. First, I step away for a few days. I spend time doing other things while pondering the problem and possible fixes. When that doesn't work, I talk to my critique partners. They're very good at helping me brainstorm my way out of a block. Sometimes, though, writer's block is simply lack of inspiration. When that's the case, I comb Pinterest and Tumblr for pictures that spark ideas, or I read a book by an author I love, or I watch a favorite movie. Often, that's enough to make me want to get back to work.

HW: What's the best writing advice you've ever heard?

KU: Write another book. Because the more we write, the better we become. Also, one of two things is going to happen with your first book: It's going to be published, or it's not. If it is, awesome—you'll be glad you have a second manuscript in the works. If it isn't, bummer—you'll be *really* glad you have a second manuscript in the works.

KISSING MAX HOLDEN
DISCUSSION QUESTIONS

1. Jill often uses baked goods to describe her friends and family. Which confection would you use to describe Jill? How might you describe yourself?

2. Jill thinks Max and Becky are terrible for each other. Do you think Becky is a negative influence on Max? In what ways is Max "the maker of his own destiny," as Jill says?

3. Over the course of the story, Jill goes from resenting the "leech baby" to wanting to be a kick-ass big sister. What do you think changed Jill's thinking? Have you ever radically changed your mind about something like that?

4. How does Jill and Max's childhood friendship shape the relationship they build throughout the story?

5. Which of Max's qualities do you think draws Jill in most? Which of her traits is he most attracted to?

6. Max's mother, Marcy, gives Jill credit for his ultimate improvement in mood and motivation, but Jill tells her that all Max needed was time. Do you think family and/or friends can influence a transformation, or do you think the desire to change has to come from within?

7. Toward the end of the story, Jill tells Meredith: "I'm just like my dad." Do you agree?

8. Throughout the story, Jill recalls times Max has come to her rescue. In what ways does she attempt to rescue him? Is she ever successful?

9. After discovering her father's affair, Jill reflects on the beginnings of her relationship with Max, wondering if genuine emotion pardons unfaithfulness. Do you think there are situations where cheating might be forgivable?

10. Kyle says that Jill holds her cards close. How does this impact her relationships? Do you think she becomes less guarded by the novel's end?

After her brother dies fighting in Afghanistan, Elise and her mother move to a sleepy coastal village where she meets Mati, who is Afghan. Can their budding relationship withstand the scrutiny of those around them—particularly Elise's family?

Keep reading for an excerpt.

elise

Aside from the predictable mundaneness of driving down the California coast, house hunting, and unpacking, the last several weeks can only be described as a loneliness-infused shit storm. Without verbalizing an objection or complaint (this move isn't about me—that's been made perfectly clear—so why bother?), I've plummeted through the first three stages of uproot-induced grief (denial, anger, bargaining) and bottomed out at depression, where I'm currently wallowing like a duck in a waning pond.

In an effort to catapult me into that final, glorious, *elusive* phase of acceptance, my mom let me pick paint for my new bedroom—any color on the spectrum. She was less than pleased with my chosen shade, Obsidian, which rolled onto the walls and ceiling like thick tar. Though the silent protest felt good initially, sitting in my deep-space bedroom now isn't doing much to improve my bleak mood.

Here's the thing: Cypress Beach repels teenagers the way citronella repels mosquitoes. After a month, I've made one acquaintance, Iris Higgins, who lives in the cottage next door to ours and is half a century beyond my age bracket. She's into gardening—like, obsessively into gardening—and she's bananas, in a good way.

My mom worries. She wants me to make friends before school starts (in a month and a half . . . *God*). She's been begging me to attend the New Student Orientation at Cypress Valley High, scheduled for a few weeks from now, and she's constantly dropping not-so-subtle hints about my needing to spend more time in town, at the coffee shop or the one-screen movie theater or the library, because those are places cool kids hang out, apparently.

Two weeks ago, in a last-ditch effort if ever there was one, she surprised me with a corkscrew-haired mess of a pup who gallops around our cottage on feet she's yet to grow into and chews table legs like they're made of rawhide.

Her name is Bambi, and I love her.

She's the reason I'm out now, at the crack of dawn, trudging down the dog-friendly beach that runs parallel to our dog-friendly town, holding a slobber-soaked tennis ball between two fingers. She's tearing around up ahead, a honey-colored ball of fluff, scaring seagulls with her ferocious *woof, woof!*

"Bambi!"

She skids to a halt, kicking up sand, swishing her tail like it's a whip. She looks at me with big cocoa eyes, trusting and adoring and expectant. I chuck her ball into the waves, exactly as she wants, and she leaps after it, crashing into the cold water like it's her job—which I guess it is. She's a goldendoodle, a golden retriever crossed with a standard poodle, a designer dog my mom undoubtedly paid too much for because the newest member of the Parker clan had to be hypoallergenic. Bambi has *hair*, not *fur*, because my niece, Janie, inherited allergies from her mama. Janie's the one who branded my dog with her name, actually, a nod to the clumsy Disney deer.

She springs out of the Pacific, neon ball clamped between her jaws, and dashes at me, sailing over mounds of slippery, stinky kelp that have washed onto the beach with the tide. She pulls to a halt just short of my shins, dropping her disgusting ball at my feet. She shakes, a slo-mo, full-body convulsion, and I scramble to block my camera from the drops of water that go flying. I should be annoyed—I'm wet now, and the morning is gray and windy, not exactly summer-balmy—but it's impossible to be frustrated with Bambi. She is at all times obliviously joyful.

I bend to scratch her wet head, and she paws the sand with an ungainly puppy paw. "Again?" I ask in the falsetto I reserve for her and Janie.

We go through the motions another dozen times. Me, hurling the drool-drenched ball into the surf. Bambi, chasing and swimming and splashing, coming to me time and again to seek a pat and another throw.

We've got the beach pretty much to ourselves. Central California doesn't get much of a summer—not on the coast, anyway. We're lucky if the fog burns off in time to catch the sunset. Thanks to so many years spent in San Francisco, I'm used to the dreariness, but somehow it was more tolerable there, haze hovering over asphalt and structures of steel and glass. Here, where building code dictates no property should rise above three stories, the constant mist feels thick and oppressive, like a damp wool blanket.

Bambi and I walk farther down the stretch of sand, playing our endless game. As much as I hate getting up early, and as much as I dislike living in tiny Cypress Beach, I've come to look forward to these mornings with my new dog. So much so, I bring my Nikon to photograph the waves and the gulls and her. It's risky, what with her shake-off showers, but worth it. I'm snapping yet another picture, Bambi bouncing over a knoll, when movement up ahead catches my attention.

I lower my camera, letting it hang from the woven strap around my neck. Absently, I toss the tennis ball, not so far this time, because I'm watching a tall figure move down the beach. He's a ways south, but I can tell he's somewhere near my age—a small miracle in this town.

He's wearing dark track pants and a hooded sweatshirt, and his hair's black, standing out in sharp contrast to the pale sand.

He strides into the surf, fully clothed.

The air is cool and crisp, and the ocean is *frigid*. He's up to his knees when a white-capped wave breaks hard against his middle, driving him back a few steps. I expect him to wade out, back to the beach, but he presses forward, undeterred, immersing his lower half completely. He uses his hands against the surging breakers like he thinks he can control them, like he's unaware of the water's absolute power.

I'm no fearmonger—that's more in keeping with my mom's personality—but the Pacific's scary along this strip of the coast. I've seen surfers in dry suits, but unless you've got a board, this isn't a swimming beach. Thanks to the California Current, the water's bitter cold and the undertows are unreal. There are sharks, too. Big ones, which normally feed on harbor seals and sea lions, but are probably ravenous for breakfast at the moment and would likely settle for a nice big bite of boy.

"Hey!" I call as he moves farther into the swells. Stupid, because there's no way he can hear me over the wind and the waves.

What he's doing . . . It's *so* unsafe.

Without a second thought, I take off in his direction, clutching my camera so it doesn't knock against my chest. Bambi chases me, nipping at my heels.

He's up to his shoulders when I reach the dragging footsteps he left in the sand. I watch him jump as waves distend, then advance beyond him in a race for the beach. His head bobs the way Bambi's ball does after landing in the surf. If he goes any deeper, he could be sucked out to sea.

"Hey!" I scream again, waving my arms.

He doesn't hear me, or doesn't want to, because he pushes off and paddles farther out.

He's an adrenaline-seeking dumbass, or he's suicidal.

I keep my eyes on his dark hair and peel off my sweatshirt, trying not to strangle myself with my camera's strap in the process. I toss it into the sand and take half a second to wrap my Nikon in its fabric, praying my beloved camera doesn't get stolen or lost to an aggressive wave.

Then I bolt into the ocean.

Check out more books
chosen for publication
by readers like you.

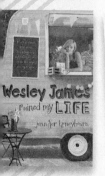